Puffin Plus
Flambards Divided

The old ivy-covered house of Flambards has seen much upheaval and tragedy since Christina first rode up the long drive as a young girl of twelve. Most important of all, her beloved Will is dead – killed in action in France – and the war is almost over. It's time, or so it seems, for Christina to marry Dick and for the two of them to settle in at the farm.

But it won't be long before Mark is back from the war and he, Will's brother, has cause more than anyone else to resent Dick's new position as master of the house. Soon it will be not only Flambards that is divided but Christina herself – in her feelings for two very different men.

Flambards Divided is the eagerly awaited sequel to K. M. Peyton's Flambards trilogy (*Flambards, The Edge of the Cloud, Flambards in Summer* – all published in Puffin) on which the popular television series was based.

K. M. Peyton

Flambards Divided

Puffin Books
in association with Oxford University Press

Puffin Books, Penguin Books Ltd, Harmondsworth, Middlesex, England
Penguin Books, 625 Madison Avenue, New York, New York 10022, U.S.A.
Penguin Books Australia Ltd, Ringwood, Victoria, Australia
Penguin Books Canada Ltd, 2801 John Street, Markham, Ontario, Canada L3R 1B4
Penguin Books (N.Z.) Ltd, 182–190 Wairau Road, Auckland 10, New Zealand

First published by Oxford University Press, 1981
Published in Puffin Books 1982
Reprinted 1982

Made and printed in Great Britain by
Cox & Wyman Ltd, Reading
Filmset in Monophoto Times by
Northumberland Press Ltd, Gateshead, Tyne and Wear

For Christine and Steven

Chapter 1

Christina had dreamed of Will again. In spite of the fact that she knew she was reconciled to his death, and the undoubted fact that since it she had rearranged her life with astonishing success, Will had a habit of disturbing her these days. She could still see his face vividly from the dream, strained and thin, gentle, the face as she had last seen it at the gates of the factory aerodrome. Aviators had to go back to France from leave in new aeroplanes; it had been part of a familiar pattern to say good-bye there. They had to replace the fighters that were being shot down. Less than a month later some other young man had been ferrying out a new plane to replace Will's. But the pilot was irreplaceable.

'Will,' Christina said out loud.

She lay looking towards the window. The November sky was heavy with rain, the big house huddled into its coat of ivy, the water-laced fields and woods spreading out to indeterminate horizons. The chestnut trees had dropped their fruits into the soggy ground year after year, but from greater heights, their flowers a greater glory every spring. Christina could remember it from a child. She had walked there with Will as a child. She had come to the house as an orphan relative, grown up there, married her cousin. Now their daughter Isobel, born after Will's death, lay peacefully in her cot in Will's old room. Which was as it should be. The sense of continuity was strong, and Christina was very conscious of it.

But harking back was a useless pastime. She had not been

guilty of it much, had been too busy building up the neglected farm. Not woman's work, they all said. But the war had
changed a lot of things, not least the place of women, and
even before it had started she had learned emancipation in
Will's carefree flying world. Will had never expected a
woman to keep at home in the kitchen; he had taught her to
fly, and to drive a car and to be a socialist. He had never,
like his brother, fancied farming for a career; the countryside
had meant nothing to him save as something to land on.
Will had belonged to the sky, to clouds and dreams and
everything that was still to come. But so much for that . . .
Christina got out of bed to face the new day. Will had been
shot down and come to earth, and died, and been buried in
it. So much for the future.

'But I have a future,' she thought. 'Now.'

She went to the window as she did every morning, and
always had done, drawn by the world outside. Flambards,
all three hundred acres of it, some cultivated, some lying
fallow, some under grass and some definitely run to seed
(particularly the poor garden) was hers. She had agreed to
marry Dick, who knew how to run a farm properly. She
reckoned she loved him. It was only now, with the marriage
date getting close, that she was getting these dreams of Will,
which reminded her uncomfortably of how she had loved
him. When she had wanted to recall him, had ached and wept
to remember him as he had been, her mind had not co-
operated, had blotted out any but the dimmest of images as
if to spare her the pain of such memories; but now she had
decided to forget, think to the future, throw in her lot with
another man whom she was quite sure she loved dearly, her
stupid brain kept producing Will with such vividness that she
felt closer to him than at any time since his death. God, how
she had loved him! Loved him still?

'You can't love someone who no longer exists,' she said
firmly, out loud.

8

She loved Dick. She admitted freely that it was a different sort of love, but it was love, nevertheless. And very lucky she was to have it. She needed him; the farm needed him; the children needed him. He needed her, the farm and the children. One of the children, Tizzy, was his sister's child, whom Christina had adopted. He loved Tizzy dearly. The fact that Tizzy's father had been Will's brother Mark had been an embarrassment and a complication that Christina had learned to live with. If she could weather the neighbourhood's opinion of her for adopting her brother-in-law's illegitimate child, she had decided long ago that she could weather their opinions when they heard that she was now intending to marry one of Flambard's erstwhile servants and drag the noble Russell lineage down into the lower realms of the social order. The banns were to be announced at morning service in four hours' time.

'And just listen to what they'll say about that!' Christina thought to herself, with a grim smile. In her heart of hearts she had not been looking forward to this morning very much, but never would she have revealed this timidity to a living soul. But to Will's ghost, his sweet face so near and real, she could say with spirit, 'Damn you, Will! To come to me today, of all days! *Go away.*'

Breakfasting in the kitchen, Christina realized that she had got into farm ways. In the old days they had breakfasted in the dining-room, she and Uncle Russell and the two boys, Mark and Will, and Violet had waited on. Violet . . . soon to be a sister-in-law . . . a qualm turned in Christina's stomach. She put down her porridge spoon.

'You all right, Miss Christina? You look right peaky this morning.'

Old Mary, the housekeeper, had turned round at the wrong moment. She was feeding Isobel in her high chair by the range, and the baby was laughing, orange egg-yolk running down her chin. When she laughed she was the image of Will. Tizzy, sitting at the table, had turned his empty egg upside down in the eggcup and was drawing a face on it with a pencil. Concentrating hard, dark-eyed, dark-haired, a proper Russell, he too looked at that moment like his uncle Will. He had nothing of his mother in his looks at all. The Wrights were fair. Dick was blond and blue-eyed. I need a change, Christina thought. I need Dick. I feel sick.

'Just because those banns are being read, doesn't mean you have to be there, not if you feel a bit seedy,' Mary said. She offered up another spoonful to Will's daughter. She said, 'Might be better not, come to that.'

'Of course I'm going. I'm perfectly all right.' Her voice came out sharper than she intended. The thought of staying at home, doing nothing, building up a fire in her private sitting room and sitting gazing into the flames, alone, while her intentions were made public, was so lovely as to cause a wavering in the last sentence. But the dream was as un-helpful as all the others.

'What's a bann?' Tizzy asked.

Christina thought, a bann means you can't do it.

'It's a public announcement in church, to say I am going to marry your uncle Dick.'

'Everybody knows that,' Tizzy said. His content with the plan was apparent in his voice, and it steadied Christina.

'Well, there's some'll have plenty to gossip about,' Mary said. 'After today's work.'

'Why?' Tizzy looked up from his egg.

'Never you mind.' Mary thrived on doom and disaster, and was probably looking forward to being a mine of in-formation concerning the present upheaval. Working with the Russell family all her life had given her plenty of practice in coping with the unexpected.

'If you've nothing better to do, young lad, go and get

yourself brushed and combed for church. Fowler will be round in ten minutes.'

Christina got up. 'And me.'

Mary would stay with the baby. Dick would walk from the village where he lodged and meet her in church. Dick was a churchgoer, and Christina, after her careless days with Will and his irreligious friends, had got into the habit again. It fitted in now, the social exchange, the feel of being settled in a community, one of the farmers. Christina had found it a comfort, this sense of belonging again, of security. But today the hen-roost was to be set by the ears; the cackle would raise the roof. Her second marriage would cause as much scandal as her first, when she had eloped with her cousin to London *in a motor-car*! The feathers were scarcely back in place after that little excitement. How slow, how unchanging was this farming round ... even three and a half years of war had done little to quicken the pulse of the land. It had made the farmers richer, a few more thistles the less, brawny young men fewer still. Dick was a farm-hand only since being invalided out after Ypres; the rest of her workers were old or half-mental. Lucas and Allison had both lost sons; even Masters' oldest boy had been conscripted now, having pulled strings for deferment for so long. The land seemed to reflect in some way this loss of its young blood. Under the winter sky it lay washed out, the silent coverts smudged out in a soft drizzle, undisturbed for three seasons by the excitement of hounds and the urgency of the horn. The foxes were getting fat and careless, the hedges were growing high, out of old men's reach. The ditches needed clearing, brimming with rain. Looking at it, Christina recalled photos she had seen of France where the fighting was taking place, the blighted landscape of craters and dead trees and churned mud. It did her no good, knowing that Mark had returned to that hell, in order to save England for fox-hunting. His

11

last letter had been from Passchendaele. The only consolation, Mark probably chased the Hun with as much
enthusiasm as he chased foxes, being aggressive and savage
by nature. If anyone could be temperamentally suited to
what was going on in France, it was Mark.

Old Fowler, who had been at Flambards since before
Mark and Will were born, drove the trap in silence. He was
as aware of the significance of this particular Sunday service
as Christina, his gaze inscrutably on the road ahead, between
Pepper's ears. They came out of the farm chase on to the
road and Christina, wishing the church were twenty miles
farther on, could see it just round the next bend, its squat
tower presiding over the ragged row of cottages that com-
prised the village, yew trees like ink-blots against the wet sky,
rooks wheeling and squawking mournfully to accompany
the single bell that tolled across the fields. A couple of traps
were converging from the farther lanes; a dribble of villagers,
answering the bell's summons, made their way under black
umbrellas to preserve their Sunday best, a few standing back
for Pepper's passage to the gateway. Fowler pulled up to let
Christina and Tizzy down. The routine had never varied all
through his life-time, even though in the old days he had
driven a shining carriage and pair and there had been a
footman to see the family down and guard the horses during
the service. These days he parked old Pepper on the side of
the lane with a nosebag for company and came in himself.
Things would never be the same again. A motor-car was
parked beyond Pepper's habitual place. Fowler looked at it
with contempt.

'God's truth, the war's done some of 'em good, and no
mistake!'

He hawked and spat.

'It's Mr Masters' new Crossley,' Tizzy said, with great
respect.

'What's wrong with his cart then? He won't find no blacksmith to help 'im with that when it falls apart and that's a fact. Stinking contraption.'

'I think it's beautiful,' Tizzy said, with true reverence.

Christina did too, but was too tactful to say so. The older Fowler became, the more he found to disapprove of. She wondered what he truly thought of her intention to marry Dick. Dick as a boy had been a stable lad under his orders. Now he took orders from Dick.

'The world's gone mad,' he said, stumping up the church path.

Christina found herself smiling. It was true. But the church had stood there for six hundred years and looked capable of standing for six hundred more, and each generation in its turn had no doubt supposed the same as Fowler. The thought put her tiny decision into context. The universe would alter little whether she married Dick or not. They would all end up here under the turf sooner or later. She passed her Uncle Russell's relatively fresh grave without a second glance. Dick was waiting for her by the church door and, seeing him, Fowler dropped back, taking his place.

Dick's smile was as uncertain as Christina's.

'These banns – it's as bad as going over the top. Between you and me, it's fine. It's telling it in public.'

She held out her hand and managed to raise a laugh. 'Think how easy the wedding will be, after this!'

Dick shook his head. He opened the door for her and the musty smell of the interior came out to meet her. She saw the congregation before her, and the mass rustle of inquisitiveness as they all turned round to see her with Dick, the careful blandness of their expressions.

'They all know,' she said to him.

They walked to their pew at the front with Tizzy between them. Dick had already worked his way over the years from the servants at the back, to the bailiff's middle position, and now, at Christina's insistence, to the Russell pew directly below the lectern, with a door to it and a stove which would have been lit except for the war. Even the Masters, with their motor-car, sat behind the Russells, and so did the Lucases and the Allisons and the Badstocks. When Mark had gone back to France after his last leave, Dick had taken his place, and the village had known, and said nothing. Today, they would have the signal to talk. Christina was aware that she had always given them plenty to talk about. It was nothing new.

The organ began to play and in the sensuous, comforting embrace of the ritual music, Christina bent her head in pretence of prayer, and in the ornate pew, pressed close to Dick, she felt her courage come back. With her hands over her face, she glanced sideways through her fingers, and saw his profile, pale against the dark oak behind, his fair hair shining out of the gloom. As she looked he turned and lifted his eyes. They were very blue and direct, and one of them winked. Christina felt the giggles coming.

'You changing your mind?'

'It's too late! I'm doomed.'

'And me. We're in the soup together.'

'There's nothing we can do.'

'We'd better try praying.'

But he was grinning, kneeling on his hassock. On the other side, Tizzy was wriggling back on to his seat.

'Ma, I want a wee!'

'You can't, idiot child. You should have said before we came in. You'll have to sit on it.'

'I can't when I'm kneeling.'

It was impossible not to believe that, amidst the tragedies, life could also be quite funny. Much better, now Dick was actually beside her, to remember the good times, and look forward to more. It will be all right, she thought. It was dreaming of Will that had given her doubts. The real Dick was already rubbing out the image of Will.

The vicar came in with the choir of five children, one young man blinded on the Somme and two elderly labourers, and the service ground irrevocably towards the moment when the banns were to be announced. They prayed for the men at the front, particularly Major Mark Russell, for all those who had been bereaved, and for all those who had been wounded. They prayed for victory, and for the King and Queen and their family. Christina prayed for herself.

The vicar read their banns.

There was a complete silence when he stopped speaking, so that the rainwater could be heard gurgling in the gutters up on the roof, and then it was followed by the rustling noise again, the turning and craning of all the stiff Sunday best, neighbour to neighbour, a great sigh of compressed astonishment.

'The *nerve* of the girl!' Mrs Lucas breathed. 'Can you imagine what old Russell –!'

'He'll be turning in his grave.'

'We're surely not that short of suitable young men?'

'Wasn't he the *stable-boy*? The one old Russell dismissed?'

'Worked under Fowler, aye. Got had for poaching.'

'Young Mark fathered a child on his sister. That little Tizzy ... would you believe!'

'And her husband only dead not a couple of years!'

'Twenty months I make it.'

'She ought to be ashamed, so soon!'

'It's her money he's after, you can see. And Flambards – she owns it all now.'

'It's to get his own back on old Russell's treatment of him, you mark my words! He'll be laughing up his sleeve.'

'She must be out of her mind, a woman in her position!'

'Whatever will Mr Mark have to say about it?'

'You mean to say he don't know?'

'Well, I don't know if he knows or not, do I? But what'll he say, can you imagine?'

'Well, they always say he was sweet on her himself, don't they? He wanted her before Will.'

'Yes, everyone knows that. But he's got a lovely wife now, and serve Miss Christina right. Perhaps she's marrying young Dick out of spite, because of Mark marrying that lovely girl.'

'Yes, could be!'

'And her mother, you know – I remember ...'

Christina, through all the rustling, sat very upright, gazing ahead. Although she could not hear anything that was said, she *knew* every last word of it; she knew even the unsaid thoughts. She was stepping out of line, shocking them. Socially, she was putting herself beyond the pale.

'But I'm a farmer,' she thought. 'Socializing is of no importance.'

Dick sat stiffly, expressionless. His face, closed down, reminded Christina of the time he had been called into Uncle Russell's study, to be dismissed. Will had always been on Dick's side. Mark had just laughed, the relationship between Dick and Mark had never been easy. But when the war was over Mark was going to live in Northamptonshire with Dorothy, in a property she owned, so there would be little occasion to meet. Life was much more peaceful without Mark. Life with Dick was going to be hard-working, straightforward, secure and comfortable. Christina had never been offered such a combination before, and had decided it would agree with her very well.

At the end of the service, after the vicar had left down the aisle and the choir had filed out, everyone waited for the occupants of the Russell pew to make the first exit among the congregation. It was the worst moment of all. Every face turned to the aisle. Christina felt as if the watching eyes glittered with malice, with deep disapproval, yet in fact they were politely masked of all emotion. She wanted to run, the stares stinging like a swarm of wasps. But she walked slowly, calmly, holding Tizzy by the hand, and looked straight ahead. At the door the vicar shook her hand and said drily, quietly, 'I trust the union will be a happy one, my dear. I shall pray for you both.'

Christina bit down an instinctive retort, smiled regally and stumbled out into the freshness of the winter rain and the wind cavorting amongst the yew trees. She held her hat, laughed.

'By gum, that'll give the vipers some ammunition,' Fowler said, stepping up behind.

Dick was pale, silent. Christina took his arm and gave him a shake.

'There, it's done. That's the worst over.'

He tried to raise a smile. 'Vipers – I'll say! I told you, give me a shell-hole in no-man's-land any day.'

Tizzy tugged at Christina. 'Ma, I've got to –'

'Yes, run behind the wall then, before they *all* come out. We'll wait by the trap.'

They went down the path and out into the lane. Someone came running after them, and they half-turned nervously. It was a young girl of about seventeen, very earnest, pink-cheeked, long fair hair falling out of its pins from under her best Sunday hat.

'Dick! Ma'am, please –' She came to a halt, flushing up shyly. 'I want to say – I do hope – I do hope you'll be very happy. I'm glad. I don't care what they say.'

Christina laughed. Dick said grimly, 'I can guess what they're saying, Rosie. We don't need your prayers!'

'I didn't mean –'

'No, Dick, she means it kindly,' Christina said quickly. 'Thank you, Rosie. It's very sweet of you.'

But the girl was rebuffed, and Dick had turned away to take off Pepper's nosebag. Christina saw something in the girl's expression that surprised her, the hurt more painful than it should have been, but she could think of nothing helpful to say before the girl ran back to join her parents at the gate. Christina recognized her father as a man who had a few acres and a cottage opposite the Flambards chase on the village side, a hard-working man of few words whose expression would not change if Dick was planning to marry Queen Mary herself.

'Someone wishes us well, anyway,' she said to cheer Dick, but her efforts were to no avail for, in waiting for Tizzy, they had to acknowledge the cool nods of Mr and Mrs Masters coming back to their motor-car. It was as embarrassing for them as for the Masters to exchange courtesies not meant. Masters, a big farmer, could obviously not bring himself to accept Dick on his level, and made no effort at civility, pulling out the starting-handle and busying himself with the mechanics, and Mrs Masters' brave attempt was worse, causing her such obvious discomfort. It would have helped if they could have driven quickly away, but Mr Masters' efforts with the starting-handle were not successful. Mrs Masters, having climbed up into the passenger seat, sat red-faced, waiting. Tizzy ran up and jumped into the trap, and Fowler picked up the whip, waiting to go.

'A minute, Fowler,' Dick said.

He sat watching Masters. Pepper, turned for home, scraped impatiently with a front hoof, pulling on the bit.

'Oh, Dick, please –' Christina felt she had had enough. Everyone was coming out into the lane, and a few were giggling at Masters' swearing. It was a nice diversion from the gossip. The morning at church was proving richer in interest than usual.

'It just needs a touch of the whip,' Fowler said, grinning.

'Why won't it go?' Tizzy asked in a loud voice.

'It's out of oats,' some wag shouted.

'Oh, let's go home,' Christina said. 'Fowler –'

'No. Wait.'

Dick got down from the trap and walked over to the Masters' car. He said something to Masters, and Masters straightened up. He looked angry, but was in no position to argue, and Dick opened the bonnet and leaned over, reaching inside. Masters peered in.

Dick said, 'Try it now.'

Masters swung the handle again and the engine fired. The bystanders cheered. Dick closed the bonnet, nodded to Masters and came back to the trap. If he was pleased he was very careful not to show it. Fowler eased the reins and Pepper moved away, eager, and everyone stood back, amused now, keenly interested in both the motor-car and the clash of personalities.

Fowler could not stop laughing. Once out on the road, he kept saying, 'That showed the old bugger! Eh, Dick? That showed him!'

Christina said, 'I thought you were a horse man? I'm the engine side of the family!'

'I started in the army with horses and got moved on to horsepower.' The incident had obviously given him some satisfaction, for the tension had gone. He smiled. 'Think he'll ask me to dinner on the strength of it?'

'Who wants his dinner anyway? It might teach him manners, the great oaf.'

'Why can't we have a motor-car?' Tizzy asked. 'They're better than horses.'

'Horses are reliable,' Fowler said. 'S'more than you can say for them things.'

Christina had a sudden, blinding vision of Will leaning over his darling Gnome rotary, cleaning something in its innards with the end of his scarf, his face grave, a lock of black hair falling over his forehead, and was suddenly dizzy

19

with her loss. It was like being punched in the stomach. She had to turn away, look out across the fields, bite her lip, to hide the shock. It was the dream come back, the haunting of her resolution which had never wavered these last few months. The wedding now so near, it was as if Will had a jealous spirit. It had a sting like a wasp.

'Are you all right?' Dick had noticed.

'Yes, of course.'

'You could have stayed at home, you know. It was brave, going.'

'And you. Gluttons for punishment, that's what we are. The wedding will be easy after that.'

'I reckon.'

'Just a little one, the family – and they're few enough. I don't suppose Mark and Dorothy will get leave. I wrote.'

'They don't give leaves for weddings these days.'

'You'd think Dorothy –' Dorothy was a nurse in the military hospital behind the lines at Étaples. But she had written to say they were exhausted coping with casualties. She had only seen Mark once since going back. They had been married three months. The start to their married life was exactly the same as her own had been with Will, for Will had gone into the R.F.C. three days after the end of their honeymoon.

'The war seems to have gone on for ever. I can't imagine what life will be like without it when peace comes.'

'We're winning!' Tizzy said. 'Uncle Mark said!'

'Now he's in the front line, of course.'

'Dick! That's naughty!' But Dick was smiling. Christina thought of something else. 'Tizzy will have to learn to call you father. You can't go on being Uncle Dick. Try it Tizzy.'

'Pa,' said Tizzy, and blushed.

They all laughed.

Christina said, 'Ma and Pa won't do, Tizzy. Mother or

father. Papa or mama. You really must learn to be a gentle-man.'

'Like me,' Dick said.

Fowler nearly fell off his seat laughing. Christina was thinking, Tizzy must call his real father Uncle Mark, and his real uncle he must call father. Life really was ridiculous. 'And another thing,' she said. 'While we're changing names, how about Tizzy being Thomas, which was what he was christened? Or Tom? Tizzy is a crazy name. Wait till you're married, and the vicar stands up in church and says Tizzy Mark Russell. Everyone will laugh.'

'Thomas,' said Tizzy, sampling it. 'It's stupid.'

'Tom. Tom and Dick. We only need Harry.'

'Give us time,' Dick said, 'and we might have him.'

Strangely, this remark gave Christina back her equanim-ity. The really stupid decision would be *not* to marry Dick. When they got home and Mary had the dinner ready, and they all sat down together in the kitchen, she felt that they were a family already. Will, the ghost, had his place, in Isobel, in her own cherished memories. He had always looked to the achievements of the future. So would she. And Harry. The thought of Harry warmed her. She had always had her sentimental dream of Flambards resounding to the cries and laughter of children, the ponies in the park, toys strewn through the hall. It was coming on well, her dream. After the war they would thrive, and the farm would bear great harvests (like Mr Masters') and the house would be painted and would shine and sparkle amid shaved lawns and rose-beds. After washing down her apple pie with a glass of port, she could see it quite clearly.

Meanwhile ... 'This wedding. There is no one to give me away.'

It would have to be Mr Saunders, Dorothy's father. Dick had no parents, no family save Violet in Rotherhithe.

'Have we got to ask Violet?'

'I don't reckon she'll come. She has no kind feelings towards Flambards, only bitterness.'

If Dick spoke without tact, it was no doubt with truth. Violet too had been dismissed, for being with child, with Tizzy.

'Does she know we're getting married?'

'I wrote, but she's not replied. Perhaps I should go and see her, explain things.'

'It might be the best thing. She doesn't like me. She won't like it.'

'We've never been close. It won't concern her. But it would be best, I daresay, to have a chat. I'll go up and see her, take Tizzy, Tom. Eh, Tom, would you like that? Go and see your old ma?'

'No, I don't want to.'

'Well, you will, so don't argue. Just for the day.'

Tizzy scowled. At six, he was twice the child he had been in Rotherhithe, brown and sturdy. Violet would scarcely know him.

'And I shall want a dress.' Christina frowned, remembering the one she had. She could not wear that dress again, rather go naked. 'I'll use one of those Hendon dresses, that I bought with Dorothy. When we were fashionable ladies! There's a lilac silk, very suitable for an old widow woman. And you, Dick – perhaps there's a suit of Mark's upstairs . . .'

Mark had never officially moved out. All his things were still in his room. Dick tried on a suit or two and they all got the giggles.

'Bridesmaids –'

'Marigold can be a bridesmaid,' Tizzy said. Marigold was a foxhound. 'Or Mary.' 'She can wear this.' Christina held out one of her old party dresses, deep pink trimmed with ostrich feathers. They laughed till they were weak.

'No bridesmaids,' Christina sighed. 'We don't know anybody.'

She folded the dresses up again, laying them back amongst the mothballs. They were out of date and too pretty; they would never be worn again.

Dick said, hesitantly, 'If you want one, there's that girl – this morning – Rosie. She would.'

Christina straightened up, serious. She remembered the flushed, hurt face, the lovely pink and gold of the girl, the dishevelled hair. A village girl, as Dick was a village boy. It was perfect.

'The only one to wish us well. She was kind. It would be lovely, Dick, if she would.'

'Of course she would!' Dick grinned. 'She'd do anything for me.'

'So that's it!'

'No. I'm joking. I'm friendly with her father. He was my father's friend, once. I've always known him. They helped my mother before she died.'

It was a lovely idea, that Dick would have someone there to link him with his past. And a village girl, to *show* the Masters and the Lucases and the rest of them . . .

Dick said, 'Your Aunt Grace won't like it.'

'She'll have to like it,' Christina said. 'She'll just have to!'

Aunt Grace did not like it.

She sat with Christina in the small sitting-room before the fire lit especially for the occasion, sipping tea from the best china, her kindly, ageing face disturbed by thoughts of Christina's future.

'I know, dear, that you have given it great thought, but I don't know if you realize how very deeply such a match upsets the natural order of things in the country community. I know you have learned your free-thinking from Will and your days out on those flying fields, but things are very different back here. I'm not saying that Dick isn't a very sound and pleasant fellow. But the fact that he was once a servant in this very place will never be forgotten by your neighbours, and any children you may bear may well suffer from it one day.'

Christina found it hard to be patient.

'But the war, Aunt Grace – and what is going on in France ... it is all changing! There's no class distinction in dying!' Seeing her aunt's expression, she tried to temper her impatience. 'I'm sure things will be different when the war is over. The men who come back – they've all been in it together ... how can they go back to the old ways? In Uncle Russell's day, here at Flambards, it was feudal. You know it was.'

'You've learned all this from Will and those friends of his. Remember, you're back at Flambards now. William never managed to change Flambards, did he, for all his liberal views? He left.'

'He left because of his father's cruelty towards him.'

'Well, I won't argue with that. But it was because he would not conform that old Russell used to get so angry with him. Mark conformed, and Russell loved Mark.'

'Russell never loved anyone,' Christina said softly.

'You only saw him as a crippled, embittered widower, my dear. There were happier days, none happier, before disaster came to this house. But that's all past history. It's the immediate future we have to talk about. I only want you to be happy, you know that. I have always accepted that you would marry again. It's quite natural. But I do want to be sure you choose the right person.'

'I have to be the judge of who is right for me, Aunt Grace. And I think it is Dick.'

'You seem very determined. I was afraid you might have made your decision through loneliness, or stubbornness.'

'I don't think so. You must see that, feelings apart, he fits in here. He is a farmer, he is Tizzy's uncle. He is a part of this place.'

'Yes.' Aunt Grace sat looking into the fire, very thoughtful. 'That is what worries me.'

'I don't understand.'

'He is a farmer, a very sound, honest man. He is intelligent, he is kind. He will run the farm very well. And what will you do?'

'I shall help him.'

'Yes. Perhaps.'

Christina was puzzled. Aunt Grace was being enigmatic, had changed her attack in a subtle manner. Christina waited, trying not to show the impatience she felt.

'What do you mean?'

'I mean this, Christina. You were given the choice of staying on at Flambards and being a farmer's wife a few years back, when Mark wanted to marry you. But you chose Will. And why did you choose Will?'

'Because I loved him.'

'And you loved him for what he was: imaginative, extremely clever, daring, very progressive in his views, always ready to take a risk. He gave you complete freedom, accepted you as an equal partner. It was his philosophy. He was no fireside man, Christina. He could never have been a farmer. And you loved him for what he was, because you are no fireside girl either. You are twenty-two now. A lot has happened to you in a short time, but your nature hasn't changed, my dear. You may well feel you want security now, but you might get boredom with it. You are very young, Christina.'

Christina, having been prepared for the first, and obvious, attack, was quite unprepared for this one. This one was clever, even unanswerable.

'But there will be a lot to do.'

'Chores, mainly. And the only excitement likely to come your way – hunting, which I know you love – is a sport not notable for its liberal outlook. The social side of it will be difficult for the pair of you.'

'The Hunt Ball, you mean? One can live without that.'

'Perhaps I'm really saying, think of it, Christina, that you are taking up that life you once turned your back on. And if it bores you, well, there is hunting. But in hunting you will not find the same attitude as you enjoyed on the flying-field. And for a girl that has flown the Channel in an aeroplane, life down on the farm might not be quite the prospect as, at the moment, she thinks it is.'

'I didn't like flying the Channel,' Christina muttered mutinously. But the argument was sound; she could not fault it. Damn Aunt Grace! As if she hadn't enough to cope with, with Will's ready ghost.

To throw a red herring, she said impatiently, 'I suppose you think I should have married Mark when I had the chance?'

'No, you made the right choice in Will, God rest him. And after that the choice was never open to you, was it?'

'Mark asked me, when he came home.'

'Silly boy. You children really are ignorant. I suppose you never had any real education down here. You should know that it is not open for a man to marry his dead brother's wife. It is against the law.'

'Really?' Christina was amazed. 'Why not?'

'Biblical, I believe. Hardly sensible. I fear this war might strain the rule somewhat, the way families have been stricken.'

Aunt Grace put down her teacup crisply. She always said what she thought adamantly, but without rancour, intending to help. She was kind, and usually right. She had always said that Will's profession was too dangerous for a girl to marry into. But it had been lovely while it lasted.

'I've said my piece. This war has put the world to sixes and sevens and no mistake. We must just pray that Mark comes home safely. Heaven knows what he will settle to after all this. He's no farmer either. He's like Will in that respect –

26

he likes his excitement too, but he never managed to find an outlet for his enthusiasms as Will did, save in his horses. A wild lad.'

Christina did not need Aunt Grace's pronouncements on Mark, for she knew Mark better than anyone alive, far better than poor Dorothy. She had had a love–hate relationship with Mark ever since the age of twelve and no doubt it would continue to the grave. And at that sentiment, she felt a shiver go through her, for grief that he might so very easily go the same way as Will. God knew, there were as many ways of loving as leaves on a tree, and she loved and had loved all three of them, the three boys of her childhood. She did not need Aunt Grace to tell her of their qualities and failings, for she knew them better than Aunt Grace, and, if Aunt Grace could see the situation from up on her pedestal of experience and wisdom, she could surely see that she, Christina, had gone into nothing without her eyes wide open.

As if to admit this unspoken thought, Aunt Grace said, 'I will say no more, Christina. You are a very sensible and brave girl. I just want to see you know what you are doing, with your head as well as your heart, and I want you to be very happy. You deserve it.'

Amen to that, Christina thought, how I do agree! She decided not to mention her bridesmaid, Rosie. A bridesmaid, in the whole context of the marriage, was nothing to worry about.

'You will come to the wedding? That is –' she smiled, pausing, 'if I do decide to get married?'

Aunt Grace laughed. 'Yes I shall travel down with Mr Saunders. He has already asked me.'

'I know, dear Aunt Grace, that all you say is true. But I shall not change my mind.'

'I feel better for having said it, and now I shall forget. God bless you, Christina. You deserve well.'

*

Dick travelled up to London with Tizzy to visit his sister Violet, and came home in the evening, quiet and thoughtful. Tizzy was full of his visit. His ma had given him a hoop and sweets and a new cap, and he had visited Charlie at the brewery and been out with the dray and had a fight with his sisters and been to the docks and seen a ship unloading ... Christina was unable to talk to Dick until he was packed away to bed, with his hoop. She had had a fire lit in the sitting-room. She did not want Mary listening in to their conversation. Christina had her bring coffee in on a tray, and leave them. They sat side by side on the big chintz-covered chesterfield, looking into the flames. It was cold outside and the long sash windows rattled every now and then in the wind, and the owls were hooting from the home covert. Familiar, secure ... boring? Christina smiled.

'Was it bad?'

'Not very good. No more than I expected. You can understand, the way she was treated here in the old days. She has only hard feelings towards Flambards and everyone in it.'

'What did she say?'

'Flambards takes everything it wants, and discards it when it no longer needs it.'

'And that applies to you?'

'She said, "Isn't Tizzy enough?" She wept over him. I wished I'd gone alone.'

'Tizzy will never be discarded. It's not like that now.' But she had no defence. She had taken Tizzy because she had wanted him. Violet was right. 'It's best for the child here. She must have seen how well he looks.'

'Yes. She said you do him proud. Because you're rich. And that is why I am marrying you.'

'For my money?'

'For your money, for the farm. Have I no pride?'

Dick leaned back, his eyes on the fire. He looked tired, drawn. Christina had come to look on him as a rock in her life and for the first time saw him buffeted. In his encounters with Mark he had been angry, stern in adversity, but now, in a similar encounter with his sister, he was hurt. She remembered his shyness as a boy, as a groom. He was only twenty-five now, and perhaps not entirely recovered from the tuberculosis he had contracted after being wounded. She needed him, but perhaps he needed her as badly. He had had very little happiness in his life up to now.

'If we listen to what everyone says, we might as well give up,' she said gently. 'Aunt Grace was as bad.'

'Did she say I was marrying you for your money?'

'No. She said I was used to an exciting life and might get bored with farming.'

'With me? Well, that's true.'

'I could have done without the excitement. It didn't make me happy, seeing Will doing his aerobatics.'

'It must have made you proud. I shall never make you proud.'

'You will make me happy, I think. And as for the money, Will was just as prickly about that . . . saying people thought he had married me so that he could afford an engine. People will always say that. It's a fact of life.'

She put up her arm and gently ruffled the hair on the back of his head. He turned and smiled.

'I never got on with Violet. I don't know why I expected her to wish me well over this.'

'You don't need her blessing, Dick.'

Dick put his arms around her and pulled her close to him, urgently. He buried his face in the thickness of her hair and said, 'I have loved you all my life! Violet knows that too. I do need you so, Christina!'

And the doubts were sealed. There was nothing uncertain in the strength of their desire, which Mary, with her penchant for timing, interrupted almost immediately with an inquiry about more coffee. Properly dowsed, they fixed the

29

wedding date and drew up a small list of invitations. Dick moved his possessions over to Flambards and two days later, on a wet Saturday morning, they were married in the parish church. It was so unlike her first wedding that Christina was spared the pain of drawing comparisons. She only knew that being united with Dick came as a great solace: a homing pigeon to its loft; she felt a sense of inevitability. They had planned no honeymoon. To be together at Flambards was all they needed.

But three days after the wedding a telegram was delivered to the door. It was from Dorothy in France and said, 'Mark wounded, desperately ill. Will keep you informed.'

Christina had gone to the door and received it, already sick in the stomach before she had opened the envelope. It looked identical to the one she had received about Will. When she had read the message and sent the boy away, she leaned against the door post and screwed the paper savagely in her hand and cried out loud, 'No! No! Oh, Mark! Not Mark!' The intrusion into her newborn security was like a spearthrust. And worse, Dick, seeing her anguish for Mark, turned away with a look on his face that was neither sympathy nor grief. It was resentment at Mark's intrusion into their happiness. Christina, recognizing it, sobbed bitterly.

But Dick came back and took her in his arms. 'Don't, Christina, don't cry. Don't cry for Mark.'

'For all of us!' she wept.

He said nothing else, but held her in his arms through the storm of tears. Once she had been brave and cool in the face of disaster, but now it seemed merciless; the injustice was more than she could bear. She wept for her own loss.

'He must be all right! I can't bear it!'

Dick held her and said nothing.

Chapter 2

'Spring is here. I can smell it,' Christina said. She could smell it in the bedroom, seeping in through the ill-fitting windows, the freshness of earth beginning to warm. Dick lay beside her, one arm holding her close.

'It's drilling weather. Lying here is wasting time.' But he did not move. Marrying Dick had been no mistake, Christina decided, for all her alarms. The sheer companionship of sharing her bed, the close warmth of a body, the endless conversations through grey dusks and dawns, was a lovely fact of life. She no longer dreamed of Will, but remembered the same times with him gratefully, without comparison.

She had had nightmares about Mark, before Dorothy's letter came, and Dick had held her again, tight and close, and let her cry. She dreaded to hear of his dying, his being mutilated; she had dreadful dreams of his injuries, and woke sweating and trembling. But, after a week that seemed three times as long, the news came through. He had severe abdominal injuries but was holding his own. The fact that he had lost neither arms, legs nor his sight, seemed to Christina a miraculous deliverance, but Dick was silent in face of Christina's optimism, and said merely, 'A limb off could well be kinder than that sort of injury, Christina.'

'At least he's *alive*!' It was all relative, no doubt; kinder to have an explosion in one's guts than one's head blown clean off. But knowing the facts calmed Christina.

'With luck it will be the finish for him, and the war will be over before he is fit.'

Dick thought it could well be the finish for him anyway, the Mark they knew, but made no more comment. He had been in hospital six months himself, and knew the score. He did not want to think of Mark. Mark was no longer the master of Flambards, having made it over to Christina, and he would not be coming back, and Dick felt nothing but relief in that respect. The two of them were congenital enemies, since boyhood, and the common ground of war-time experience had changed nothing. Knowing how he thought, Christina said gently, 'He's got Dorothy to look after him now. He will need her, to get through this.' Mark had never been a patient invalid.

'For better or for worse, eh?' Dick smiled again. 'I thought of you a few times when I was in hospital, Christina. Never thought I'd ever do this again.'

He kissed her.

'Some farmer you are! Six o'clock and still in bed!' But he kissed her again, and she loved his gentle body and his strength, and thought she had nothing to worry about.

The farm imposed a pattern, which they slipped into without effort. Dick worked outside all day, ploughing with the horses, harrowing, drilling, setting tasks for the men: Wilhelm, the German prisoner, Harry, the stupid village boy, Fowler, and a new man called John, invalided out with the loss of an eye and proving very useful. Christina saw to the children and the house and Mary did the cooking, but it was too much for them and a housemaid was sorely needed.

'The place is no better than it was in old Russell's day – there's too much of it to keep clean!' Christina complained.

'You'll have to hire another Violet then,' Dick agreed. 'Shall I write and ask her?'

'That's a joke, I hope?'

'Never fear, yes. Hire what you please – if you can, that is. All the girls prefer to work in factories these days.'

'Well, I don't blame them, now they've got the chance. But

I might be lucky. I'll ask around. Mrs Masters might know someone.'

Dick raised his eyebrows. 'Does she speak to you then? Are you on her visiting list?'

'Don't be so touchy. Yes. She's not as bad as some. I'll get round to asking them to dinner one of these days.'

Dick made a face. 'No hurry is there? I haven't noticed her husband going out of his way to pass the time of day with me.'

'Well, we'll wait till his Crossley starts playing up, and he'll not resist an invitation then, to get some free advice.'

Dick laughed. 'It was luck before, that I knew what to do. I'm no mechanic. I'm still a horse man.'

'If I ran this farm –'

'Don't you?' he said, wide-eyed.

'No. You're too bossy to let me.'

She spoke in jest, but with the scent of spring in her nostrils she was also aware of a faint regret in the loss of her responsibility. It was no good reminding herself that it had been too much for her, that she had been desperate for Dick's help; it was not a reasoned feeling, just an instinct. She had been so ridiculously proud and happy when things had worked, out of all proportion.

'The trouble is, Isobel Russell,' she said to her baby as she dressed her on her knee, 'I'm not used to being domesticated. I must learn to be a good housewife, and make jam.'

Isobel was one year old. She had a birthday cake, but no icing for there was no sugar. Tizzy insisted on putting a household candle in the middle, pressing it down into the soft, risen top and lighting it with one of Mary's tapers, so that it was a positive beacon of a cake, flaming in the middle of the table. Isobel loved it, holding out her hands to the flames.

'God almighty, it's a lighthouse!' Dick said, coming in as daylight faded into dusk.

'It'll soon be iced with candle-grease, that rate, Mr Tizzy,' Mary snorted. 'My cake –'

'Tom,' said Tizzy. 'You're to call me Tom.'

'Really? Well, you're perverse and no mistake. At least it's a name. Just you get your dirty boots off that bit of floor, Dick now. I've scrubbed it this afternoon and it won't get done again for a week.'

Christina glanced up and saw the look come into Dick's face which she had seen before. He did not like Mary treating him as if he was still the stable-boy, and was going to be sharp with her if she persisted. Christina thought she must have a private word with Mary before there was any ill-feeling. Their ranks had got badly confused since her return to Flambards, and it was largely her fault. Dick was much stricter with his men than she was in the house with Mary and Fowler. It had surprised her, how quickly and surely he had taken command.

He said, 'I met the postman coming up with a letter. It looks like Dorothy's writing – it's from France.'

He gave it to Christina.

'Oh, I hope it's not bad news!' Christina tore it open and read it rapidly, her face lighting up. 'No, it's lovely! Dorothy is coming to see us – she's got leave. She's going to call on – hey, what's the date? The twenty-fourth. It's tomorrow! She's coming tomorrow! She says all the news when I see you. Oh, how splendid!'

'If she's got leave you'd think she'd spend it with Mark, nursing him,' Mary said.

Dick gave her a sour look. 'No doubt she's got leave because they reckon she needs rest from being up to her elbows in blood twenty-four hours a day. Those nurses crack up, same as the men. There's things they do every day, take for granted, that would put you in a dead faint at the mere sight.'

'Dick, don't!'

Christina took his cap and jacket, and pulled his chair out at the table. 'Perhaps Mark has been sent to hospital over here, and she's coming with him. We'll find out tomorrow.'

'Is Uncle Mark coming?' Tizzy asked excitedly. 'Uncle Mark as well?'

'No, he's not. Sit down, Tizzy. Mind the milk, for heaven's sake!'

'Tom.'

'Tom then. Perhaps Tom's got better manners than Tizzy.'

'No he hasn't.'

'Pity. I thought we could demonstrate for your Aunt Dorothy.'

'I suppose that means the spare room doing up and the bed aired,' Mary grumbled. 'And a smart dinner in the dining-room?'

'Yes, it does.'

Dick said, 'I don't see why now the weather's getting warmer we shouldn't eat in the dining-room every night. It's a right rubbish tip in here. A smart dinner every night, in fact.'

Mary put down her pan of eggs on the range with a crash and turned round like a vixen defending her cubs. 'That's nice from you, young man! I remember how *you* lived in that filthy hovel before your ma died –'

'Mary!' Christina leapt up in a panic. 'Stop it! You –'

'A rubbish tip he calls it! Well, if he wants to be the fine gentleman now let him get some more servants then and play the part properly! An old woman like me – working my fingers to the bone – I remember you, young lad, when you –'

'*Mary!*'

Christina took her by the shoulders and shook her hard to prevent the fearful words spilling out. Dick sat with a face like thunder. Mary, shocked by Christina's force burst into a great flood of tears. 'I know when I'm not wanted. I'll go tonight. I'll pack my bags and go. I'm not working for a trumped-up stable lad –'

She nearly bit her tongue at Christina's final shake, and broke off. Christina marched her out of the kitchen and down the passage into the hall and sat her down firmly on the settle under the window. Never had she seen the dour, redoubtable Mary in tears, save of compassion at deaths and weddings, and it upset her nearly to tears herself.

'Hush, hush, hush. Don't, Mary. Of course you won't go! Dick didn't mean to criticize. You *are* overworked and we shall get another girl. I promise you. Please, Mary, don't upset yourself.'

The old woman calmed down at the rush of sympathy, Christina talking as if to an animal, soothing, non-stop. But when she had grudgingly agreed to stay, Christina knew she had to have the last word.

'And you must never talk like that to Dick again.'

Mary gave a contemptuous sniff. 'He –'

'Be quiet. He is the master here now, and you must serve him. And if you won't, then you must go. You must obey him like you used to obey Mr Russell.'

'His mother was a *housemaid –*'

'It's no matter. What he said was quite right. We shall eat in the dining-room in future, and you shall have a girl to help you and she shall wait on. And you will call Dick "Mr Wright".'

Mary positively wailed at this, and Christina took her up to her room, holding her firmly by the elbow.

'I will bring your tea up later, and you can tell me if you wish to stay. If you think about it, Mary, you will see that it must be like this. We have let everything get slack, because life has been such a mix-up. It has been my fault as much as anybody's. But now it must be as it used to be, in Mr Russell's day, and Dick – Mr Wright – is the master. And he'll be a far kinder one than ever Mr Russell was, you know that.'

She marched out firmly, but found herself much more shaken than she knew. She blamed herself bitterly for not forestalling the situation. She went hesitantly back to the kitchen and found that Dick had taken over the eggs and was scrambling them in male fashion, standing at the range.

'She must go,' he said, 'unless she can keep a civil tongue.'

His words stung Christina, compelling a rush of loyalty back to Mary, who was a cornerstone of Flambards, had been there all her life. She had been at the wedding of old Russell and the mythical Isobel, Mark and Will's mother, whom Christina had never known; Mary remembered, when she was a girl, Russell being born, and Aunt Grace, and Hettie, who had been Christina's mother. She was Flambards' history. But Christina knew better than to defend her.

'It's my fault,' she said briefly. 'I will see that things are organized better.'

'You were talking earlier about asking the Masters to dinner. I've got to get some practice in at using the right knives and forks and passing the port, so we'd better start now.'

He spoke curtly, for the first time in their married life. Christina was tactful enough to let it pass. She took the eggs off him and served them out, forcing herself not to be upset.

'They're hard,' Tizzy said. 'Burnt.'

'Just like you get in the army,' Dick said. 'I thought you wanted to be a soldier?'

Tizzy could not answer that one. 'Has Uncle Mark got bullets in him?'

'Shell splinters, more likely.'

'Is that what you got?'

'That's right.'

'Did they take them out?'

'Yes.'

'Have you still got them? Did you keep them?'

'No. I don't like that sort of souvenir.'

'I would. I'd keep them. They'd all be covered in bl—'

'Tizzy!'

'Tom.'

'Oh, stop it! I've had enough! It's Isobel's birthday and I want to enjoy my tea.'

Christina longed to see Dorothy again, her mad friend from her flying days, with whom she had shared excitements and griefs that Dick knew nothing of. She fixed her mind on the coming visit to block out the clash between Dick and Mary, and later made up Dorothy's room herself, to show Mary that she was sympathetic. The next day she dusted and polished the dining-room and put some catkins and daffodils on the sideboard, and made her first real attempt in the village to find a girl who would come and help, to wait on the table and call Dick 'sir'. There was a young woman with two children whose husband had been killed; she said her mother would mind the children and she could come up every day.

'The hours will be long. You will have to stay until after supper. Will that suit you?'

'I've not much choice, ma'am. I'll do my best.'

Her name was Amy and she looked sturdy and resigned. Christina went home and told the subdued Mary, and Mary said, 'Amy Partridge that was? She was in the same class as Dick at school.'

'As Mr Wright,' Christina said sharply. Mary's information made her heart sink – she should have guessed! She must impress upon Amy that she was not to be familiar; she had not thought of it when she had interviewed her.

'She's starting tomorrow,' she told Mary. 'So you won't have so much to do. You will feel better about everything.'

Having achieved justice on this front, she went to meet

Dorothy at the station in a happier frame of mind. She drove in the trap, alone, remembering this same journey in other circumstances. Journeys in her life seemed to have been connected with changes of fortune, or death, not ever with going to the seaside for a holiday or up to London for a spree. She had come on the train as a child to start her life at Flambards; she had come back years later for Russell's funeral, after Will's death; she had met Mark when he had come home from being a prisoner-of-war a mere few months back. All of them occasions of momentous importance in her life . . . no wonder the station gave her an instinctive feeling of uneasiness! She felt it even now, driving Pepper up the approach beside the station-master's vegetable garden, a feeling at variance with the innate peace of the place, where everything happened to time, the fruiting of Mr King's vegetables no less than the arrival of the down train. The day was mild and still. Empty milk churns were being loaded; some calves bellowed from a van in the siding. There is nothing to upset me now, Christina thought. I have Dick, Dorothy will be here in a minute. Mark is going to live. She sat waiting, persuading herself into tranquillity. The grass verges were full of cowslips, opening to a milky sunlight. The whistle of the approaching train could be heard far away across the ploughed fields. She put down the reins and climbed down.

She would scarcely have known Dorothy if she had not been expecting her. Even as they embraced and Dorothy was laughing – 'Christina, you look marvellous! Why, you're getting plump! Country living –' she knew better than to try dissembling with similar exclamations of admiration. 'They made me come home, I had no choice,' she was saying, and Christina, seeing Dorothy's gaunt face and strained eyes, knew that 'they' were right. Glamorous, radiant Dorothy . . . she was a shadow of her earlier self, too thin, with a brittle animation that suggested shattered nerves. 'I wanted to wait and come with Mark, but they wouldn't let me. I suppose what happened to him broke me up rather. I was all right till then. Tired, but – well, I was coping. We have to.'

Her brightness faded suddenly. She looked anguished, close to tears. Christina took her small suitcase from her and put her arm round her.

'You must need a rest, away from all that! You will love it here – however long you wish to stay. It's so lovely to have you, and wonderful that Mark is going to be all right.'

They climbed up into the trap and Dorothy settled herself quietly. 'Yes,' she said. 'It will be all right for us in the end. I keep telling myself that.'

Christina picked up the reins and Pepper turned for home. 'He is all right, isn't he? There's nothing you haven't told us?'

'No, but it's bad enough – touch and go whether he came through for a few days. He still can't be moved. He wasn't sent to our place, but they gave me time off to go and see him, just quick visits. There was nothing I could do, and so much to do in my own place ... oh, you can't imagine! It seems so unreal here, I just can't get used to it, being here – and knowing that over there –' She shrugged and broke off. 'Everyone says, when they've been on leave –' She broke off again and made a great effort to wipe the bleakness from her face. 'Well, perhaps now Mark is out of it, and you're safe with Dick ... it can't last for ever. We shall come through, and forget.'

Christina did not think that Dorothy would ever forget, but did not argue. She could think of nothing adequate to say. Their friendship had been established in the old days, before the war, with Will and his friend Sandy who had been killed in a flying accident, and later with Mark; Dick had never entered into the circle. It had not occurred to Christina before, but it did now, as Pepper drew steadily up the long drive to Flambards, that Dick and Dorothy might not have a great deal to say to each other. They overlapped nowhere, save through Mark. And that, to Dick, was no recommendation.

She was right.

Dorothy, in spite of her weariness and despair, was still a highly sophisticated, far from country girl, a type Dick knew nothing of. Mary and Fowler thought she was wonderful and dazzling and, as Mark's wife, could do no wrong; they revered her, rushed to do her slightest bidding. But Dick, who had to treat her as a familiar, could find no common ground at all. Having washed and changed for dinner into his good wedding suit, he sat at the head of the table in silence. Christina could see that Dorothy was too worn-out to make the effort to coax him into conversation and it fell to her to try to include him in it, which she found a great strain. With Mary waiting on and butting in, Dick out of his element, and Dorothy with little on her mind save Mark, Christina longed to be alone with Dorothy in her own sitting-room, just the two of them together as it had been in the old days – and this thought brought with it the guilt feeling of disloyalty. Nothing was right. She asked Dick to open a bottle of port, hoping to improve the atmosphere, and after a glass or two Dick and Dorothy found their one common subject on which to discourse: hospital life in France and the nature of wounds, the damage inflicted on human flesh by the explosion of a shell. Technical it might have been, but with the searing memory of the irreparable damage Will had suffered in this way, Christina found that the port and the ensuing conversation moved her only to utter grief. The dessert course ended in a more dismal silence than the earlier silence of embarrassment.

Dick put his spoon down and folded his napkin.

'I reckon I'll go down the farm and see if Nellie's started calving. I might have to stay a while, Christina, if she's under way. You'll excuse me . . .'

He went out, no doubt to change back into his farm clothes. Christina felt the tension go out of her, a feeling of caving in, a rush of relief. She glanced up and knew that it was the same with Dorothy. They were together in their old way, as if the last year or two had been blotted out, as if Will and Sandy would breeze in at any moment to laugh and tease, as if nothing had come between. The sweetness of it was the worst of all: they were both crying now, reaching out hands across the table. But there were no other words to express these ridiculous sentiments, and a feeling that to linger on this quaky ground was dangerous; they were both of them realists by nature.

'Strong coffee, don't you think?' Christina suggested, wiping her eyes. 'We'll sit by the fire and talk knitting.'

'The very thing. Recipes and how hard it is to get servants.'

'Marrow jam. Exactly.'

Christina loved the balm of her old – her only – friend's company, who had been with her through all her best and worst times. They talked on into the night, sitting by the flickering firelight, and for the only time in her life Christina could admit the hopes and the doubts she felt for her future, and could listen in return to those same hopes and doubts expressed by Dorothy for her future with Mark.

'Whom I scarcely know, if the truth were told. Even now, we have lived together for only three days. And it frightens me, knowing how fickle my nature is. I shouldn't have married, Christina. I'm such a flibbertigibbet, and I'm not like you, strong in the face of – well, all these awful things that happen. I just can't see what will become of us.'

'But who can, with what is happening? I am supposed to have done a crazy thing too, from what people say. You saw the worst of it this evening. Dick for me is just as risky as Mark for you. And you underestimate yourself, you know. You might have been like that once, but now you have proved your strength by what you are doing. When you have come through this, anything afterwards will seem easy by comparison.'

'But not with relationships, and coping with people at home, being difficult. That's what I'm so bad at. If men get difficult, you see, I've always tended to drift on to another one. But now I can't. You know that's true, if you cast your mind back. Look how many men I went through while you remained steady with Will.'

Yes, Christina remembered, that was quite true. Dear Sandy had suffered dreadfully through loving Dorothy and seeing her going out with all the others.

'And now, with Mark, it's not going to be a good beginning, now that this has happened. We neither of us have much patience, and we shall need patience before Mark is well again. I know his sort. They're bad invalids.'

'That's true.'

'The quiet ones, your sort – like Will, and Dick – they're the ones that put up with it. I've seen them. Oh, my God, I've seen them . . .'

She started to cry again in a soft, hopeless way, and Christina sat and listened to her tales, not wanting to know, not daring to stop her. The fire fell into embers and they wept for the dead men, and went to bed and cried some more. Dick did not come back and Christina lay exhausted through the still, moonlit night, wondering at the despair released in Dorothy, remembering the effervescent creature that she had been. But in the morning, although white and hollow-eyed, Dorothy was her old, hard-edged self, the bright, funny, brisk business girl, hospital sister, organizer of staff and households. She organized Amy the new maid while Christina saw to Isobel, she made Dick his breakfast when he came in from the farm, almost asleep, from his difficult calving – 'Really, you should have called me, Dick. Delivering babies in air raids is one of my specialities, and

I'm sure I could cope with a mere cow!' – and she charmed all the farm-hands by producing hot tea when they came down to collect their wages in the kitchen. Away from the dinner table, Dick was easier and Dorothy found new energy to include him in her charming, so that he relaxed and in the afternoon took her at her word to help him with another calving. The change seemed to do Dorothy good, for within a few days, the gauntness went out of her face and she did not speak again of France, nor cry, but played with great gentleness with Isobel and read stories to Tizzy like a born auntie.

On the morning Christina took her back to the station, she was quiet and resigned and said she was ready to go back.

'You can't imagine – how much better I feel after these few days, knowing that there is still sanity in the world. I shall remember these days when things are bad, and it will see me through.'

'It can't be much longer.'

'No. There aren't men enough.'

'When you come home . . .' Christina had thought a good deal about what would happen when life became normal again for Mark and Dorothy. Dorothy owned a property in the Midlands that they had said they would make into a home and as they no longer had ties in Essex or London, she presumed that was what would happen. But she knew she would love to have Dorothy near her; the knowledge that there was no real future in this rewarding friendship made saying good-bye much harder than it might have been.

She amended her remark. 'When Mark comes home . . . I suppose he will be sent back when he is ready – do you know where he will go?'

'No. But I suppose one of the London hospitals first, then to a convalescent home somewhere. It worries me rather, as I don't suppose I shall be allowed home to look after him. He'll have to go to father in Kingston, perhaps.'

'I shall visit him, of course, as soon as he comes back. I will do what I can. But you know how it is between Dick and him. I shall have to be tactful.'

Dorothy laughed. 'Yes, to make up for Mark. Tact and being sensitive about other people's feelings are not his strong points. He really is incredibly selfish.'

'Yes. He's fine if everything is going his way. And I suppose now it isn't. Poor Mark.'

'He's well out of it, Christina, even at such cost. He could well prove to be one of the lucky ones in the end, like Dick.'

'I hope so. Give him my love when you see him, and if there is any way I can help, do let me know.'

The parting was painful, and Christina tried not to give in to the blanket of depression that descended on her on the way home. She had enjoyed Dorothy's lively presence; there was a common wavelength between them which made words, explanations, unnecessary. It was perfect comradeship, built on past experiences both physical and emotional; it could not be shared with anyone else. When she got home she was aware of standing away from Dick, harking back to Dorothy with childish longing, their past painfully alive. She wanted to be on her own until the feeling died. It was disquieting and aroused in her the guilt feeling of disloyalty to Dick, but it was too instinctive to be stifled. She went out, taking the foxhound Marigold, and walked through the home fields and coverts, avoiding the farm boys, finding the old paths through the tangled, unkempt woods where no one went now. It was difficult going, but it was what she needed, tiring herself in struggles with bramble and eglantine, dragging herself through ditches and over banks and under wire fences. It was cold, the sky grey and dismal, and her steps disturbed dank odours of fungus and roots, elemental and satisfying. The first primroses were thick by the stream as they had always been and evoked – as always – a sense of optimism, that they showed so early out of the cold ground, and would always do so, a part of nature's unchangeable pattern. 'We change,' Christina thought, 'we change our allegiances, our plans, our motives, but out here . . .' Mere ground – empty fields and woods, the cawing rooks, the first pink flush of new bud on the bare twigs – put her disquiet into perspective. She was tired, comforted, and turned back hopefully, wanting Dick now. It was beginning to go dark and she was hungry. She came out in the top of the horse meadows facing the house, and walked down the length of the long hedgerow, climbed the iron fence at the bottom and crossed the drive. Fowler was just going in for his tea.

'Where's Dick, Fowler?'

'Why, ma'am, he's looking for you. Sent me to fetch you.' He was laughing and looked excited. 'He's got something to show you, ma'am. You go along to the stable now. You'll get a surprise and no mistake.'

'What is it?' His excitement was infectious.

'I'm not saying. You go and see for yourself.'

Christina, postponing an urgent desire for hot tea, picked up her muddy skirts and swung round for the stable yard. No longer, as it had been once, the hub of Flambards' life, the yard housed only Pepper, the all-purpose nag, and Pheasant, Christina's temperamental young thoroughbred which was out of action after an accident in some wire. Christina missed her riding. She did not find much joy in riding the stolid Pepper, but loved Pheasant. Dick considered Pheasant dangerous and did not like her riding him, an argument held in abeyance by the horse's injury. He had preferred her on Woodpigeon, but Woodpigeon had had to be put down, growing infirm in his old age. As she went under the archway into the yard, she heard Pheasant whinny, an excited note, and another horse answered. It did not sound like Pepper.

'Dick!'

A light was shining through the stable windows. She

crossed the cobbled yard and Dick shouted, 'In here!' For a fleeting moment she thought he had bought her a gorgeous hunter, to show her how much he loved her, but when she went in she saw immediately that the new horse was not a gorgeous hunter. It was a desperately broken-down old mare, once a roan but now almost white with age. It stood in one of the big hunter boxes, its nose deep in a bucket of gruel which Dick was holding. Its spine stood out all along its back, all the vertebrae showing; its neck was caved in and weak, the mane in unkempt ropes to its shoulder, and its belly swollen.

'Dick, whatever –?'

Dick looked up, smiling. 'So you don't recognize her?'

Christina looked again.

Dick said, 'You got me sacked, once, for the sake of this mare.'

'Sweetbriar!'

'I bought her before the knacker got her. Your money, but I knew you would want it that way.'

'Oh, Dick, of course! How awful –'

Christina felt that the past was coming up to clobber her with a vengeance, seeing the poor mare standing there, remembering the drama they had all been involved in as children, when Uncle Russell had ordered her to be destroyed after she had been injured in an accident. Christina had persuaded Dick into taking her into hiding instead of to the knacker's and when the deceit had been found out Dick had been dismissed. She had stood in this very spot after Uncle Russell's brutal decision, and cried, and Dick, for the first time, had taken her in his arms to comfort her. He had been fifteen then; she remembered clearly even now the feelings of that moment, of having a breast to cry on after her bleak childhood, of Dick's calm and pure sense after the demented arguments back in the house, of Dick going to answer for his disobedience like a Christian to the lions. The sad strawberry-roan mare brought it all back as if there had been no years between.

'How strange!'

'Brings it all back, eh? Things best forgotten, I reckon. Save me kissing you that night.' He grinned. 'The only good bit. I remember that best.'

'Yes. And you saying – how right you were! – that sometimes it's best for a horse to be shot than sold off when it's old and unsound. Whatever's happened to her, that she looks like this?'

'Well, it's not as bad as it looks. An old boy had her over Danford way, and he bred a foal or two from her, but this winter he died and his stock was neglected, just this last three months, they say. And his nephew come along and sent the lot to market, and I happened to look in there this morning. Nobody was bidding much and I knew you'd have wanted me to do it. She's in foal, you know, so it's not money thrown away.'

'Oh, how lovely! It's wonderful to have her back! She taught me to ride – I owe her everything.'

'Well, there was a lad alongside, if you remember, telling you what to do.'

Christina laughed. 'Funny lad – I remember him well. He was a very good teacher. I wonder what became of him?'

'He made good. Got what he wanted in the end, that lad.'

Christina went to him. 'Me, you mean?'

'That's what I mean, yes.'

He put the bucket down in the straw. 'Just like old times.' He put his arms round her and kissed her. Christina felt the same sense of haven as she had the first time, laying her cheek against his hard collarbone.

'You smell just the same.'

'Manure and hard sweat.'

'Yes.' She paused, remembering. 'Will used to smell of oil. Always.'

'There's something about you, likes the smell of honest endeavour.'

'That must be it. I like workers.' The day had been a day of mixed emotions. Thinking back to its beginning, she said, 'And Dorothy too – she smelled of carbolic. She said so herself. She's a worker. When I think what she does, it makes me feel inferior. Guilty that I can still enjoy myself here. And have Sweetbriar back. And you.'

'In that order?'

'Well, naturally.'

'I'm hungry. I hope you've been slaving over my dinner.'

'No such luck. But perhaps Mary has. We'll go and see. It's lovely to have Sweetbriar back.'

'Well, she's got a soft billet here. I've given her hay and a good bed. She'll be happy tonight. We've done her a good turn, I reckon.'

They walked back to the house, Dick with his arm round her. Christina felt drained, but soothed by the Sweetbriar incident. Animals were always a solace after the things humans did to each other; she had proved it many times. At the back of her mind she was uneasy about Mark coming back to England with no home to come back to. The uneasiness was provoked by the knowledge that it was she who had bought him out of Flambards and paid off the mountain of debt that Uncle Russell had left; she had taken his place as owner of Flambards. But walking back towards the old creeper-covered house, seeing the new leaves ready to break on the chestnut trees down the drive, and the sloping home paddocks with their trim hedges and repaired railings fading into the evening dusk, looking towards the lights that gleamed faintly behind drawn curtains, she felt a powerful surge of affection for the place. And she knew that Mark had the same streak of sentiment, for all his brave, rough ways. He had never known another home. And when he was drunk he would reveal an astonishingly tender core, fixed on the ways and places of his boyhood, and on the rambling house and the old hunters he remembered, everything that added up to Flambards. Mark had never been the one for change, for progress. He liked things as they were. And Christina could not help thinking of this now that he was on the scrap-heap. The Northampton property of Dorothy's, un-inhabited for several years, was going to take a deal of putting right. If Dorothy was unable to leave France, someone was going to have to make decisions for Mark. She hoped very much that it would not have to be her.

Chapter 3

Christina followed the nurse nervously up the wide, carved staircase, clutching her bunch of lilac and a couple of books on hunting out of the bookcase at home. The hospital was a commandeered house in Highgate, still very gracious in spite of being stripped of its normal trappings, no sign of wards with rows of beds, but civilized rooms like private bedrooms, with curtains and carpets. The sun streamed in through the long landing windows and through the branches of beech and silver birch a hazy blue view of London shimmered to the far horizon, skylights glittering here and there like jewels. A pair of thrushes were singing their heads off. The carpets muffled the nurse's brisk tread. Christina could not help wondering at such elegance embracing mortal suffering; it made the agony of war unreal, yet the evidence was only too plain that it was real. There were men in the garden with limbs missing; another passed on the arm of a nurse, his head and eyes swathed in bandages. Christina, thinking of Dorothy, knew that a good deal of her nervousness was for finding Mark in such a condition. She was such an amateur when it came to physical suffering, knowing it only by hearsay. Even Will, who had died a minute or two after being dragged from his plane ... she had suffered only the pain of the telegram's message, never known his physical pain at all. She looked closely at the nurse, for evidence of her distress, but the girl's face was fresh and untroubled. The resilience of human nature amazed Christina, her own included. She walked on, feeling she was in a dream.

'In here.'

The nurse opened a door into a small, sunny room with a large bay window. There were two beds in it, one empty. In the other, Mark lay propped on pillows, his head turned towards the sunshine. He did not move to see who it was, until the nurse withdrew and Christina was forced to say, 'Mark –'

Her voice was shaky, and the lilac shivered in her hands.

He turned and looked at her. He said nothing, and neither did she. What emotion moved in him she could not tell, but she was shocked by her own strength of feeling, which she had great difficulty in hiding. It was as if he was not Mark alone, but Mark and Will together, the tangled loves of her childhood distilled in the dark Russell eyes. Mark had a way of looking, when he was low, which was just like Will concentrating over a tricky bit of mathematics; the dear familiarity of that expression speared Christine. And worse, it was not particularly the remembrance of Will that hurt, but an instinctive pang for Mark, companion of wild galloping days through the winters of their youth, brought to such a pass by politics he would never understand, an outside world that he had never tried to know. Will had been the political animal. Mark had joined the cavalry merely to keep on galloping. The war, it appeared to Christina, had done for him almost as completely as it had done for Will.

'You're alive, at least,' was all she could find to say, when her tongue would work again.

'Kiss me, Christina. Prove you're real.'

She walked to the bed and bent and kissed his forehead. It was very hot, and his breathing was rapid and painful. He reached for her hand.

'Sit here, close.'

'I'm not running off. I've got all day, I'll stay with you if they'll let me.'

Once before in her life she had sat at Mark's bedside when he needed her, after Dick had beaten him up for getting Violet pregnant. He must be remembering it too, she was sure, by the way he smiled as his hand took hers.

'Don't tell Dick!' He found speaking exhausting, she could tell, but even in his present condition there was the old mockery in his expression.

'Hush, stupid. It's not like that any more. Dick is just as sorry as I am, you know that. We've all been worried to death about you since we heard the news.'

She felt she had to talk on, for sitting in silence was painful, and it was obvious that Mark could contribute little. He was terribly weak and thin.

He said, 'I can't breathe. I can't eat and I can't sleep ... the trouble – is – I can't die either.'

'No, well, you've always been awkward.' She had to cover up with banter else she would have broken down. Mark, of them all, had always been the one with immense physical energy. Even in repose he had generated a restless atmosphere; one never relaxed for long in Mark's company. He acted first, thought later, and accepted the consequences as they came, good with laughter and bad with a shrug. He invoked great passions: of anger as much as love; he was utterly selfish, and equally charming. Christina knew that he would never surprise her again, having in ten years gone through the whole gamut from elation to despair in his company, having loved and hated him with equal force. She saw him now as one of the children, needing her loving care, Tizzy's father needing her as Tizzy himself needed her. But she was no longer in a position to give it. He drifted into uneasy sleep while she talked, still holding her hand. Unconscious, he moaned and muttered, and his lips twitched continually. Once he threshed out with his arms, throwing off the blankets, and she saw that his whole body was a mass of bandages.

Christina went and stood at the window, looking out over the peaceful gardens and the haze of London, feeling bludgeoned and sick. The garden was full of shattered men. Not long ago it had been Dick ... Will. Now Mark. But her experience was common enough. Some women had lost four, five sons. How did they go on living? She felt very tired.

A nurse came in. She was young, and had the same taut, brittle look that Christina remembered in Dorothy, compounded probably of too little sleep and too much responsibility.

'Oh, I didn't know – I'm sorry ...' She glanced towards the bed. 'I'll come back later.'

'No. It makes no difference, now he's sleeping.'

'He needs it. Are you his wife?'

'No. His sister-in-law.'

'I see. You're his first visitor – I didn't know – he's so ill, it makes little difference at this stage.'

'Is he going to be all right?'

'Well –' The nurse paused, sighed. 'Yes, I daresay. He should have been dead right from the start, you see, but having got so far, one can be optimistic. He must be lucky. A shell exploded amongst six of them, and the other five were killed. It's all relative, you understand, that with injuries like his one can be considered lucky.'

She gave Christina a wan smile.

'If you wish to stay and see him again later, the Red Cross ladies downstairs will give you a cup of tea.'

Christina felt annihilated by her day when she got back to Flambards late in the evening. It was hard to answer Mary's eager questions, and Tizzy's childish curiosity. It was all mixed up with the excitement of Sweetbriar's having produced a foal. They dragged her out to see, and in the flickering lamplight all she could think of was Mark facing the same Sweetbriar at a monstrous hedge out hunting and somersaulting to disaster. Now the mare nuzzled protectively at the little thing lying in the straw, all legs and long, inquisitive ears, and Christina was moved to sentimental snuffles at the sight of Tizzy, Mark's son, sitting in the straw with the colt that was Sweetbriar's son, the generations repeated, the story unwinding with the capricious inevitability that was real life, nothing ever finished and rounded off, but new growth springing from the old. Oh, the mawkish wanderings of her weary mind! She went back to the house and slumped wearily on the best chesterfield before the remains of the fire. Dick came and sat by her.

'It was awful,' she said.

'Yes. I guessed. It is.'

They stared into the embers, and he put out a hand and rested it on the back of her neck, his fingers gently stroking her cheek.

'Poor Christina.'

'Poor Mark.'

But Dick showed no resentment, merely a brother-soldier's pity, perfectly genuine.

'It will be a long time for him,' Christina said, and she was glad she had no decisions to make, for she knew she was not fit.

She was in a difficult position for, much as she felt she should visit Mark, it was not easy to spend the long day away from Flambards and the children. At first he was too ill for it to matter much, but as the summer progressed and he grew gradually stronger, with his returning strength came the characteristic demands.

'You're the only one I've got, Christina. Everyone else has wives and sweethearts and sisters and mothers. You're supposed to do your bit, you know, stroke my brow and all that. Stand in for Dorothy. I need you.'

'Being speechless became you,' she said bluntly. 'I might have known, when you got your breath back, you'd want things. Ask, annoy. It's an eighty-mile round trip for me to visit you, and I do my best. I can't do more. I can't help it if you haven't got a mother and a sister and a grannie. Aunt Grace comes, doesn't she?'

'Yes, once a week. And Dorothy's father.'

'Well then.'

'They're not very pretty.'

'Nor are you. You get what you deserve.'

'The war has made you hard, Christina.'

'Yes, I'm pleased to say.'

'What will happen when they discharge me? I've nowhere to go.'

'No. But the sister tells me it will be some time yet. You have to go to a convalescent place, once you're out of bed.'

'I'm having another operation next week. You'll be sorry if I die.'

'Yes, I will, but I'll buy you nice flowers.'

He laughed, groaned. Christina smiled. 'Perhaps the operation is so that you can laugh.'

'It's so that I can eat.'

'Well, first things first. The laughing one comes later.'

'You're really cruel.'

Christina knew better than to give in to Mark's appeals. She knew him too well, herself as well, for she felt a great tenderness towards him for his painful condition, to which he had resigned himself far more patiently than she would have guessed. Wartime experiences had not left him unchanged either. He had matured as fast as she had, in the subtle way that only the experience of death can provide.

She inquired about his future prospects of the tight-faced sister.

'He will go to a convalescent home as soon as he is able to cope with his food sufficiently. His lung has healed up well. The other will take time and require patient nursing.'

Christina knew that her own great uneasiness was caused by the certain knowledge that Mark wanted to spend his convalescence at Flambards. Flambards was the only home he knew and although he no longer owned it Christina had no doubt that he felt he had a right to come and stay. If Dorothy had been home there would have been no problem but Dorothy, in spite of the situation, was unable to leave France.

'In a strange way,' she wrote, 'I do not want to come, as I know Mark is in good hands, whereas the boys here need all the help they can get. We are desperately short-handed. When it eases I will do my best to come. I think Mark understands. I write to him as often as I can and he has not tried to persuade me otherwise.'

Christina did not mention her doubts to Dick, for her worry stemmed entirely from her appreciation of the impossible relationship between the two men. Too much bad blood had passed between them, and now that the tables were turned and Dick was master in Mark's old place it was transparently asking too much of human nature for reconciliation under the same roof. Well apart, with occasional visits, it might work.

Mary, with her blunt peasant unawareness of finer feelings, said, 'Well, ma'am, we could nurse him here until Miss Dorothy comes home. We've got the room.'

'He's going to a convalescent home.'

'When people are ill they like to be at home.'

'This isn't his home any longer.' Christina was sharp. 'And don't you talk like this in front of Di – Mr Wright. It will make him very angry. The situation between them would be impossible. Can you imagine Mark remembering all the time that he is a *guest*? Use your brain, Mary!'

'I remember him being born here, Miss Christina, poor little mite.'

Christina had been witness to Mary's maudlin reminiscences many times, and had no patience now, flouncing out of the kitchen and taking refuge in her garden, the only part

57

of her estate where she had any authority. In truth, part of her trouble, dwelling on situations that had not arisen save in her imagination, was due to boredom, since Dick allowed her no part in running the farm, not even doing the books.

Now it was summer Tizzy was out with him all day; Mary did the cooking and Amy the cleaning; the house ran smoothly. Christina entertained Isobel, but found her mental energy, for the first time in her life, frustrated. For the first time in her life, she realized, she had no problems, and for that reason she was looking for problems. She went out into her garden with Isobel and lay on the lawn which she had scythed with her own hands. She had cleared the terrace and rosebeds of weeds and the house was now free of the old jungle of overgrowth which had lapped at its back doors and windows for several years. It gave her a basic satisfaction to see the new, strong growth on the old bushes, and the first roses flowering, pearl-white, papery petals unfolding their intricate globes to expose trembling gold stamens to the June sky. There was no wind, no cloud. Dick was hay-making in the home meadows and the men were all out turning and loading. She could smell the mown grass and the roses together. Isobel, plump and brown-limbed in her white frilled dress, picked daisies out of the grass with great solemnity, bringing them to Christina to thread. Christina thought: 'This is the epitome of peace and young mother-hood: the golden child, the flowers, the harvest . . .' It was a picture-book, a dream. It was the second anniversary of Will's death. Mark lay sweating with the pain of his mangled innards in London. If the war did not end soon, Dick would be recalled, for his health was restored. He was due to go before a medical board in November. The crump of the guns in France echoed to the British shore in the soft, still days of summer; the whine of a trio of Sopwith Camels taking off from the near-by airstrip blotted out the clack of the reaper. Nobody knew when the war would end, and nothing made sense while it lasted. Perhaps, now the Americans had come in, the end was in sight. But the end had been prophesied may times before. Dick said that Mark had received his injuries only a mile or two from the place he had got his over two years earlier. 'It makes you wonder,' he said, 'what it's all for.'

'It's so that the Huns won't take over the whole of Europe.'

'Politicians' games! Put them in the front line and the war would have finished long ago. Your Hun soldier is no different from the rest of us, when you get talking to him. Like Wilhelm. They don't want it, any more than we do.'

Wilhelm, the prisoner who worked at Flambards, was a gentle, elderly peasant, who longed to get back to his farm and his family in Bavaria.

Christina sighed. She could feel very depressed at times, remembering Will, not able to forget Mark. If she had something more positive to do, she thought, it would help a lot. Gardening did not seem enough, somehow. She needed a challenge, something difficult, to stave off her useless pre-occupation with problems she could not solve. She tried to think of something difficult, something that needed to be done. She lay on the grass with a daisy chain round her neck, screwing up her eyes to the flawless sky.

After a few minutes she got briskly to her feet. She called Isobel to her, took her fat, sticky hand and marched into the house. The big perambulator, brought down by Fowler from the attic where it had languished for over twenty years, stood in the hall, refurbished and relacquered for Isobel's use. It had carried both Mark and Will, and been banished after the birth of their still-born sister a few years later. Their mother had died ten days after the little girl's birth.

'You can't use that!' Mary had cried, scandalized. 'After all that tragedy! You must be out of your mind!'

'Stuff!' Christina retorted.

Now she lifted Isobel in, tied on her sunbonnet, fetched her own straw hat and lace gloves.

'We're going visiting,' she said to Mary.

'Lord love us! Who to?'

But Christina did not reply. She walked rapidly down the drive in the thick shade of the chestnut trees, and the old foxhound Marigold came with her, casting backwards and forwards into the covert.

It was not far to the Masters' farm, but far enough in the heat, with the pram heavy in the gravel. The lane was better, hard beaten, and the elms making a roof over head. The Masters were haymaking too, with little boys hired from the village to turn the cut hay. A couple of old women were taking out the beer; Mrs Masters was making bread in her kitchen, looking hot and tired, strands of hair sticking to her forehead. When she saw Christina she was dismayed.

'Why, Mrs Russell! It's not my afternoon for callers!'

'Mrs Wright,' Christina said sweetly.

'Oh, my dear, excuse me!' The woman blushed scarlet. 'I am so sorry! But as you've made the journey ... it's so hot – I shan't turn you away without refreshment. Please give me a moment to wash my hands. Take a seat on the bench there and I'll be with you in a moment.'

'I have called to invite you and your husband to dinner,' Christina said, arranging herself where she was told.

Mrs Masters blushed once more with embarrassment, but made no comment, telling a maid sharply to put the kettle on, and withdrawing to tidy herself up. Christina could picture her frantically trying to work out excuses while she repinned her untidy coiffure. We have to face these fences, Christina thought to herself, not without a quiver of excited anticipation; the confrontation had already given her the quickening of her heart beat which she so badly felt in need of.

Mrs Masters returned and invited her into the cool of the

parlour, where the maid brought tea. Isobel was asleep and stayed outside and Marigold lay guarding her from the prowling farm dogs. Mrs Masters talked about the harvest and the war and the shortage of sugar and Christina made polite replies and passed up her delicate teacup for a refill. They discussed Mark's progress, Dorothy's noble self-sacrifice in France and the eldest Masters' son's letters from the front. Christina, after the polite length of time, got up to go.

'And I do hope you feel able to accept my invitation, for a fortnight today. Mr Wright and I are both very anxious to entertain you. The hay should be got in by then and the men will have more time.'

'Well, Christina, I don't know if –' Mrs Masters was deeply embarrassed. Christina watched her without sympathy. 'My husband, you see, might not – he might feel –' She stopped, gathered herself together. 'He might not –'

'Wish to come?'

Mrs Masters was silent, studying her teacup.

'Mr Wright is a farmer too, you know. They have a good deal in common, to discuss. I can't see any impediment myself.'

'No, Christina, you wouldn't,' Mrs Masters said, caving in abruptly.

Christina was silent, uncertain. 'Things are different now.'

'Not here, Christina. Nothing changes here. You should know that by now. You have been away and you see things differently.'

'Perhaps you should have been away too! Dick nearly lost his life to defend your right to go on here, unchanging. Will died, and Mark almost – how can you say nothing is different?'

Her surge of anger was almost her undoing, threatening total breakdown. With a great effort she stopped herself, took hold, apologized. 'I beg your pardon. I didn't mean –'

'Oh, my dear, you are right! You mustn't be sorry! We are wrong. But I cannot change other people's attitudes. I will come to dinner with you gladly, and I will do my best to bring my husband with me. Can we leave it like that? I will truly do all I can.'

Christina felt weak and drained, the fight knocked out of her. She had meant to keep totally polite, distant and contained, and emotion had got the better of her.

'Yes, whatever you please. I'm sorry. I shouldn't have asked.'

'It's right that these things are faced. You have courage, more than most. I will see what I can do to make amends, dear. I will do my best.'

'Thank you, Mrs Masters.'

Christina went home with less ebullience than she had set out, blaming herself for her stupidity. Worse still, three days later a note was delivered to the effect that Mr and Mrs Masters would be pleased to accept the kind invitation of Mr and Mrs Wright to supper on the evening of the twenty-fifth of July. She passed the letter to Dick immediately, before her courage should fail. They were having breakfast in the kitchen at the time, and Dick read the letter slowly. Christina could see that its news brought no joy.

'You *invited* them? You never told me.'

'No. I didn't think they'd accept.'

'What are you trying to prove?'

'Nothing. I just want to be friends.'

'Well, I don't. I've never tried to hoist my friends on you, have I? My village friends, like Enoch and Simeon. What if I asked them to dinner? Would you like it?'

'It's not the same.'

'Why isn't it?'

'Because you – you've come into a different place. You accept the habits of the new place.'

'A new class.' He said the word with scorn. 'That's what you mean. I must learn to be a gentleman.'

'You choose to put it like that. It's not how I would phrase it.'

'And how would you put it?'

'Through marrying me you have become a landowner. Quite a big landowner. Landowners ask each other to dinner. It's one of their customs. So you should abide by the customs.'

'To be patronized? How can it work? That man Masters had me for poaching once. Took me up before the magistrates. He said things to me I shall remember all my life.'

'You are in a position to put all that behind you. If anyone should be embarrassed, it seems to me it's more likely to be him. And he's ready to start afresh.'

Dick did not reply, but looked miserable. 'I should have thought of all this –'

'Before you married me?'

'That's right.' He smiled wryly.

'And then you'd have thought better of it?'

'Well, perhaps for you, Christina,' he sighed, shrugged. 'We can talk farming, I suppose. I'll ask him how much money he's made out of war.'

'And why he's still got two sons at home, active and healthy. Splendid conversational gambits. It will be a great success.'

Christina realized that she wasn't looking forward to it any more than Dick, and cursed her moment of boredom out in the garden. She went to see Mark after his operation, and found him deeply depressed and pulled down.

'They're sending me to convalesce in Derbyshire or somewhere crazy, as soon as I can stand the journey. But they're short of beds, might be quite soon. I don't want to go.'

She tried to cheer him up. He had never been farther north than Oxford in his life.

'If I'm better, I want to go home.'

'You haven't got a home.' Christina had to steel herself to say it, and her voice shook slightly. She felt desperately tender towards him, so limp and drained. Not only did he not have a home, he did not even look better to her anxious eyes. He was so thin she thought she could quite easily pick him up. Her own distress disturbed her in a strange way. She felt almost panicky for a moment, reaching out for his hand and closing it in both hers. He was cold, and she had a sudden fear that, even now, he was going to die.

'You are a bitch, Christina,' he said, and smiled, and the cold hand pulled hers to his lips and he kissed it.

'What did you do that for?' She was startled.

'Because I love you.'

She snatched herself away and flounced over to the window, turning her back. This situation had arisen before between Mark and herself; he had always professed to love her, even when she was married to Will. His admissions had never moved her before, save to impatient anger, but this time she felt a surge of tenderness that surprised her. She was not sure if she had hidden her reaction sufficiently, for Mark was watching her closely, with his old mocking expression.

'Nothing changes,' he said.

'It most certainly does.' She spoke firmly. It did not do to weaken before Mark.

'Not for me.'

He was going to say something else, lifting himself on one elbow, very serious, but the movement set off one of his spasms of pain which put everything else out of his head. Christina instinctively reached out for him and he took her hand not with any intention of wooing but merely as something to hold on to in his agony. They clung to each other through his compulsive need, an entirely necessary embrace through which, after a few moments, they were able to regain a grateful equilibrium.

'You'd think I was bloody pregnant!'

'Triplets at least.' Christina's voice was shaky.

'God almighty, if I could just deliver and have done!'

He lay back, wrung out by the pain. Christina sat and watched him, feeling his despair with an equal misery. She could not leave him, although he fell into a sleep of exhaustion: he needed her, she thought, far more than anyone at Flambards. Her emotions quietened as he slept. She felt very close to him, almost as if it were Will she was guarding. The two brothers, beneath quite different outward characteristics, both had the Russell driving force that she had found so stimulating, a compulsion to go their own ways without recourse to outside opinion. She saw its strength now in Mark's fight merely to go on living. The nurses had given him little chance, she discovered, on arrival, and still presumed he lived to plague them mainly by willpower. The sister came in, but Mark did not stir.

'Are you all right?' the nurse whispered.

'Yes.'

'I'll bring some tea shortly, and then we'll have to wake him.'

'He says he's going to a convalescent home – will that be soon?'

'We can't do any more for him, I'm afraid. He just needs rest now, to gain strength, and that will be easier in the country. They nearly all go on from here.'

She did not sound very convincing, and spoke with the sorrow and resignation that Christina had come to accept. A nurse brought the tea, and pulled up a table by the bed. Mark's ration was a sort of gruel which reminded Christina of old Uncle Russell. Mary had brought him gruel every night which he had laced heavily with whisky. The hospital did not appear to supply the spirits. Mark groaned when he opened his eyes to the feast.

'You see what I have to suffer, Christina? If you get your

arms or legs blown off, everyone's really sorry for you, but at least you get a square meal. Eat like pigs that crowd, and get all the sympathy. There's no justice. I don't want that awful stuff.'

'I'm sorry but you've got to take it.'

'Worse than the sergeant-major ... I want roast beef and yorkshire pudding.'

The nurse laughed. 'Kill you off, that would! Good as another bomb. Talk sense now, and do as you're told. I'll come back in ten minutes and see it's all gone.'

She went out and Mark said, 'See how they treat you? Do you wonder I want to come home?'

'I can see the sense of it, if you want to get better.'

'Even that stuff – makes me throw up. I'm in an awful fix, Christina.'

'Yes, I can see. I thought you said the operation was so that you could eat?'

'Yes, but it's all relative – all that just so I can eat that rubbish a bit thicker than it was before.'

'What did they do?'

'I think the general idea is that they prune away the damage and join together the remains as best they can. They provide a basic service. It's like keeping the railways running after an air-raid. It still works, but the refinements are missing.'

'Oh, Mark –!'

'But nobody in here is any better off. If you were to see, Christina. It's all so depressing. I want to get rid of all these horrors. I've had enough.'

'You're going to be all right, that's the main thing. And when Dorothy comes home – you've got so much to look forward to –' Offering up the grey mess, remembering Mark eating his dinner after a day's hunting, head down, elbows out, fork shovelling, Christina was aware of the cold comfort she offered, words and meal alike. He did not mention again coming home to Flambards for which she was eternally thankful, for she did not think she could have resisted him again. She had not realized just what he had to endure. She stayed as late as she could, and got home only a few minutes before midnight and found Dick waiting up, worried and irritable.

'Surely you didn't have to stay so late? I thought something had happened to you.'

Tired and emotionally spent, Christina found it hard to keep the irritation out of her voice.

'He just needed me – I felt I had to –'

Dick made an effort not to nag, biting his lip angrily.

'I'm sorry. It's just because it's Mark, I suppose. Anyone else –' He shrugged.

'I know!'

'Is he bad then?'

'Well, yes I think he is. He seems to accept it, that eating is agony and he's just got to make the best of it. I suppose it will improve gradually. He's not going to get much sympathy, not as if he's been blinded or lost a leg, but it's just as tough really. I feel terribly sorry for him.'

Dick sighed. 'I wouldn't have wished it on him, but – well, I'll never be sorry for him, put it that way. He'll get better, if I know him, and live to plague the life out of you all, as he always has done. Just as long as he doesn't cross me, that's all.'

Christina knew better than to stick up for Mark, remembering how badly he had treated Dick when they were boys. All she could think, falling wearily into bed, was how right she had been to resist him. The two men under the same roof would be impossible, as it always had been. As Mark had said himself, 'Nothing changes.' The fact that he was referring to his own love for her was something she was not going to think about. He was married now and things were different. He must learn to accept it. Exhausted by her day of conflicting emotions, she fell into a deep and dreamless sleep.

Dick lay for a while looking at the dark, starless sky. It was close and still, not a night of moonlight and beauty, but a night, he sensed, of sombre reality. His dear Chrissie lay beside him still as a corpse, distant as the hidden stars. He felt uncertain of the future, for what reason he could not tell.

What have I done, he thought?

Chapter 4

Christina assuaged her conscience by writing to Mark, kindly, sanely, wishing him well in Derbyshire, holding back her sentiment because she owed her first allegiance to Dick.

'Surely Dorothy will come home when he's finished with hospitals?' Dick remarked. 'I can see that there's no point at the moment, but when he's discharged they'll have to find a place and settle down together.'

'Of course.'

It was fruitless to go on worrying about Mark, and Christina turned her attention to the immediate hurdle that faced her: the evening with the Masters. It was no good pretending she was looking forward to it any more than Dick was but she was hopeful that, by going through with it, the path would be smoothed for future relationships amongst their neighbours. After all, Dick might want to hunt when sport was resumed, and he was going to have to meet his fellow farmers at market and around the village – far better to broach the subject sooner than later.

She took trouble with planning the dinner and arranging the dining-room and the table, with what to wear, what to drink, with the flowers in the sitting-room, the position of the lamps. She thought, if it was all perfect, she would have nothing to worry about. Save Dick.

'God almighty!' he sighed. 'This awful evening! I haven't got to carve, have I?'

'No. I've seen to that. You'll have to pour the wine. That's not difficult. I've shown you. And talk about cows. Keep your elbows in.'

'Feet off the table. No spitting.'

'Don't sit down till the ladies are seated.'

'Does that include you?'

'Yes. I'm a lady.'

'Not always.'

'Today I'm a lady.'

'Very well. I shall try and live up to you.'

'If we get a bit drunk first, we shan't worry too much.'

They had a couple of glasses of port downstairs, standing in front of the long windows which were opened on to the terrace. It was a soft, still evening. Christina had put on one of her old Hendon dresses, a pinky-grey crêpe de Chine which she had bought with Dorothy for one of Will's looping-the-loop demonstrations, dated now, but as flattering as it had always been, one of her favourites. Farmers' wives could hardly expect to be any smarter after four years of war.

Dick looked at her doubtfully.

'I don't know – sometimes I think I'm going to wake up . . . all this. You.'

'And such charming guests for dinner.'

'Even dinner.'

'When did you go without dinner?'

'After I lost my job, often. My mother didn't, but I did.'

'I'll give you big helpings, to make up.' Christina looked at him over her port glass. He looked very smooth and clean, his lovely blond hair flattened smartly down, white collar, dark tie and best suit in perfect taste. He was so uncomplicated, she thought, after the Russells, predictable and safe. She put down her port glass.

'You are lovely,' she said.

He put his glass down too and took her in his arms and they kissed gratefully. Christina felt her carefully pinned-up hair giving way, wriggled away, laughed, kissed him again.

Somebody coughed loudly in the doorway.

'Ma'am, sir –'

They sprang apart. Christina felt hairpins dropping down her bare nape, hot colour flooding her cheeks. Mr and Mrs Masters stood in the doorway with frozen expressions on their faces, Amy beside them, flustered and embarrassed.

Christina tried to smile graciously, but felt dangerous giggles rising, the port having done its job only too well. A lock of hair slithered down on to her shoulder and lay across her décolletage in another small cascade of hairpins.

'How lovely that you've come,' she said, advancing with her hand out. 'We're so pleased to see you.'

Holding herself very steadily, she was able to contain her coiffure while greetings were exchanged and the Masters took their seats on the proper chairs. They were plainly doubly embarrassed by their reception and in a worse state than Dick. Christina knew she had to retire to see to her hair, knew that the three of them would sit in total silence till she came back, knew that the evening was a disaster from the word go . . .

She made her excuses and went out. Amy was still in the hall close to tears.

'I'm terribly sorry, ma'am! I knocked and you didn't answer –'

'Oh, heavens, Amy, don't worry! It's going to be a perfectly lovely evening!'

Amy looked at her doubtfully, and departed to the kitchen, and Christina scooped her hair together as best she could, picking the hairpins out of her bosom and skewering them back in. She felt she could well burst into tears of despair, and equally of laughter: the situation was farcical; they were all aware of it.

'But we're all human beings,' she thought savagely, staring into the mirror. 'We're all as vulnerable, as stupid.'

It helped to be angry, giving her back her nerve. She made her entry briskly and promptly opened the conversation by inquiring after the health of Edward Masters, now in the front line. The war was a conversational gambit free for all; death knew no etiquette, and Christina was at home with the subject, Dick no less.

Over dinner, with Christina kicking Dick sharply on the ankle to keep the glasses well-charged, the war and farming proved fertile ground for the two men, and Masters unbent as his belly filled. Dick kept calling him sir, but as he was so much younger it was fitting. Mrs Masters was as anxious as Christina to smooth the ground, and Christina found herself being genuinely grateful towards the woman who could, so easily, have blasted her advance from the outset. The dinner was satisfactory; Amy waited on as if she had been in service all her life, and Christina began to relax. She realized she felt very tired. The meal was finished and Dick fetched the port from the sideboard, having been well primed by Christina.

Christina got up and Mrs Masters pushed back her chair. Dick remained standing, glanced at Christina and winked. At that moment the noise of a motor engine came plainly from the front drive and the glare of a pair of headlights lit the dusk through the uncurtained windows. It was unfamiliar enough to startle Christina and Dick, and Mr Masters got up anxiously.

'Someone's tampering with our motor, dammit! Or have you got callers?'

'We're not expecting anyone.'

'No, that's not our engine. Too powerful. Well, you've got callers, I'd say. Strange time of night to visit.'

'Somebody lost, I daresay,' Mrs Masters said.

They were all curious enough to listen for the knock on the door, the surprised mutterings of Mary and Amy in the hall, the voices as the door was opened. They heard a man's voice, urgent and authoritative, a shriek from Mary. Christina felt the cold, sick heave of fear in the stomach, legacy of wartime telegrams, and saw that Mrs Masters was having the same qualms. She glanced at Dick.

'Dick, please –'

They all went out into the hall. It was too much to wait, affecting disinterest. The man at the door was in uniform, a Red Cross uniform, and Mary and Amy were taking his message with obvious amazement.

'Oh, ma'am, he says –' Mary turned to Christina, her hands up to her face, her lips twitching with excitement. 'He says it's –'

'Major Russell, ma'am,' the man said. 'He said to ask for Mrs Wright.'

'Yes? I'm Mrs Wright. What do you mean?'

'Major Russell, discharged from hospital, ma'am. I had instructions to bring him here. We had some trouble with the motor, ma'am, and I apologize for arriving so late. Wasn't sure if I'd got the right place, to tell you the truth. Flambards, is it? He told us Flambards.'

'Yes, but –' Christina found the words would not come out. She felt as cold and stricken as if the man was in fact announcing a death.

'They needed the beds so bad, ma'am, and this was the address he gave us. Perhaps if the gentlemen here could give us a hand with the stretcher?'

The man turned away and shouted something outside. An ambulance stood in the drive, with another man opening the back doors. The cross on its side gleamed in the dusk, like the crosses on the German bombers. Christina thought she must be dreaming.

'Oh, my dear,' Mrs Masters said to her softly.

'He – said – he said Derbyshire! Dick! Oh, Dick!' Christina turned in a panic, terrified of Dick's reaction. 'I never said! Dick, I never told him he –' Her voice broke as the full significance of the situation took hold. The old familiar surge of rage against Mark and his casual injustice, so typical, so characteristic, took hold of her so that she choked on the words. Dick's face was like a stone.

'Be glad to give a hand,' Masters said. 'Least we can do.'

'Of course,' Dick said.

'Oh, Miss Christina, Mr Mark's come home!' Mary babbled. 'What bed shall we put him in, the poor boy? I never thought I'd see him back here again! What a night, to be sure! What –'

Christina rounded on her furiously. 'For one night! He can stay for one night, until we sort out what's to be done. Go upstairs and take Tizzy out of his bed and put him in the spare room, and straighten the bed for Mark. Light the lamps!'

The men went out to help with the stretcher. She forced herself to go forward, to try and raise a grim smile for her brother-in-law.

But Mark was beyond smiling in return.

'I'm afraid the journey's done him no good,' the ambulance man said unnecessarily.

If she could have raged at Mark, Christina would have felt better, but to have him treat her like this, and then be compelled to feel sorry for him, was almost more than she could take.

'What shall we do?' she hissed at the complacent ambulance man. 'We've no nurse here! I've no experience in – in all this –'

'You can call in your own doctor, ma'am.'

'He's eighty-five! He needs a doctor himself.'

'Well, I daresay he'll cope in the morning. I'll give the gentleman a shot of morphia before I go, and that will see you through the night.'

Mary was at the top of the stairs with a lamp, Tizzy hovering beside her, pop-eyed with excitement. Their stumbling, tangled shadows flared against the wall, manoeuvring the turn of the stairs. Masters grunted and groaned, but Mark, grey-faced, was silent. They got him to his room and lifted him into bed, where he lay beneath the stony eyes of his mounted foxes' masks, as very nearly defeated as his trophies. To Christina's surprise, it was Dick who pulled the blankets up and tucked them in, and made the pillows comfortable, while the ambulance men went downstairs to fetch what they called their 'bag of tricks'. Christina went out to cope with Tizzy, who was capering about in his nightshirt, and by the time she had got him settled in the spare bedroom, Mark had been drugged, the ambulance men had departed and Dick was downstairs in the hall with the Masters. Christina went back to Mark and bent over him, driven by compassion for his state. She put out a hand and stroked the hair back from his forehead. He opened his eyes. They were hazy, wandering, the pain muffled, the senses adrift. He focused on her slowly, smiled.

'Don't – have – have me ...' She waited, watching his lips forming the almost soundless words – 'have me put down.'

'Oh, you –'

Anger was easier than the awful tenderness his stupid joke inspired. It was an effort to do a cool, Florence Nightingale act with the emotions clashing like cymbals.

'Dick will do it in the morning,' she whispered. 'Quite painlessly.'

Mark had the right idea, to turn Dick's dislike of him into a joke, for his intrusion into their life at Flambards was bound to be catastrophic. Christina could see only storms ahead. First shock settled into resignation, and the dread of her nursing duties began to overtake her anxieties for the men in the drama. She went downstairs, into the excitement that had been generated by Mark's arrival – Mary's near-hysterics, the Masters' eager interest in this new aspect of the scandal that was her life at Flambards, Tizzy's capering. Only Dick was apparently unmoved.

'Oh, my dear, what a shock, coming without any word!' Mrs Masters burst out. 'The authorities should never have allowed it to happen like that!'

'We'll be getting along,' Masters said. 'You've got too much to think about now to want to make chat.'

They were kind, concerned, offering help, disappearing into the night. Christina had to see to Tizzy again, Mary and Amy were dispatched back to the washing-up; Isobel awoke with the disturbance and had to be cuddled and made comfortable. By the time all was sorted out, and Amy gone, the house locked up, Christina was so tired she could scarcely raise her arms to do her hair. To her amazement, Dick seemed relatively unconcerned.

'We'll send a wire to Dorothy in the morning,' he said. 'She will have to come home and decide what is to be done.'

For some reason this simple resolution of the problem had not occurred to Christina. She realized she had given Dorothy very little thought.

She wanted Dick to understand her innocence plainly: 'I told him he couldn't come here. I made it very clear. That's why it's been such a shock.'

'Well, since when did Mark ever do anything to suit other people? Only himself.' Dick hung his best suit on a hanger in the big mahogany wardrobe and closed the door. 'I imagine he arranged it with the ambulance men, gave them a good tip.'

'I thought you'd be so angry!'

'But he won't be staying. I'm not brute enough to turn him away in that state, for heaven's sake!'

Christina slept as if she, too, were drugged, and woke in the early hours to Tizzy's cries and shouting across the landing. Dick was getting out of bed. She came awake suddenly, frightened.

'What is it?'

She followed Dick out of the bedroom to collide with Tizzy.

'Uncle Mark's shouting – all about a man in a shell-hole! He keeps shouting! He says there's a sniper! He says –'

'Oh, Tizzy, hush!' Christina was impatient, jerked into frightened awareness. 'He's ill, he's dreaming! Don't worry!'

But she was worried sick. She was no nurse, and had never seen the effects of shell-shock and delirium. Tizzy was frightened and so was she, but Dick sat patiently on Mark's bed, talking softly: 'They've gone to fetch him in, don't worry. The stretcher party are bringing him and he's all right, there's nothing to worry about any more.'

'Why's Uncle Mark like that?' Tizzy sobbed. 'What's he shouting for? What's wrong with him?'

Christina had to sit with Tizzy, take him back to her bed and hold him in her arms, and Dick sat on with Mark till he slept again. In the morning they sent a telegram to Dorothy, and Fowler went for Dr Porter, and Mary told stories of death and disaster in the kitchen, all the war horrors she could remember. Dr Porter came with his black bag, as he had come through the years to the Russells, but this time his age was showing and Mark's injuries were beyond his rustic experience. As he started cutting and tearing away the dreadful stained, stiffened wads of gauze that were glued to Mark's body from chest to hips, his hands were trembling and his eyes watering. Mark sweated and swore and raged and Christina felt the panic rising with every snip of the scissors.

'Go and fetch me some more hot water from the kitchen,' the doctor commanded her, and Christina ran. She went for Dick out in the yard and clung to him.

'I can't do it! I can't bear it! I can do everything else but I can't do that. Will you go?'

She had never felt so hopeless, so inadequate. Dick gave

her a little shake, and went, without a word, and she went out on to the terrace into the sunshine, burying her face in the heavy overblown roses, shaking with self-pity. It was still anger she felt towards Mark, and for herself for being so thrown by the situation.

'I will be better after a good night's sleep, after I've got over the shock,' she thought.

But a good night's sleep did not seem a likely proposition. She was Mark's nurse, whether she wanted it or not and, even if she could not stand the sight of what lay under the bandages, she was perfectly capable of the rest of the routine, the making of meals, washing and bed-making and emptying slops and dancing attendance. After twenty-four hours Mark was decidedly better, verging on the apologetic.

'We've sent for Dorothy,' Christina told him crisply. 'She'll be here shortly. Meanwhile you'll have to put up with my nursing.'

'That will suit me very well,' he said meekly.

'If you were on your way to a convalescent home, I take it you can do quite a lot for yourself? Get out of bed and fetch things, go to the bathroom? Now you've got over your journey, I mean – I can see that that set you back, obviously –'

He looked surprised. 'I haven't been allowed out of bed yet, no. Don't think I could, to tell you the truth.'

'But convalescent means –'

'It only means there are a whole lot nearer dying than you are, so make the best of it. Times are hard, Christina.'

'You mean –'

'I'm sorry. I'll try. But I can't eat enough to get my strength up. The spirit is more than willing but the flesh – that's the problem.' He looked genuinely sympathetic. 'I'm terribly sorry.'

'*You're* sorry!' Christina flounced down to lunch with Dick.

'I hope Dorothy won't be long! He has to be fed every two hours, everything sieved, and during the night as well . . . and he can't get up at all.'

'I'm surprised, quite honestly, he's here to tell the tale, having seen what the damage is.'

'Oh, Dick, I shall never be able to cope with that part of it! We should have got an answer back from France by now!'

'I daresay it will come before evening.'

It came at four o'clock. The boy came to the front door with the little brown envelope and Christina tore it open.

'Regret Sister Russell contracted salmonella. Will be unable nurse several weeks. Letter following.' It was signed by Freda Smith, Matron, Military Hospital, Étaples.

Christina took in the news with a feeling of dread. The failure of the longed-for relief was almost worse than the initial shock of Mark's coming. She could cope with looking after him, no doubt, but whether she could cope with the clash of personalities under the same roof was another matter altogether. Even Dick's calm was disturbed by the news. Christina saw the look come over his face that she remembered only too well from past encounters between the two men, but he said nothing.

'What shall I do?' Christina appealed to him.

'Whatever you have to,' he said coldly. 'There's really no choice.'

He was right. Christina tried to hire a nurse, but no one was available. Even when Mark was being accommodating, looking after him was very nearly a full-time job, and when he was not, when vomiting, pain and boredom got the better of him, Christina found that he needed almost constant attendance. They quarrelled incessantly, Mark's impatience with his condition provoking him into fits of bad temper or long hours of sulkiness and self-pity, and Christina's resentment at being forced into the situation she had dreaded spurring her to a remorseless goading of her patient.

Knowing only too well his natural physical hardness and energy, his state grieved her as bitterly as it did himself. She did her utmost to help him, even when they were exchanging insults and injustices without pause for breath, forcing him to take his insipid meals, the hated warm milk, to shave himself, to get out of bed to sit in a chair while she banged the pillows into shape. She willed him to get better without relenting.

'To get rid of me,' he said.

'Yes! How right you are! There's no place for you here any longer.'

'Dorothy will come soon and save me – the sooner the better! She says she is longing for me, and she can't wait to see me again.'

'She's welcome. You can run *her* off her feet, shout at *her*! *She* married you! She doesn't know you like I do.'

Dorothy, still infectious with the germ that was fatal to contacts with open wounds, was stranded in an isolation hospital somewhere near Boulogne. She wrote weary, impatient letters. 'For me to come near Mark in this condition could well prove fatal to him and there is nothing to be done about it. It could be two or three months, so I cannot give you any consolation, dearest Christina, only my love and prayers for you to find the courage and patience for the job. I know just what his condition is and what a difficult time you will be having and I shall never be able to thank both you and Dick sufficiently for your kindness.'

Christina showed the letter to Dick. He read it without comment. The harvest had started and he came in late and tired, as often enough to find Christina behind with the dinner, waiting on Mark. She had no time to go out to the fields with the beer and his bait and was hard put, sometimes, even to appear at lunchtime, amid her mashing and sieving and measuring of the exacting diet which could be entrusted neither to Mary nor Amy. Dick never complained.

He just said nothing at all. He continued to help Dr Porter when he came in for the dressings, until they were gradually discarded; he sat with Mark through the nightmares and he sometimes went in for a brief chat early in the morning or at lunchtime, but these contacts were made out of the barest courtesy. When Tizzy chattered about Uncle Mark, he did not reply; when Mary rambled on about 'the poor lad' he cut her short, and he made no answer to any comments Christina made about the condition of her patient, until she too learned to say nothing. At night, when she came to bed, Christina knew that she would have to get up twice before morning to wake Mark and feed him. She knew better than to complain, but often felt deathly tired, especially as Isobel was teething and needed her as often as Mark. When Dick turned to her in the soft, early dawn and she opened her eyes to the feel of his arms taking her, she felt more like weeping than responding, caught in the impasse of divided loyalties.

She tried not to let it show, but Dick said in a low voice, 'I hate Mark. I hate him.'

'What can I do?'

Dick flung over on his back and said, 'It's this bloody war. I'm not blaming you. But I hate you being with him all the time, doing all those – those intimate things for him. And yet I know it's got to be done. It's what a family is all about. It's not your fault. Even him – I can't blame him for coming back here, and I can even admire him for what he bears without any complaint – not to me, at least – but it makes no difference to how I hate him.'

'Yes, I understand that.'

'I hate his guts.' He lay with his hands behind his head, frowning at the ceiling. 'What's left of 'em,' he added.

Christina laughed. She preferred to hear Dick complaining than to suffer his cold silences. He too was overworking, and it did not help in the evening, their mutual exhaustion, when they came together over supper to spend their brief time together – more often than not interrupted. It seemed to Christina months since she had given the farm any thought, or the animals.

'I'm sorry. I'm so sorry the way it's worked out. But it won't be for ever.'

'No. That's what I tell myself. Meanwhile ...' He glanced towards the clock, and pushed the covers back. 'It's nearly five o'clock. We're starting on the Silver meadow this morning – I am, that is, and Wilhelm's going to finish the barley at Tar Bottom.'

'Have you managed to get extra help?'

'Only from the village. Some of the girls and the women. Enough.'

'I don't know if I trust you, down in the Silver meadow surrounded by village ladies.'

'No. Nor me you, sponging Mark's fevered brow.'

'It isn't fevered any more. I nag him. I'm not nice to him. He has to try to get back on his legs, and I drive him and nag him and he hates me. He says it hurts and I say good, and nag him some more. I tell him the sooner he's walking again the sooner he can go.'

'Mmm – that makes me feel better. Poor devil.'

'Cheered you up, have I?'

'Yes.'

When he had gone Christina lay back and thought over what she had said. It was the truth, but sometimes she wondered at the motives that drove her where Mark was concerned. She had a feeling that it was something best not diagnosed. And for that reason she very shortly got out of bed herself and turned her thoughts to practical matters.

Chapter 5

The women moved after Dick's reaper, standing the sheaves up into stooks of four, ears up, in rows across the shaved field. Their toddlers and babies slept and played and fought in the hedgerow shade, and the women gossiped as they worked, discussing their employer and his wife, and the return of young Mark, and the likelihood of Christina getting pregnant.

'But who by, I should like to know?' said one woman, smiling to show broken, brown teeth. 'She's in the bedroom all day with that brother-in-law of hers, by all accounts, and him out here –' She jerked her head in the direction of the reaper.

Her companion laughed, but Rosie, working down the adjoining row, straightened up furiously.

'That's a wicked thing to say! He's been wounded something dreadful, and he couldn't –'

'Couldn't what then, young Rosie?' The woman stood up, laughing. 'He was always a one for –'

'He's married now! It's not like that at all!'

'Well, where's that pretty wife of his then? Why doesn't she come home and nurse him? It's a woman's duty, I would have thought, when her husband's as bad as that.'

'I don't know that, do I? I don't know everything! But you are wicked to talk like that.'

'No, you don't like it, my lass – and we all know the reason for that, don't we? You and Dick now – we all know when he came round to talk to your father you were dancing attendance, making sheep's eyes. We all know that, don't we?'

The women stood with the sheaves under arms, laughing, and Rosie went scarlet, pushing back her hair from her sweating face. The village women, bored, were always coarse, ready to smear honest, tender feelings. Rosie hated them, as much for what they said about Christina as about herself. They only spoke of what went on in bed. She was used to their crude gossip and hated it when it touched herself.

'Dick never had eyes for me, all the same. So don't you dare suggest otherwise. He loved Miss Christina right from a boy.'

'Aye, and her money and her farm!'

'No! It's not like that!'

Rosie flung her sheaf of barley furiously at the woman's head and the others stood round whooping with laughter. Dick, coming back up the field, shouted at them, and decided to stop for a break, to rest the horses. He felt uneasy with the older women and their venomous tongues, aware of what they had to wag about, but was on easy terms with Rosie because her parents were old friends. They had been friends of his parents when they were still alive, when his father had been horseman at Flambards in the days of old Russell. Simeon Deakin, Rosie's father, was in fact more of a father than Dick could remember his own being.

'What are they on about, Rosie? Don't let them fret you.'

She crimsoned up again, so that he could guess, and felt himself going the same way. It made him angry, to be defenceless against the tongue-wagging.

'Go and get your bait then. We'll have half an hour.'

He would rather have kept on, but the horses needed the rest. He sent one of the women for water for them, and got their nosebags out, and then went and sat in the shade apart, to take his bottle of cold tea. Once Christina had been in the habit of coming out into the fields at midday and making a picnic of it with the children, but now she had no time to come, and Tizzy got bored, and would go back home to listen to Mark's stories or to fetch and carry for him. Dick could see how it was for Christina but understanding made him no happier.

Rosie came over shyly. She held out a hunk of bread and dripping.

'I don't want all this. You have it.'

Her voice was soft, with the Essex broadness, like his own. Dick smiled, accepting, for he was hungry.

'I should've got my own. They're that busy at home, all that dancing attendance, and the children to see to, they forget about me.'

'It's a shame!' Rosie was delightfully indignant on his behalf, which he found comforting. 'If you want some more help,' she added, 'my sister's come home from Canada. Her husband's been killed and she didn't like it over there. She's got to find work.'

'We tried to get a nurse, to look after – Mr – Major Russell.' He was never quite sure how to refer to Mark in company. To himself, he called him 'that bastard'. 'But we couldn't find one. Would she do that?'

'Oh, I don't know about nursing. Only the children. She was a nanny once, before she went to Canada. She might be a nurse for your children.'

Dick considered the proposition. It would certainly take a load off Christina, perhaps give her time to come out into the fields with his dinner. He hated to see her so tired with her disturbed nights, and irritable by bedtime, dark shadows of weariness under her eyes.

'That might be an idea. Perhaps I should come and see her.' It was a long time since he had met Clara. She had emigrated as a girl of twenty. He did not fancy sending for her without seeing what sort of a woman she had grown into.

'Perhaps I could call in, after I've put the horses away tonight.'

'We'll be pleased,' Rosie said politely.

He went, riding over on Pepper. Christina's horse, Pheasant, was a useless animal, he decided, too small for him and too dangerous for Christina, in spite of her denials; he would sell him, he thought, and get a big hack they could both use. Sweetbriar and her foal were doing well, but Christina scarcely had time to visit them either. She had christened the colt Moonshine, having caught a glimpse of him one night from the bedroom window, galloping through the paddocks in the summer dusk, but no one had time to handle him. He would grow up wild and they would live to regret it.

Dick rode out of the Flambards chase on the village side of the farm, and came to the Deakins' place a few hundred yards down the lane, a small weatherboard cottage set back amongst a cluster of barns, approached by a grass road under some fine old elms. White ducks up-ended themselves on a pond just outside the garden gate and some Wyandotte bantams scratched on the path, panicking out of Pepper's way as Dick approached. The cottage garden was a profusion of flowers mixed with cabbages and runner beans, of roses and lettuces, herbs and early dahlias, a long run of potatoes edged with lavender, a few beehives set behind. Deakin had the minimum of land but extracted from it the maximum of produce, both in the garden and from the fields, a man of infinite patience and pains, of attention to detail, a man after Dick's own heart. The place had been all thistles and docks twenty years ago.

Dick got off Pepper and tied him to the gatepost and went up the path. The door was open: the sun had nearly gone down beyond the far hedgerows and the newly shaved fields behind the garden were warm purple-brown in the twilight, scored by the patterned rows of cut stalks, silver-white. Dick

paused at the door, taking in the landscape for the deep
pleasure it gave him: everything as it should be, even to the
bees going home heavy from the throats of the gladiolus
spikes, and the smell of baking coming out of the house. He
knocked. Mrs Deakin called to him and he went in, taking
off his cap.

'Why, Dick!'

Nell Deakin looked up from the oven, where she was
taking out a pie, and her hot face smiled up at him. She had
a face like a big currant bun, shining, with dark, quick,
currant eyes, and dark hair scraped back. She was always
cooking or cleaning or doing the hens or weeding the garden
or dollying sheets; he had never set eyes on her idle.

'Why, we don't see enough of you these days, Dick,
since you moved up the big farm. It's nice you calling. Sit
you down and you can have a bit of new bread here. It's
just ready. I'll call Simeon. He's out the back getting the
eggs.'

Simeon came in, a tall, quiet man, greying, but ageless –
he had always looked the same to Dick from a child, and
Dick could not imagine him ever changing. He was ready to
talk, to listen, sitting down over his dinner. Dick refused to
eat, not intending to stay, but by the time they had discussed
the harvest and the prices and the war, and Clara had come
in with Rosie and been introduced and the possibility of her
coming to Flambards had been touched upon, the evening
was well on its way. Dick had not realized how quickly the
time had passed. Riding home in the warm dark across his
shaved fields, he was surprised to feel so content with his
visit, slightly guilty, in fact, to have enjoyed it so much.
Evenings at home had not been restful of late.

He put Pepper away with his feed, and went into the
house. Mary was washing up in the kitchen with her usual
clatter. She looked at him, disapproving, and said, 'Your
dinner's all dried up. We thought something was amiss.'

Dick said sharply, 'The only thing amiss is your manners.'

Mary, remembering, muttered, 'Yes, sir. I'm sorry, sir. I'll take it into the dining-room at once.'

If she had said 'sir' for the third time, Dick thought he would have hit her. He washed in the scullery and went down the passage and across the hall to the dining-room. The lamps were lit and he could hear Christina talking to someone, laughing. He went in, and saw Mark sitting at the table with Christina. He stopped dead. A barely controllable anger rose up in him, which he had to stifle as best he could. Seeing Mark's face, half-amused but uncertain, his instinct sensed the old relationship between Mark and Christina which excluded him. Perhaps it was a figment of his jealousy, he could not tell. But coming so unexpectedly, when he wanted to sit and talk to Christina alone, Mark's presence infuriated him.

Christina got up. 'Dick, you're so late! Where have you been? Your dinner has been ready for ages!'

Dick explained, trying to keep civil. Mary brought his meal and he sat down. He thought he was being unreasonable, and made the effort to turn to Mark and say, 'Congratulations on getting downstairs! Is this the first time?' He still had to make a conscious effort to prevent himself from calling Mark sir.

'Yes. But I won't make a habit of it, don't worry. It was only because you were late, and it seemed worth trying.'

Looking at him Dick doubted whether it had been wise. He got the impression that it was only willpower that was keeping him sitting upright in his chair, and Christina confirmed the truth of the situation by saying, 'I'm afraid you'll have to help us get him back up the stairs as soon as you've finished, Dick. I'm not sure that it was a good idea.'

Looking at Dick's dinner, Mark said, 'It would have been worth it if I could actually have eaten anything after the effort.'

Dick supposed afterwards that he should have been gratified to play out the reversal of their respective positions in life, loathing Mark as he did for past injustices and his innate arrogance, but when he was alone again with Christina downstairs he could feel only an intense dejection at the pass they had come to, the senseless killing and maiming over the years that seemed to have no end. In Mark, his worst enemy, it was as bad as if it had been his brother, the waste of a man's life having no fine distinctions. Mark bore his lot with a desperate anger that was far tougher on his attendants than patient acceptance, but which Dick understood and admired. To admire Mark was no help to his confused state of mind, and the evening was doomed – what was left of it. Christina was played out, exhausted by her responsibilities. When Dick told her about the possibility of Clara coming to work as a nanny to the children, she was furiously angry, and Dick was in no mood to be patient.

'What is it coming to, that I have to sit out in my own fields and take my meal from what my own workers offer me, because there is no one here with time to bring it out?'

He had not foreseen that the decision would annoy her. His own neglect took precedence, and his indignation clashed with Christina's. They quarrelled angrily, both goaded by weariness, and went up to bed in furious silence to lie well apart, careful to make no contact at all, not even a toe. In the morning Christina said miserably, 'It will be all right when Dorothy comes. She can't be much longer!'

Dick would not reply. Christina determined to see that Tizzy took out his bait at lunchtime, and went to the kitchen to prepare it, but Mark was shouting for her. She went up. He wanted to get dressed, but could not bear the feel of trousers round his waist.

'Don't wear trousers then!'

'Don't be stupid! You can alter them, can't you? Make them looser?'

'Look at them! They're like sacks already, the weight you've lost! There's nothing I can do, save put the dressings back on again.'

'Fetch some then.'

'And you can do it yourself! I can't bear to look at it. I shall be sick.'

'Some nurse you are! God, I can't wait for Dorothy to get back! Go and get them then, and find me some braces as well. There must be some old ones of father's around.'

'And don't come downstairs again, else we'll never get you back up. You can't wait for Dick every time.'

'I'll get back up if it kills me.'

'It probably will! And after all the work I've put in – you've no consideration!'

The arguments, waged nearly every day, scoured them both. It must end, Christina thought desperately, before we all go under, and she went downstairs and saw the postman standing at the door.

'Morning, Mrs Wright. Here's one from France.'

Christina tore it open. It was from Dorothy.

'I am cleared and coming home immediately. Expect me at Flambards Thursday.'

Christina leaned against the porch. Tomorrow! The relief flooded through her, bringing with it a great anguish at what she felt was her failure as well as a fantastic longing for the peace that was promised. She looked out into the sunshine and saw the tranquil fields and the great canopies of the yellow-touched chestnuts and felt optimism creeping back into her system.

'I must tell Dick,' she thought. 'I must send a message.'

It seemed more important than telling Mark. But at that moment Tizzy came running round the corner bawling hideously, having lost his pet mouse when introducing it to a wild one in the fodder room, and Fowler came in to say that a man had called to have a look at Pheasant and did she know where his bridle was.

'What man? Why's he looking at Pheasant? Be quiet, Tizzy – he'll come to no harm, in the fodder room, of all places! He'll love it there.'

Mark was standing on the landing in his dressing-gown.

'What about fetching the stuff for me then? Or am I to sit here all day? Believe me, if I could trot up and down stairs like the rest of you I'd not trouble a soul –'

'I'm *coming*! Tizzy, be quiet! I'll come and help you look for him when I've seen to Uncle Mark.'

She went and fetched a stock of cotton-wool and bandages that were stored in the linen cupboard and went back to Mark.

'Dorothy's coming home. She'll be back tomorrow. She can do all this for you.' She dropped the stuff on the bed. Mark was sitting there in his dressing-gown. She saw his expression change, but not to joy. He looked startled, nervous even, and said nothing. 'I shall have a rest. I was never meant to be a nurse.'

She started to gather together his spare breakfast things on a tray.

'Aren't you pleased?' she asked.

He was watching her. She turned, because he said nothing, and saw his expression. He was suddenly defenceless and vulnerable, and looked dreadfully ill. She saw him as Dorothy would see him after all these weeks, and felt a suffocating panic rising in her insides, at having failed him, and Dorothy. And alienated Dick. Nothing had gone right.

'No,' he said.

'I am.'

'You're lying. Tell me the truth, Christina. We fight each other to cover up our real feelings.' He lay back on the bed, all the determination gone, gaunt-faced, hollow-eyed. She had never seen Mark make any sort of plea before, ever since she had known him, and she knew this was the nearest to it he would ever come. 'Tell me you feel the same as I do.'

She was exasperated.

'Mark, don't go over all that old ground again! Yes, I do love you, but not the way you mean. I care terribly that you should be better, that you should be happy, but I don't love you as I loved Will.'

'As you love Dick?'

She paused. It was very difficult to define such an infinite range of affections, but it seemed the moment for honesty.

'No one will ever be the same as Will.'

Saying the words made her suddenly aware of that bleak loss with an unexpected emotion. And worse, looking at Mark and seeing the dear Russell expression looking back – the rare tenderness in Mark making him more like Will than usual – gave her a weak longing to look to Mark for comfort. She did love him, yes, and knew she had shared Mark's life far more closely in many ways than she had shared either Will's or Dick's, especially through his hardships, but she knew just as well that what he was asking of her now was impossible. She steeled herself, putting down her own sentiment, and said quietly, 'I shall always care for you very much, but you must look to Dorothy for what you are asking of me, you know that. And for my part, it is Dick, and I don't want it any different.'

She turned away, not wanting to face Mark any longer, and started to tidy the wash-stand, emptying the water into the pail, wiping down the shelf and arranging the shaving-brush, the razor, the toothbrush, all with great care. It seemed to matter very much, to keep busy. Mark had always been a great one for stirring up conflict.

'You say all the right things,' he said. 'Stop doing the bloody housework and come over here. Come back.'

She turned again. It seemed right to go through with it,

to set the record straight, whatever it was. Just at that moment, she was not quite sure how it stood.

'Come here. Look at me.'

She stood before him, obedient. She looked at him. She felt nervous, the pulses thudding uncomfortably.

'Look me in the eyes and tell me you don't love me.'

She did not answer. She had said her piece earlier and there seemed no point in saying the same thing all over again.

'Kiss me.'

'No.'

'Like a sister. To wish me well – with Dorothy. I need you to help me, Christina. Please.'

He was smiling now, and put his hands behind his back to show his innocence, and lifted up his face to her. She could see the old tease, his old endearing habit of turning whatever hurt him most into a joke, covering up. She had never seen him show weakness: only anger or mockery towards hurt. One could only capitulate – laugh or cry: there were no half-measures with Mark.

She bent down and kissed him on the lips, holding her hands round his head, her fingers in his hair.

He did not move. She stood upright. 'First and last time,' she said. 'We won't talk about it again.'

He was not teasing now. 'No,' he said. 'It's best.' And for the first time she saw him laid bare, without a defence of any kind. He lay back on the pillows and shut his eyes to hide it, and she went downstairs, not at all sure of the wisdom of what she had done, more disturbed than she should have been. As always, indignation took over, and she was angry that he had caused the situation to arise, and that she had not cut it off at the beginning. She went into the kitchen and found Tizzy still going on about his mouse, Isobel in her high-chair banging the tray with a spoon. Mary was sorting the washing and Amy was making out a shopping list.

Christina went back to making Dick's lunch, finding a basket and a linen cloth, fetching bread out of the crock, lifting Isobel down and taking off her bib.

'Can I have some cheese?' Tizzy asked. 'If I take it to the fodder shed my mouse might come.'

'Very well. Here you are. Take Isobel with you.'

'Shall we have pork tonight, ma'am?' Amy asked. 'Mr Deakin sent a leg over with the master last night.'

'Keep it for tomorrow. Dorothy – Mrs Russell – will be coming tomorrow. I've just had a letter.'

'Oh, my dear!' Mary's face lit up. The excitement was all as Christina had foreseen. Fowler must be told; the room must be got ready. What room? 'Will she be sleeping with Mr Mark?'

'No, she will not.' She tempered the unexpected sharpness of her reply: 'Well, they must decide. They will want to be together, but –'

'We all understand how it is, ma'am,' Mary said, with the old woman's all-embracing acceptance of the human situation. 'I will wait and see what Miss Dorothy – Mrs Russell decides. You look poorly, ma'am. You'll be able to have a good rest at last when Mrs Russell comes. He's kept you on the run, has Mr Mark.'

He has indeed, Christina thought.

She thought it best to avoid him until Dorothy came. She made his next meal and sent it up with Amy. Amy said he looked very poorly. He wanted the pain-killing tablets.

'They're in the bathroom. Give him two.'

'He shouldn't have come down last night,' Mary said. 'That was very foolish. I told you it was.'

'I told him it was too.'

'Well, that's Mr Mark. If he wants a thing . . .'

'Are you going to take them to him, ma'am?'

'No, I'm not. You fetch them, and a glass of water.'

The morning was nearly gone, and Christina had lost all

track of time. She went out with Dick's lunch. She looked for the children and could not find them. Fowler said Wilhelm had taken them in the cart down to Tar Bottom, so Christina set off along the track with the dinner, but she felt too tired to continue, seeing the beaten, dusty ruts stretching ahead in the shimmering heat as if forever. She had not been out with Dick's lunch for weeks. She felt disorientated in a strange way, both mentally and physically, and felt obliged to sit down in the hedgerow, in the shade of the long grasses and the hawthorn. The conversation with Mark had disturbed her more than she knew, probing into her own muddled affections, and the stab of jealousy she had felt when Mary had asked where Dorothy should sleep had shaken her. In the past, she could remember exactly the same sourness of that ungodly emotion when she had noticed how Violet, Dick's sister, had loved Mark, and how Amy Masters had pursued him both literally and metaphorically in the hunting field. But she had never before felt it towards Dorothy, her dearest friend. In fact she felt only gratitude towards Dorothy for coming at last to free her from the complex burden of having Mark in the house – perhaps more complex now than she had supposed. The sooner they set up house on their own the better. Christina realized that she was tired to death. She curled up in a ball like a cat and slept.

When she woke up she was ashamed and confused. Dick's lunch was dried up, the bread hard, the butter and cheese melted. She looked at it with a feeling of deep failure. Everything I do, she thought – even a simple thing like Dick's bait – I am a failure. All the time and energy she had expended on Mark, and Dorothy was returning to find him a haggard scarecrow scarcely able to stay on his feet for more than an hour . . . she started for home dejected, and as tired as when she had sat down.

When she got back to Flambards she was amazed to see a motor-car standing outside the front door. If it had been a normal machine she would have assumed it was Dorothy's, but it was a weird, vast ungainly thing which was all bonnet and – presumably – engine, with two cramped seats right at the back, low down behind an enormous steering wheel. It reminded her of her Hendon days, when rich young men had turned up in such monsters to watch the flying. She thought it was a Mercedes. It was certainly not the local farmers' choice of safe transport.

She went in the front door.

An extraordinary noise was coming from upstairs, like a jazz band practising. A trumpet and a piano vied for ascendency, struck several wrong notes between them, stopped; the piano groped around for another key, somebody laughed and the trumpet blew several raspberries. Christina heard Mark's voice, then more laughter.

'Whatever – ?'

She dropped her basket and ran upstairs.

There was an old piano in Mark's room, put there out of the way years ago and now used as shelves. Christina had never seen it with the lid up in her life. Now, not only was its lid up, but it was launching into an amazingly accomplished syncopation. The player's back was to the door, a lean figure in shirt-sleeves; standing at the window, framed against the strong evening sunshine, was the man with the trumpet, now poised uncertainly at Christina's interruption. She saw a wide grin, a halo of untidy hair gilded by the sun. She blinked. A row of empty beer bottles stood on top of the piano.

Mark was sitting on the bed, an empty glass in his hand, laughing.

'This is Christina,' he said, 'Jerry –' he waved an arm towards the man with the trumpet. 'And Fergus –' to the man at the piano. 'Friends of mine.'

Christina found it difficult to adjust. Coming at the end of her hard day, the strange intrusion of this other outside world into the present inbred ferment of Flambards came more as a relief than a liability. In fact, the atmosphere was familiar: it took her back with an agonizing wrench of nostalgia to her days at the airfield and Will and Sandy – the crazy music, young men who apparently had no ambition beyond beer and enjoying themselves, an indefinable anxiety to turn everything that was most dear and serious to them into a great joke – it was something she understood and had lived with all the time she had been away from Flambards.

'Pleased to meet you,' she said.

'Enchanted,' Jerry said, and started to play 'If You Were the Only Girl in the World'. The piano took it up. Mark came over to where Christina stood, took her in his arms and started to dance. It seemed the most natural thing in the world. Christina, stiffened instinctively for attack, shut her eyes and abandoned her scruples without a murmur. She was so tired! She hadn't the will to resist. Mark held her very close and she laid her head on his pyjama shoulder and loved him like a sister, questioning nothing. She was totally happy, and wondered momentarily why she had to go through life fighting. To drift with the tide was so much easier. The music finished. Mark went on holding her; she felt his lips touch her forehead, and she pulled away. She would not look at him.

Jerry said, 'I thought your wife was some hospital matron all dressed in starch, old fellow! You never told us –'

'This isn't my wife. This is my sister-in-law.'

'Oh, frightfully sorry! What a gaffe, eh? Got the wrong impression. Do excuse me, Miss – er –'

'Mrs Wright. I used to be married to Mark's brother Will, until he was killed, and now I'm married to someone else.'

'Oh, pity. Yes, I'm with you now. Mark's brother Will was the fellow Fergus used to fly with. Isn't that right, Fergus? You were in France with Russell's brother?'

The man at the piano turned round. 'Will? Yes. We were in the same flight.'

Christina turned round eagerly, felt Mark put a quick hand on her shoulder. 'Steady on,' he murmured, and Christina sensed the warning, although there was no time to act on it.

'Will used to talk of you. I'm very pleased to meet you. Sorry I'm so shocking looking.'

His voice was soft, very cultured, with the hint of a stammer. One half of his face smiled, but the other half was a rigid, livid desert of burnt skin, stretched taut and shining, hideous. There was no eye, only an eyelid that merged with the puckered flesh below it. Christina looked on it, smiled back. She could not speak.

Fergus said, 'I tell 'em how handsome I was before, but no one believes me. You'll just have to take my word for it.'

Being burned alive was the great fear of all the pilots, Christina knew well. Will had had sick leave, once, after a near squeak, with minor burns and had spoken, one sweating, memorable night, of his horror. In spite of what had happened to him, she had always been grateful that it had not been what he had so dreaded, what they all dreaded.

'The Huns are given parachutes, so they can jump out, but our lot aren't allowed to have them, in case it encourages surrender. Isn't that correct, Fergus?' Mark's voice was dispassionate, conversational.

'Quite correct. We just jump out without 'em, which gives one a worse profile than this, believe me.'

He gave Christina another of his half-smiles. The one half of his face was thin and sad, a sensitive, academic sort of face, Christina would have said, not the usual boyish face of the fighter pilot. There was grey in his hair – on the side that it grew. Christina could think of nothing to say, for sympathy for such a state seemed futile. She latched on to the obvious conversational gambit.

'You knew Will? You were stationed near St Omer?'

'I was. He was a splendid chap, your Will. He was shot down two days before this happened to me – we'd only just heard. It was rough – rough all round, not least for you.'

'But if you were in the R.F.C., how did you meet Mark?'

'In hospital,' Mark said. 'We were all in together. Jerry here is a signaller, got kicked by a mule on his way to the latrines.'

They all laughed. Jerry looked very young to Christina, clutching his trumpet as if he could not wait to play again. It seemed suddenly to Christina that it was a long time since she had heard the sort of laughter she was hearing now. Jerry said he was fit and going back to France in three days' time.

'We're celebrating,' Mark said.

Celebrating what, Christina thought? But it was infectious. She switched her mind, laughed, called for Mary to bring up some tea. There was a big cake she had made, and some honey from Deakin. Mark could not eat cake. They all laughed. Jerry was going to form a dance-band as soon as the war was over; he had earmarked his recruits, but the pianist had just had his arm blown off at Cambrai. 'Just my luck, eh? He's been in Chicago, before the war, been around with Jimmy Yancey and his brother Alonzo – they can play the blues like nobody's business! There's nobody can play like those guys ... but this mate of mine was good – before he stood on a land-mine.' Very funny; they all laughed.

'You go back in the lines and you might find yourself a real Yankee pianist now they've come over to win the war for us.'

'No. You need a black man for music. They don't read a note, but it's just in them – they make beautiful music.'

Mary brought up a bottle of port. Christina lost all track of time. She could see that Mark, lying on the bed, was suffering from over-exertion. Thank God, she thought, that Dorothy was coming tomorrow! She asked Fergus and Jerry to stay to dinner, but they declined.

'We only meant to breeze in for ten minutes,' Fergus said, looking at his watch. 'You have been very kind, but we've got to get back to London. Mark is fagged out with us.'

It was almost dark, Christina noticed. She went downstairs with them. Mary was drawing the curtains.

'Hasn't Dick come home yet?' she asked her.

'He came in a couple of hours ago and went out again,' Mary said.

Christina was surprised, but too tired to give it thought. She went out to the beautiful motor-car, reminded poignantly of Will and the Rolls-Royce he had borrowed to collect her in, to take her away from Flambards. The sound of its engine gave her a great nostalgic longing, so powerful that she could not help but recall Aunt Grace's warning words before her marriage. Its lamps were electric, more piercing than the old acetylene ones, picking up the bright alarm of rabbits' eyes down the drive.

Christina had to shout. 'It was lovely to have you! Do come again!'

They waved and smiled. Christina wanted to shout after Jerry, 'Don't get killed!' The great machine swept away across the spattering gravel, its throaty revs shattering the still autumnal night. Christina stood and watched it go, following the stab of its lights away down the lane beyond the home meadows. The memories evoked by the noise, the smell, the pure euphoria of engine-power, swept over her already fragile state of mind. She remembered Will with shattering, agonizing clarity, and wondered if she was losing her mind. 'How can I love them all? And yet it is true! I love the three of them, and them me.'

The noise faded, the lights disappeared, the rabbits came back. She realized that she was overtired, overwrought and downright stupid. After tomorrow she must sleep for a week, and then life would come back into perspective. Now, for the last time, she would see Mark to bed. She went indoors and made for the stairs. Dick, coming from the kitchen, met her at the bottom. She looked up, startled.

'Where have you been?' she asked him.

'I went out to get some supper.' His voice was icy.

'But – why? Why didn't you come up? We had company.'

'Yes, I noticed. Mark had company.'

'But –'

'I had no company, not even my own wife. No supper ready. No lunch brought out. I was treated better when you employed me.'

'Dick!'

'We might meet in bed, I suppose, if you're coming up.'

'I have to see to –'

'If Mark is capable of coming downstairs for supper, he is perfectly capable of putting himself to bed.'

'Tonight he –'

'No.'

They went upstairs together and Christina went straight to bed. She knew Mark would be ill in the night, having taken alcohol which was forbidden. She slept like a dead person. Attuned to night emergencies, she woke when Mark started vomiting, but did not move. Dick got up without a word and went to Mark's room, and Christina slept again, dreamlessly. When she woke in the morning, it was like coming up from the bowels of the earth. Dick had already gone; she knew Mark was still asleep.

She went downstairs and said to Amy when she came in, 'You are to attend to Major Russell today. I have too much to do.'

'Very well, ma'am.'

Mary was full of the events of the day before. 'What a right time you had up there! It was a treat to hear you all laughing like that. And that poor man's face! I nearly dropped the whole tea-tray when he turned round! I told Amy – I said –'

'What happened when Dick came home? Why didn't he come up?' Christina asked.

'He was that hungry, and nothing was ready, ma'am – he got really angry. You could hear all the goings-on down in the hall, you see, and he said, "What the devil's going on up there?" And I told him it was friends of the Major's and he got funny – you know how he is sometimes. And he sat and had a cup of tea, and then just went out, without a word. Very quiet, he was. You know, Miss Christina.'

'Yes. Where did he go?'

'I don't know, ma'am. To the Deakins, I daresay. They're his friends.'

'He should have come up.'

But she knew a trooper did not easily go into a room where three officers were drinking together, even when he owned the house. Everything had gone wrong, and she had behaved hopelessly. She was appalled at her own behaviour.

She got ready to go to meet Dorothy, feeling that everything depended on Dorothy's arrival. She got Dick's lunch ready and gave it to Tizzy with strict instructions to see that it reached Dick.

'If it doesn't, you'll be in trouble. You're to pretend it's vital ammunition for the front line. If it doesn't get through you'll get field punishment.'

His eyes lit up. 'Yes, I shall take it!' He knew all about being spreadeagled on a wagon wheel for six hours, tied hand and foot.

'Good man. I shall give you the Victoria Cross if you make it. It's dreadfully important.'

She sent orders for Fowler to get Pepper harnessed up, and went upstairs to fetch her hat and coat. When she was dressed and came out on to the landing, Mark came to the door of his room. He was white, and had to lean against the doorway.

'Are you going to fetch Dorothy?'

'Yes. She's due in forty minutes.'

'I'm terrified of seeing her again.'

'It will be all right. She's probably thinking the same. It's quite natural.'

'I can't even remember what she looks like.'

'No, perhaps not, but I know it will be all right. Don't worry.'

'I don't love her, Christina.'

'Mark, you're not a child! You've got to work at it, like everybody else. You need her, and it will be all right, I promise you. Go back to bed and rest until she comes.'

She would not weaken, even hearing the shrewish, scolding tone of her voice and recognizing Mark's unaffected despair. She drove to the station. The train came in and Dorothy got down, as white as Mark. They embraced.

'Christina, you look so tired!'

'Yes, well, I'm going to get a rest now, aren't I?' Christina forced a smile. 'Are you fit to take the job on? You don't look so marvellous yourself.'

'I've got the most awful butterflies. I'm so nervous about seeing him again. It's terribly hard to believe we're married, somehow.'

The porter loaded her cases into the trap, and they climbed in.

'He's still bad, you know. I hope you won't be dreadfully disappointed. Worse today, because he had two pretty lively visitors yesterday and it's tired him. I'm afraid I'm a rotten nurse, and Dick – oh, heavens, Dorothy! – Dick hates him being here! I'm torn in two, trying to cope. That's the worst thing, not the work, but the *people*! Dick is so jealous of

103

the time I've spent with Mark, and I've neglected him ...'

'We will leave as soon as we can,' Dorothy promised her. 'I can guess how it is – Mark and Dick. You have been wonderful to put up with it.'

Pepper's hooves pounded on the hard dust. Every time he flagged Christina touched him with the whip, and the familiar lanes spun past. Flambards crouched in the shade of the big chestnuts, its shroud of ivy giving the timeless impression of the house having grown, like the trees, an impression of ageless tranquillity. How wrong! Christina thought. The house to her was a stirring-pot of ingredients that should never have been put together.

The trap came to a halt at the front door and Fowler came to unload Dorothy's cases and take Pepper. Christina ran up the stairs, Dorothy hurrying behind.

'Mark!'

Mark came out on to the landing. The afternoon sun streamed out of the open door so that he stood in silhouette; he had got dressed and was wearing the old, patched Norfolk jacket and breeches which he had always worn about the house before the war. Christina could not see his face against the sun. She stopped and Dorothy went past her and held out her hands. They stood for a few seconds looking at each other, and then Mark drew Dorothy to him and started to kiss her passionately. Christina went past them to her own room and went in and shut the door. She flung herself backwards on the bed and lay looking up at the familiar patterns of the cracks on the ceiling, studying every major course and all the tributaries that sprang out and travelled from cornice to cornice. She remembered something that Dick had said recently: 'We must get the electric,' and she lay thinking, 'Yes, we must get the electric.'

It seemed desperately important at the time not to think about Mark and Dorothy. She did not know why. Only this instinct overwhelmed her: to concentrate on the cracks, on the electric, on what to get for tea. There was to be no drifting with the tide, not now nor ever.

She took off her hat and coat and put them firmly away and went down to the kitchen, averting her eyes from the closed door of Mark's room, to put the kettle on.

Chapter 6

Christina put on her riding habit and found that it was too big for her; she was wasting away. She swore, laughed, remembering how once she had tried to pull her waist in when she was too fat – 'before I suffered!' she added to her image in the mirror – visually pinpointed where the buttons needed moving to, and went down to fetch her horse.

The harvest was in; Clara had taken the children down to the village; Mark and Dorothy had gone out in the trap and Dick was working. Christina had nothing to do.

'I have nothing to do!' She said it first with incredulity, then with joy, then with a slight doubt. It felt very strange. It took her some time to remember how she used to pass the time when she had had nothing to do before. She had to think back years. The horses, she remembered . . . Sweetbriar and Woodpigeon and Drummer; Treasure and Goldwillow . . . knee to knee with Mark across the winter grass with hounds running like fury . . . oh, God! Start again! Hacking kindly across her acres on Pheasant, wild funny little Pheasant. He must have got over his bad leg by now, she decided, and reached for her habit.

She went down to the kitchen. Mary and Amy looked at her in amazement. Mary said, 'Lawks, Miss Christina, just like old times! You look a treat.'

'Where's Fowler? He can get my horse ready for me.'

'He's gone out, ma'am. He's gone to the village.'

'Whatever for? Clara's gone to the village, if he wants anything.'

'That's it, ma'am,' Mary said, and exchanged glances with Amy who was cleaning the silver with great concentration.

'Whatever do you mean?'

They giggled.

'He's sweet on Clara, ma'am.'

Christina was dumbfounded. '*Fowler* – !' Fowler was *old*! How old, Christina had no way of knowing, for he had looked the same ever since she could remember. His wife had died fairly recently, but he had a daughter to cook and clean for him and had not seemed unduly put out. Clara was about thirty, a quiet, kindly, unexceptional woman of tidy habits who came in every day and departed after putting the children to bed. Christina had accepted the arrival of Clara to look after her children meekly, after the initial row, but now she was no longer worn out and had time to herself, she resented her. She knew she was being unreasonable but she could not help it. She was jealous of her when she saw her with Isobel in her arms, when Tizzy ran to her with one of his discoveries. It was a feeling she knew she must overcome. People in her position employed nannies; Dick was right. So she said nothing. But the thought of the woman *courting* in the village whilst amusing the children –

'Oh, really!'

'Now, don't get me wrong, Miss Christina,' Mary said hastily. 'Mrs Munrow – Clara, that is – she don't have no truck with 'im. She's not that sort of person. But Fowler – he just makes an excuse, like, to go the same way.'

'But Fowler is supposed to be working.'

'Well, that's as maybe. I don't know.'

'Hmm. I shall have to speak to him.'

Meanwhile she would have to get her own horse ready. She went out to the stables but there were no horses there. Only one box looked to be in occupation – Pepper's. Sweet-briar and her colt were out at grass, and of Pheasant there was no sign. Christina, annoyed, went out to see if he was turned out with Sweetbriar, but the big paddock held only the mare and foal. She sat on the fence for a while, trying to get the foal to come up to her, but he was shy, hanging back. He was pale-coated, patchy, his winter coat growing through, darker than his first growth. Amazingly, he appeared to be sired by a thoroughbred, although good stallions were short in the area. They had not hoped for anything much, and had been gratified by his looks; more so now that he was growing.

'You are a handsome lad and no mistake, Moonshine,' Christina said to him. 'I wish you were four years on and ready to ride.'

Sweetbriar cropped steadily, and Christina, thwarted in her desire to ride, sat on the fence and watched her. It was a still, sunny day with the intangible flavour of autumn. Christina sniffed the clear air and felt an autumnal nostalgia for everything that October had once meant: cubbing in misty dawns with the excitement of hunting proper to come, getting the horses fit, the corn threshed. Now there were no horses, no men to hunt them. October was the month of another offensive, of German withdrawals. The news was optimistic, but one was wary, now, of optimism. It did not seem possible that the war might, in fact, be drawing to a close.

She was interrupted by the sound of the trap coming back up the drive. She climbed down off the fence and walked back to the stableyard to coincide with Pepper going through the archway.

'What's all this? All dressed up and nowhere to go?' Mark was laughing at her, throwing down the reins. 'I haven't seen you in a habit for months.'

'Yes, and now I am, I've no horse to ride. Pheasant seems to have disappeared.'

'Old-fashioned things, horses. Dorothy and I are going to buy a motor-car. We've been talking about it, haven't we?'

108

Dorothy laughed. 'You have, yes.'

'You promised to buy it for me. Didn't you?'

'Yes.'

'She holds the money-strings,' Mark said to Christina. 'She's like you. Dick and I have got to touch our forelocks and ask nicely.'

Christina laughed. 'I can see you! Is that how it is, Dorothy?'

'No, of course not. He tells me how *we* are going to spend *my* money.'

'I knew it.'

'There's a house down the road,' Dorothy said. 'We've been looking at that. He says I'm to buy it.'

'We want a place of our own,' Mark said. 'It's quite clear that the quicker I remove myself from Flambards the better.'

'But I thought you were going up to Northamptonshire?'

'Oh, I belong down here,' Mark said carelessly. 'I can't see myself anywhere else. This place used to belong to old man Dermot, Will's mate. It's a nice house and some good paddocks. You know it, Christina – you used to go there with Will.'

'Yes.'

Mark had done it again, Christina thought weakly, dropped the sky on her and expected her to take it in her stride. She was counting the days until he went away – far away, she had thought – so that Flambards could drop back into its old groove, its quiet ways, and she could stop being the buffer between Mark and Dick. But Dermot's place, Marsh House, was only a mile away, less across the fields. Mark would loom as large in their lives as he did now. Christina could see Dorothy looking at her anxiously, signalling sympathy, too wise to say anything out loud. She could not think of any remark to make at all. She shrugged, and went to Pepper's head while Mark got down. Mark had improved rapidly since Dorothy had come home, whether out of sheer perversity or because of Dorothy's skilled nursing Christina could not guess. He went out in the trap quite often, which was inconvenient as it was the only transport they possessed.

'Where's Fowler then?' Mark asked.

'I don't know,' Christina said, not wanting to tell him.

Mark turned and bawled, 'Fowler!' and said, 'What's the good of keeping a groom and doing it yourself, for heaven's sake? You aren't very good with servants, Christina.'

At that opportune moment Dick came into the yard, as if he were a player on stage waiting for his cue. He had obviously overheard the remark, but said no more than, 'I'll take Pepper. I want to go down to see Murray.' Murray was the corn merchant in the village. Noticing Christina's riding dress, he added, 'You weren't going to ride him, were you?'

'No. I was going to ride Pheasant, but I can't find him.'

Mark said, 'I'm not surprised. He's been sold.'

He had got out of the trap and was sitting on the edge of the trough. Christina swung round in amazement.

'What do you mean – sold? He's mine. How can he have been sold?'

She turned to Dick, expecting the remark to have been a joke, but Dick, getting up into the trap, merely said, 'It's quite right. I sold him three weeks ago.' His face was cold, the face Christina had come to know since Mark's arrival.

This time it was more than Christina was capable of, to take the blow and remain calm.

'Dick! You can't – you don't mean –' She was stunned, and the words did not make sense. She appealed to him, almost in tears, 'You haven't sold him? Not Pheasant?'

Dick was not cool enough to stop his expression faltering momentarily. Christina saw the soft flush of guilt, perhaps shame, but he said stiffly, 'He was useless, and eating his head off. He went to a good place – a lady who thinks we'll be hunting again next year.'

110

'He was mine, Dick.' Christina's voice was shaky.

They were both of them acutely aware of Mark watching the argument from his perch on the trough, frankly amused.

'It's not fair!' she said bitterly, hearing herself like a child, her lips trembling, wanting to hurl herself at Dick and beat at him with her fists, but seeing Mark's enjoyment and knowing how wrong it was to give him so much pleasure.

'I'll buy you another,' Dick said sharply. 'Something a good deal safer. Or you can use Sweetbriar – the foal can be weaned.'

'Sweetbriar! Oh, *Dick*!' It was impossible to stifle her rage at the suggestion. Sweetbriar was well into her twenties, and looked it. But Dick was driving out of the yard, belting Pepper's reluctant rump with the end of the reins. Christina felt as if she was going to choke on her rage and ran blindly into the stable to be on her own. The afternoon's blows, both delivered with the force of a steam-hammer, were too much for her equanimity.

Dorothy came after her.

'Don't, Christina. I know it's bad, but there's nothing to be done about it, not with either of them.'

'What do you mean?'

'Mark and Dick, showing who's boss. I don't want to live in Marsh House either – it's too close. But I can't argue with him. I've tried to make him see, but I think he enjoys – oh, I don't know. He said, "We can all have fun together."'

'He's so *insensitive*! And Dick too – how could he do that?' And even as she asked the question she knew that Dick had done it in retaliation at her being bound up with Mark's well-being, ignoring his own. It was fair, in a sense. She let out her breath in despair at their ways, and said to Dorothy feelingly, 'At least *we* can enjoy being close to each other, you and me! That's the only good thing I can see that will come of it. I dreaded you going away. But Mark and Dick – oh, heavens, I want to knock their heads together!'

'Mark hates Dick being the master at Flambards, his old place. It's natural, I suppose. I have the devil of a job to make him behave like a guest. It's bound to be better when we move out.'

'It might work.' Christina was a born optimist and, having survived the shock, felt her pleasure in the thought of Dorothy's continuing presence growing. She found she could force a smile.

'I don't know about buying me a new horse – I reckon I'll ask Dick for a motor-car! After all, as Mark says, it's my money, isn't it? And we've the neighbours to compete with. If I can't buy a horse –' She broke off in exasperation, remembering dear Pheasant. She had never felt more in need of a good gallop to relieve her feelings she did at that moment. 'I *must* have a horse! We can't possibly manage with only Pepper.'

'Mark was talking about riding again as soon as he can. Now the war is going so well he thinks hunting might be on the horizon. He wants me to learn to ride. He says he'll have me hunting too, can you believe!'

'Yes, I can,' Christina said soberly. 'They're mad, the Russells. Just what happened to me. If anyone is going to teach you to ride, Dorothy, make sure it's Dick, not Mark. Dick is a lovely teacher, and Mark is terrible.'

They went back to the house together, Christina reconciled to her lot for the time being. Christina made a pot of tea and they carried the things into the little sitting-room and sat in the window bay, the late sun streaming in. Mark joined them, bringing the newspaper. They did not normally sit together when Dick came in, Mark and Dorothy using this little room as their own, and eating there separately. Christina had made the arrangements, to keep the peace, and joined them now only because Dick was out. She realized suddenly how much easier life would be when they were gone, the servants not having to answer Mark's calls or tidy up after him, everyone off tenterhooks. Even herself. Looking across at him, absorbed in the newspaper, she knew that he was the cause of all the trouble, both in Dick and herself. She did not want to analyse it and said, 'What's the news then? The Germans still running?'

'Yes. Very good. We've taken Bruges, Courtrai, Tournai. We're really moving at last. They are talking here about the end being in sight. That lady that bought Pheasant might be quite right about hunting after all.'

'Is that all you think about?' Dorothy asked.

'In winter that's all there is down here. Ask Christina. Isn't that right?'

'Well, there are a few little distractions, like earning a living, for example.'

'That's what I tell him,' Dorothy said.

'What living? We're living on your lovely money, darling. That's what I married you for.' He grinned across at his wife. 'And my disablement pension. Don't forget that I've a contribution to make. Fair's fair.'

'Oh, yes, that will keep you in hunters, I'm sure! It will stop, I presume, when you're fit enough to ride a horse?'

'We won't tell them. Hey, Christina, that bitch Marigold –' he gestured to the indolent hound scratching her fleas in a patch of sunlight – 'When is she due to come on heat? If we put her to Lucas's old Bellman, we could breed the beginnings of a pack for next winter. We could hunt 'em ourselves. Lucas says he's not starting up again, and there's no one else.'

'Well, it's an idea, yes.'

'And I'll look out for some horses.'

'You're nowhere near ready to ride yet,' Dorothy said. 'It will crucify you, you idiot. Was he always like this, Christina? Insane, I mean?'

'Yes.'

'Insanely in love with you, my darling,' Mark said to her.

'With my money.'

'Oh, you grasping women! You're all the same. Dick and I have something to put up with!'

Mary knocked and came in with the children. Tizzy flung himself on Mark, so that Christina instinctively sprang up and pulled him back. 'Be careful! Tizzy, you –'

'Tom. I'm called Tom. You said –'

'Thomas Russell, behave yourself!' Mark said in his army voice, holding the boy at arm's length. Thomas Russell wriggled and fought.

Mary stood there smiling. 'My, he's a right chip off the old block,' she said.

Christina exchanged fraught glances with Dorothy and felt her responsibilities settle heavily. She swung Isobel up in her arms, crossed over to Mary and said furiously, 'You are *never* to make remarks like that! Haven't you any sense?'

Mark laughed and said, 'The woman's right. We've a winner here, haven't we, Thomas?'

'What's it mean?' Tizzy asked.

'Never you mind,' Christina snapped at him. And to Mark, 'Have you *no* sense of responsibility?' She wished desperately that she had waited a few months and had Tizzy's adoption made out in her new surname. When it was changed to Russell, she had been newly a widow, Mark had been missing for more than a year and was presumed dead, and the name was precious, the boy being the sole heir to it, even if illegitimate. But now there was quite likely to be a string of Russells and she hated to see Mark acknowledging Tizzy as his son. Biologically it was true, but not in any other way. Admitting the truth was painful to Dick and now, Christina presumed, to Dorothy, and upset the façade she was anxious to show to the neighbourhood. God knew, their history was unorthodox enough; it needed no underlining!

'Leave your uncle alone,' Mark said severely to Tizzy.

'He's a walking wounded and to be treated with respect.' To Christina he added, 'That better?'

'He's a sitting wounded,' Tizzy said. 'What's a chip off the old block mean?'

'Have some cake,' Mark said amiably, and stuffed it in his mouth. 'Shut up,' he said. 'You're annoying your mother.'

Christina withdrew to simmer down, and went to her room to change. When she sat alone with Dick over supper later, anxious and cast down by the day's events, Dick, having eaten in silence, said when he had finished, 'I'm sorry if you are upset about Pheasant. I shouldn't have done it.'

'Why did you?'

'He's not a safe animal. I didn't want you hurt. And as you never went near the horses, I took the opportunity. It's taken you nearly a month to discover I'd done it.'

'I was too busy before. I loved Pheasant.'

She spoke without rancour. Dick seemed to be waiting for her to be angry, and when she said no more, he said softly, awkwardly, 'You know why I did it.'

She said nothing.

'I wanted to hurt you. I was jealous. I'm still jealous.'

'Of Mark?'

'Yes.'

'It's over now.'

'I hear he's going to buy Dermot's?'

'So he says.'

'I can't wait for him to go. I only wish it was a lot farther away.'

'He can't hurt you, Dick, whatever happens. And for my part, the attraction of their staying in the area for me is my still having Dorothy, not Mark. She's a very good friend to me. My only, I suppose.'

'Yes, I can see that. But I still feel – I shall always feel, and always have done – at a disadvantage with Mark. The past went too deep for it ever to change. And he hasn't changed.

Nor me either. And I think he hates me more now, not only because I've taken his place here but because you chose to marry me.'

'What do you mean? I couldn't have married Mark!'

'You couldn't legally, no. But feelings don't obey the law. I'm not a fool, Christina.'

'What are you suggesting?'

'There is something between you and Mark – always has been – that goes very deep. I am jealous of it. I think he has always been in love with you. He asked you to marry him, didn't he?'

'Years ago, before I went off with Will. And I laughed at him.'

'And after Will died, did he ask you again?'

'It's not possible – you know –'

'He wanted it though, didn't he? Before Dorothy, before me, he wanted it, whether it was lawful or not. Isn't that true?'

'Yes. And I laughed at him again.'

'And now, after all that you've been through with him, done for him, are you still laughing? That's why I sold Pheasant.'

Christina, deeply disturbed, groped for honesty. 'It has been hard because – because of – of his being so ill, and seeing him so bad, in pain – it brings out deeper feelings, of compassion, tenderness ... it's like loving a child. It's not anything that you should be jealous of. I would have had those feelings for anyone in his condition, forced to nurse him. But now he's better –'

'But the experience you have been through together – it has added to this – this whatever it is between you.'

Dick had never attempted to diagnose relationships in his life, and Christina recognized how deeply he had been hurt by the situation. His perception came as a surprise. She was not sure if she had answered him with perfect honesty, but it was a good way towards it. On the deeper implications in this relationship that he revealed he was so acutely aware of she had no wish to dwell, neither for Dick's benefit nor her own. It was an area of agonizing uncertainty which she hoped would disappear if not investigated.

Dick's face was tense, his eyes very blue and direct. 'I think you married me out of sense, for Flambards, for the children. It was right all ways round, and with love of a kind, and it works. But I can't compete with Mark.'

'Dick! Please! Oh, Dick –'

Christina flung her chair back and went to Dick and put her arms round him, pressing his head against her breast, leaning over and hugging him in a great rush of pity for what she had done to him. The truth of his appraisal speared her.

'I do love you, Dick! I didn't want Mark back either –'

'No, because you know you –'

She kissed him, forcing back the words, furious at what he was saying. He put his arms round her and pulled her down into his lap; two glasses fell on the floor and broke.

'I *do* love you!' she raged at him, and he picked her up and took her over to the sofa and they collapsed together in a wild embrace. Mary came to clear away and Dick lifted his head and roared at her, 'Get out! Get out, you wretched woman!'

'Kiss me! I love you!' Christina pulled him down again, laughing and crying at the same time, and Mary banged her tray and said tartly, 'I don't know what things are coming to, in the *dining-room* –' and went out with a disapproving slam of the door.

'In the *dining-room*, Dick, I love you even in the dining-room,' Christina said, and pulled him against her and kissed his hair, his eyes, his nose, his mouth, 'I love you. I love you everywhere.'

Chapter 7

Christina went with Dorothy to Marsh House to look over it, wanting to get the business over with. The house was so inextricably bound up with Will that she had thought going back there would be painful in the extreme, but in fact, an empty shell, it had been wiped clean of memories. Everything was gone, the flying-machines in the hangar, even the hangar; the gap they had cut in the trees to let the aeroplane through had grown over, the mown grass for take-off and landing was high with thistles.

'He spent all his time here, working with Mr Dermot. Mr Dermot was lovely to Will. He treated him like a son. Will hated Flambards, but he was happy here.'

The ghosts having been found wanting, she was happy wandering through the bare, sunny rooms with Dorothy, arranging what was to go where, which room was the main bedroom, the spare bedroom. 'And the nursery,' Christina said. 'This must be it.' The back bedroom looked over the old airfield to the south, and the November sun lit its faded wallpaper, the polished floor.

'Nursery! That's not for me,' Dorothy said, standing in the doorway.

'Why, you're not serious? Surely you want –' Christina turned round to see Dorothy's face, and saw no sign of a joke in its expression.

'I don't want to be tied down. I've only just got my freedom, for heaven's sake! I want to have some fun.'

'Yes, but later?'

'I'd be a hopeless mother. I'm much too selfish. I shall never have a child, Christina.'

Christina was startled. 'But what will Mark –'

'Mark can hardly expect me to produce a child when he has no intention of working for a living,' Dorothy said calmly.

'But he will find something, when he settles down, when he's better. He –'

'He's going to be a master of foxhounds, he tells me. Nobody pays you for that, not that I know of. And in the summer he thinks motor-racing might pass the time agreeably. His friend Fergus builds racing cars, I understand.'

Dorothy spoke ironically, but Christina was relieved to see that she was smiling.

'Well, it sounds fun.'

'While the money lasts, it will be.'

'He'll grow up eventually.'

'He's the same age as Dick, and Dick has grown up. Will grew up years ago, and he was younger.'

Christina was puzzled by Dorothy's implied criticisms. 'Don't say I didn't warn you,' she said. 'Nobody would marry Mark for security.'

'No, I'm quite happy with the situation, but you asked why I didn't want a child. That's the answer – that and my own lack of stability. I'm no better than Mark. You know what I'm like.'

'Yes.' But their dizzy times were over now, Christina thought. She had reconciled herself to settling down; she thought that was what marriage was all about – in peacetime, at least. And peacetime had come at last.

'Does Mark know how you feel about it?' Mark's last proposal to her, she remembered, had been followed in the same breath by the suggestion of what he obviously thought the natural consequence: have lots of children.

'No. He's never talked about it.'

119

'Taken it for granted?' Christina suggested anxiously.

'I daresay.' Seeing the gravity of Christina's expression Dorothy continued: 'We knew right from the start that this marriage was going to be a fighting partnership, didn't we? It was an act of bravado, when we were both going back to France. I love Mark as much as I've loved anybody but, to be honest, Christina, how much is that? I've no illusions about my character. I'm used to getting my own way, I like my freedom and I like to enjoy myself, and it's too late for me to change now.'

Christina stood looking out of the window, taking in what Dorothy was saying, surprised by how clearly she was able to delineate herself. She was surprised by what a selfish character she drew, and thought she was being hard on herself, but when she thought back to the days at the airfield before the war she remembered quite clearly her brittle affairs, her self-indulgence. Somehow, she thought the war had changed things.

'Have I shocked you?' Dorothy asked. 'I know you are very fond of Mark. I'm not going out of my way to hurt him, Christina. I'm only being honest and you might as well know. I've agreed to live here and I'm perfectly happy for him to enjoy himself spending my money – two generous concessions on my part. I don't want to hurt him. But children, no. For their sake. I've got to be free.'

'When you put it like that, it does make sense. You both want to have your own way. If it's the same way, everything will be all right.'

'Exactly.'

'And if it isn't, and you both fight, I'd say you were pretty equally matched.'

'In selfishness, aggression, waywardness and whatever other sundry undesirable characteristics you wish to name, I agree.'

'Dorothy!' Christina could not help laughing, although

the subject was serious enough. It was, in fact, what she had foreseen, but she now felt far more fearful for Mark's happiness than she had before. Earlier, she had felt more fearful for Dorothy's. She was convinced that Mark was expecting to have children. She respected Dorothy's argument but she doubted if Mark would. She wanted to say to Dorothy, 'Please don't make him unhappy,' and was disturbed by the strength of will required to prevent herself from saying it.

They closed the door on the little bedroom and Christina said, 'For visitors then. It's a lovely house.'

'Yes, apart from the fact it's miles from anywhere. We're going to have a car each though, did you know? I don't know who is going to look after them, but perhaps one employs a sort of groom?'

'Chauffeur.'

'But we'll be our own chauffeurs. If we have hunters, perhaps there is a new forward-looking worker who can handle both? That would suit us. Mark is out looking for horses now. He's gone over to Willington Park.'

'He'll be lucky if he finds anything that isn't too old, too young or broken down. There's just none to be had. Dick has been looking.'

'I told Mark to wait. He can't do it yet – but he won't be told. He rode Pepper – did I tell you? It nearly killed him; he was in agony all night. Then he rode again the next day. He said his innards had got used to it. And he was in agony all night again. I have a nasty feeling he thinks it's merely like getting muscles acclimatized. He's dreadfully stubborn.'

'Oh, don't tell me! Russell characteristic number one: do it if it kills you. Will was a fine example. I'd concentrate on getting a motor-car if I were you.'

'Yes, I think that's wise. And how about you? Have you told Dick you want one?'

'Do I want one?'

'I have a feeling . . . yes, I think you do.'

Christina considered. 'Yes, I think I do too.'

'It's your money.'

'Hmm.'

They walked back across the wintering fields to Flambards. When Mark was out and Dick was working they had tea together in the little sitting-room. It was worth a lot, Christina thought, having Dorothy close. The friendship was very dear to her. Fowler and Clara were sitting in the kitchen laughing and the children were helping Mary make cakes. It was going dusk. The house was decorated with paper flags for the armistice, and the thankfulness and the grief were bound up together in Christina's mind so that she did not want to be alone to think about Will left in his grave in France. She had never been there.

'You know, I ought to visit Will's grave sometime next year. It doesn't seem right not to have seen it,' she said to Dorothy.

'I saw it,' Dorothy said. 'There were five together, in a village churchyard somewhere near Bethune, as I remember. There was Will, and four soldiers, under some trees. Will's grave had roses on it, and a vase of buttercups.'

Christina was silent, remembering all he was going to do. Fly the Atlantic. She would have lived in fear all her life.

'I did love him,' she said.

'Have a nice cup of tea, dear,' Dorothy said. 'There, there, and all that. I loved Sandy too. We could go on a jaunt next summer, take the children. Have a jolly time. Visit Will's grave. Stop getting maudlin.'

Christina smiled feebly. How profligate she was with her love, she thought! Dorothy was right to mock her. Please don't hurt Mark. She still had the urge to say it, watching Dorothy's smile, the light accentuating the coppery-red of her hair. She was very beautiful, flashily beautiful like a bright chestnut filly, all movement and life and wanting to go. Anyone would want her for a wife.

'Mark is late. It's his feeding time,' Dorothy said, glancing at the clock.

'I'd better go and see about the dinner.' Christina started collecting the tea things together. 'Do you know when you'll be able to move to Dermot's?'

'Quite soon, I think. Tell Dick. He'll be so glad for us to go. He's been good about it, all things considered.'

Christina stood up with the tray. There was a hooting noise outside on the drive and the sound of an engine. 'Heavens! I think Mark's bought a motor-car, not a horse!'

'Oh, no!' Dorothy leapt up. 'I was going to choose it!' She went to the window. 'There are two cars, and lots of people – one, two – six! Looks like the army. Whatever –'

Christina looked out and recognized the big Mercedes; a smaller open tourer was pulling up beside it.

'It's that friend of Mark's I told you about – Fergus. The one with the burned face. And the other looks like Jerry. They came before. Oh, heavens, Dorothy, I'd better go and see that Dick doesn't get funny about it! He was awful before. You entertain them in here. I'll tell Mary to make some more tea, and Fowler can fetch some drink.'

'Oh, what larks! What fun!' Dorothy jumped up from the sofa and went to the mirror to improve her coiffure. 'Are you going to leave me all alone with them?'

Christina made a face at her. 'What do you want, a chaperone? I'll send Mary.'

She went out into the hall as the doorbell rang. She put down the tray and opened it. Fergus bowed deeply from the waist.

'Madame, ve'ave taken se liberty off calling! Permit me to introduce mes amis – Jerry, you've met, Herbie and Clarence, Madam Christina, the enchanting sister-in-law of our brother in convalescence, Major Russell. I trust he is in, well, thriving?'

'Thriving but out. We're expecting him back any moment.

Do come in, I'm delighted to meet you! Come and meet Mark's wife. She will entertain you until he gets back.'

'The hospital matron?' A certain alarm overcame the inebriated features of Fergus and his friends.

'That's right. You can hear starch crackling? She's in here, this way.'

Christina hurried them through the hall and opened the sitting-room door. She had time to see their expressions change as their eyes lighted on Dorothy, then she scurried away to waylay Dick.

'No, ma'am, he's not back yet,' Mary said. 'Major Russell's just come in though. I saw the trap go past. Fowler's gone to see to him.'

'Oh, thank goodness for that! Those friends of his have come, six of them —'

The kitchen door opened.

'Fergus and Jerry here?' Mark was pleased and excited. 'I saw the cars. That's great —'

'There's six of them. They're in the sitting-room with Dorothy.'

'Aren't you going to join us? Come on, we should have a little celebration – the armistice, our new house, Flambards getting rid of me – cheer up, Christina! Can't we all have dinner together? What have you got, Mary? Will it go round?'

'There's a pork leg cooking, Mr Mark. Yes, it'll go round nicely if we just do some more vegetables. And some apple pie. I've been baking this afternoon.'

'I'll go and tell 'em. And that port father laid down, there's still a few bottles of that in the cellar. Tell Fowler to fetch it up. We'll have a good evening, eh? What's the matter, Christina? Come and enjoy yourself!'

He flung his coat over a chair, dropped gloves and muffler on the floor and made for the door. He paused there – 'Six of them, you say? We'll have to use the dining-room. Is that all right, Christina? Dick will join us, won't he? Tell him he's invited to the party!'

He slammed the door behind him. Christina tried to keep cool, but the situation horrified her. Dick would be in within the half-hour, tired, cold and wanting his dinner. Mary was already flustering around the kitchen like a mother hen, getting out more vegetables and chivying Amy. When Fowler came in he was sent scurrying for the port.

'Come on now, it's for Mr Mark's gentlemen! We want the best.'

Christina did not want to offend her guests, and knew they must stay to dinner, knew they must use the dining-room, but equally well knew what Dick's reaction would be. He could no more sit down to dinner as host to six officers than Mark could milk a herd of cows before breakfast. Already she could hear laughing and shouting echoing from across the hall.

'Mary –' she started.

At that moment Dick came in. Simultaneously Fowler came up the cellar steps with six bottles of port on a tray. Dick stared.

'Since when have you been employed here as butler?' He shut the kitchen door and leaned on it ominously. 'You were supposed to cart hay this afternoon. What happened to you?' he asked Fowler.

'I had to get the trap ready for Mr Mark, sir.'

'Who gave those orders?'

'Major Russell, sir.'

'And the port – who told you to bring that up?'

'Major Russell, sir.'

Dick did not move, leaning against the door with his head back, the rain still running down his face. He looked at Christina.

'Dick, it's Mark's friends – they've arrived to see him. I'm sorry, there's nothing I can do about it, but there's no need for you –'

'I don't want to see them.'

'No. I know. I thought we could eat separately –'

'To spare you embarrassment?'

'No! I don't want to join the party either! We can eat here together –' Christina could see doom descending; there was no way out.

'Eat in here? I'm not eating with the servants.'

'Dick!'

'They're none of them worth their keep as it is. They can all clear out and dance on Major Russell when he goes, as they've got into the habit, and the sooner the better. You're sure that's the best port, Fowler?'

'Yes, sir.'

'Good. Major Russell will send it back otherwise. Now just you carry on – I can see you're all doing a good job.'

Uproarious bursts of laughter filtered through the door from the passage. Dick pulled his cap on again.

'Where are you going?' Christina crossed over to him and laid a hand on his arm. 'Please, Dick –'

He shook it off angrily and opened the door. A furious blast of wind blew in and a spattering of rain.

'I'm going where I'm welcome,' he said curtly and went out, slamming the door behind him.

'Oh, my, what a temper!' said Mary, opening the oven door.

Christina spun round in a rage. 'How dare you talk like that! He's entitled – he's right! You don't take your orders from Major Russell, you take them –'

'But you saw how it was, ma'am!' Mary stood up, all wide-eyed innocence. 'You heard him ask for the port! You didn't tell Fowler not to go!'

'Oh!' Christina was bitterly angry, not least with herself,

but had no idea of how to handle the problem. 'It's my fault!' She saw them all looking amazed, amused, enjoying the crisis. 'And you're all as bad!' she shouted at them. 'You're all tactless and stupid! You ought to know better! You know how it is in this house –' And she broke off, knowing, even as she spoke, that with the instinct of their kind they resented Dick rising above them to be the master and enjoyed seeing him taken down. They still preferred to obey Mark; they preferred his insolent handling to Dick's more sober approach. And what was more, they were enjoying preparing for a party.

'Oh, ma'am, he's old sobersides, Mr Dick, don't take on!' Mary said briskly. 'We should've had a party for the armistice, and the harvest, but Di – Mr Wright, he doesn't like parties, you know he doesn't. He only thinks about work. He'll be all right in the morning. Don't upset yourself. He doesn't know how a big house should be run yet, but he'll come to it, he'll learn. Come on, Miss Christina, don't upset yourself.'

Christina, aware that Mary was far overstepping her bounds as a servant, nevertheless found her words very practical. There was a good deal of truth in them. Dick had never been one for fun; not having had anything to make fun of in his youth he had never learned the habit. Even amongst his village friends he was known as hard-working and sober. He did not drink and roust about with men his own age; his friends were the older, hard-working men.

'He'll have gone down to the Deakins, miss, they'll look after him. You go and join the party and enjoy yourself.'

'That young Rosie, she'll look after him,' Fowler said wisely.

Christina wanted to scream.

Dick hurried through the darkness and the driving rain, pleased that the elements were in accord, the wind flaring his anger, the rain beating on his hot face. The injustice he felt could not have been contained by sitting down and eating his dinner; he needed to stamp through the flooding ruts, shove against the tearing wind. They had all combined to ostracize him, even Christina, to diminish him, running round like hens after Mark and his high-powered friends. He had not been unprepared, having seen the cars in the drive and seen through the sitting-room window the officers' uniforms; he had gone into the house belligerent, aggrieved. He worked on the land from dawn to dusk, sweating out his guts to bring it back to shape, make it productive, something to be proud of, but the people whose inheritance it was had no respect, no pride in seeing it thrive; they frittered their time away enjoying its fruits, its sport, and giving back nothing. He only knew work, he realized; he had done nothing else since he could remember, and bastards like Mark knew only pleasure; even the war to him had been a bit of excitement, like hunting. Mark would live his life out on other men's work just as his father had before him, and laugh, and never see the injustice.

'I hate him! I hate him!' Dick raged to the storm, and turned away down the hedgerow that led to the Deakins' cottage, like an animal to his lair.

'Why, Dick!' They were all astonished by his arrival, pushing back their chairs, standing up. The fire in the hearth belched out smoke as he pushed the door to behind him. Now, in the lamplight, in the quiet, he felt ridiculous. Mrs Deakin came up to him anxiously.

'Is anything wrong? Come in the warm and take off your wet things. Come on, lad, you're soaked through.'

He stood against the door as he had stood at Flambards, head back, frightened by what he had done. He had run away.

'No,' he said.

God knew, he had known it wasn't going to be easy. They had all said ... the Deakins had said ...

'I'm – I'm sorry. I shouldn't have come.'

'Nonsense. We're always pleased to have you.' Nell took his coat and his cap and hung them by the fire, pulled up a chair. 'Sit here where you'll dry out. I'll give you some soup, and some bread. You've not eaten, have you?'

'Bide a bit, lad,' Simeon said. He sat calmly, wiping his plate round with a chunk of bread. In the smoky, humble cottage room Dick felt back in the womb, closed round with familiar things, rock underfoot. Everything was as it should be.

'You can have my chair,' Rosie slipped down and pushed the hard chair across to the fire. There were only three in the cottage. She sat down on the rag rug in the hearth, looking up at him. They fed him, took his boots to dry and gave him slippers, asked no questions, brought him ale. He sat opposite Simeon across the fire, and the women did the mending at the table under the lamplight, and waited on. Later, when all was done, they invited him to sleep on the hearth.

'The rug's thick, and we've a spare blanket. Simeon will make the fire up. If you wish.'

'Yes.'

He lay watching the fire smouldering under the damp logs, listened to the wind wittering in the eaves and moaning in the chimney. He felt at home, calmed, and did not want the night to pass.

Christina, having no alternative, joined the party. Uncle Russell's port was up to standard; the company was wild and hilarious. She remembered dimly at one point dancing on the dining-room table with Dorothy to a great tumult of clapping and cheering. She remembered the bed being empty when she went up; she remembered looking underneath it for Dick, and in the wardrobe, and crying because she could not find him, and falling asleep without taking off her clothes. Later she woke and took them off and got under the covers, and it was cold without Dick and she cried some more, and then she remembered nothing until she was woken by someone shaking her shoulder. She opened her eyes and groaned as the light split her head.

'Christina! Wake up!'

'Dorothy – don't –'

'Listen, Christina. You must help me. It's Mark. What fools we were! He's in a dreadful state and I must get Dr Porter – or at least I must get some drugs off him – but I can't leave Mark. Oh, wake up, Christina!'

Christina felt as if her head was coming off. 'What is it?'

'For heaven's sake! Can I take the trap? Or send Fowler? Or will you go? I must do something.'

Christina came awake, coldly. She got up and wrapped her dressing-gown round her and followed Dorothy across the landing.

'Mark shouldn't have had anything to drink,' she said. 'You ought to have known.'

'Oh, don't tell me! But it's done now and I can't undo it! Someone must go to Dr Porter. Look, I can write down what I want – will you go and ask him? Or Fowler?'

Christina stood looking at Mark, dispassionately, trying to work out what she felt. He was as bad as she had ever seen him. She wanted to lie down on the bed and hold him in her arms, but she turned away and took the written prescription from Dorothy and said, 'I'll go and find Fowler and tell him to take it. If he rides Pepper, he'll be back in under the hour.'

Fowler was in the kitchen with Clara who was making the children's breakfast. He should have been outside doing the horses. Christina gave him Dorothy's prescription and made him tuck it safely into his pocket.

'Now, go, quickly. Mr Mark is very bad and every minute you save will help him.'

He went. Christina sat down at the table and buried her head in her hands, her hair falling in a thick curtain behind which she could hide. She felt terrible, almost in a state of shock, not knowing who she was most sorry for: Mark, Dick or herself. Her head was splitting. Tizzy – Tom, she must remember to call him Tom – Tom was shouting at the top of his voice, 'I'm a chip! I'm a chip!'

'Ti – Tom, be quiet! What do you mean, a chip?'

'A chip off the old block.'

'Don't say that!'

'I asked Fowler what the old block is, and he said Uncle Mark. It's a block of wood, you see. And the chip is like a wood-shaving. And it means –'

'Be quiet!'

'Shall I make you a nice cup of tea, ma'am?' Clara asked solicitously.

'Please.'

'Eat your egg up now, Tom, and stop annoying your mother. She's not feeling very well this morning.'

I want to die, Christina thought.

The door opened and Dick came in.

'Where's Fowler gone?' he asked. 'I saw him going off down the drive on Pepper.'

'He's gone to Dr Porter's. I told him to go.'

'For Major Russell, I presume?'

'Yes. It will cheer you up, no doubt, to hear that his eating and drinking last night has brought him his just reward. He is very ill this morning. Dorothy wants some stuff for him.'

'I wonder *you* didn't go.'

'I feel much the same as he does.'

'Has Fowler done anything at all this week save dance attendance on Major Russell and waste Clara's time?'

'Dick! That's not fair. *I* asked him to go to Dr Porter's. Have you had your breakfast?'

'No. You're not actually offering me a meal, are you?'

'Clara, do eggs and bacon for the master.'

'The master? I like that.'

Tom turned to Dick and said, 'Fowler says I'm a chip off the old block.'

Christina got up and left the room. She could face no more. She went into Mark's room to tell Dorothy that Dick was back, and that all was disaster in the kitchen.

'And Fowler's gone,' she said. 'I told him to be as fast as he can.'

'Good. Oh, Christina, I'm sorry! It was a celebration for our leaving – do tell Dick. I'll talk to him. He must understand.'

'Tiz – Tom has just told him about being a chip off the old block. I would avoid him for the moment if I were you, Dorothy. Just keep out of his way. I'm going back to bed.'

Mark opened his eyes and through his exhaustion Christina saw the spark of amusement. He had no strength to speak, but he could still see what was funny.

'Oh, you –!'

She flounced away, and saw Dorothy looking shocked, and remembered that Dorothy had never witnessed her gruelling nursing relationship with Mark. She could not explain it now; she went back to her room to bed, and fell heavily asleep.

When she woke up, she had no idea what the time was. She got up, feeling much better, and washed and dressed and did her hair. The house was quiet, the rooms dark with the grey skies outside. She looked into Mark's room and saw that he was sleeping peacefully, the ashen look gone from his face, his features serene. She stood watching him, full of tenderness. For a child, as she had told Dick? He behaved like one. For a lover? It was impossible. But she was drawn to stand there for a minute or two. It was very quiet, only the sound of his breathing, and a trickle of rainwater from the gutter falling on the ivy outside. She went out, closing the door noiselessly.

From downstairs came the sound of hysterical weeping and wailing, like some peasant wake. She was startled, and started down the stairs, heavy with anticipation of yet more doom. It sounded like Mary. She went down the corridor to the kitchen.

'Whatever –'

'Oh, ma'am –!' Mary was sitting in the chair by the range, wracked with sobs. Amy was standing over her, stark-faced. 'Oh, ma'am, he's given Fowler the sack! Told him to go! Told him never to show his face here again! And when I told him it was wrong, after fifty years, he turned on me and said I'd go the same way if I didn't hold my tongue!'

'Oh, no!' Christina was horrified. 'Where is he? Where did he go – Dick, I mean?'

'I don't know, ma'am. He went out. I hope he rots in hell, after all Fowler did for him –'

'Mary! *Mary*! Be quiet!'

Christina felt much like expressing her feelings in the same way as Mary, by wailing and wringing her hands. She would have to have it out with Dick, and could not contemplate losing the argument. He could dismiss the men on the farm, any of them, or Amy or Clara; but Fowler and Mary came in another category altogether. It was akin to dismissing her. It was perhaps what he was trying to show.

'I'll speak to him when he comes in. But be quiet, Mary. You can make me something to eat –' She glanced at the clock and saw that it was already afternoon. 'Bring it to me in my sitting-room.'

She went there and sat by the fire, gazing into the flames. Marigold lay at her feet, comfortably unaware that she was to found a dynasty. Christina felt as wretched as she could remember for a long time, knowing that this was going to be a fight to the death, and afraid, torn in pieces. When Mark and Dorothy left, would there be an armistice at Flambards, she wondered? All she could do was sit and wait for the clock hands to inch round until it was time for Dick to come home again.

Mary brought her some food, and told her that Dorothy had gone to Dermot's, and taken the children, Clara was mending in the nursery, Fowler had gone home. The house was silent and gloomy. Outside it started to rain.

The back door slammed suddenly. Christina sat and listened. She heard Mary set up her sobbing again, and then the kitchen door slammed. She got up and went out into the hall.

'Dick!'

He was just starting up the stairs and turned round at her voice.

'Dick, come in here – there's a fire and you can dry out.' He was soaked through. 'Have you finished for the day?'

'I'm not going to work myself to the grave in this weather, no. Nobody else does any round here, so why should I be any different?'

His voice was rough and angry. For a moment Christina thought he had been drinking, but then she knew that that was not Dick's way. A spark stirred inside her, the same feeling as facing a big fence out hunting. But this fence was her marriage.

'Come in here. I want to talk to you.'

'Yes, and there are a few things I could say to you while we're about it.' Dick came back abruptly, flinging off his coat. He came in and slammed the door and stood with his back to it. 'Who's going to start?'

His manner was the light to Christina's tinder, exactly what she needed to find her courage.

'I will. I hear you've given Fowler the sack?'

'That's right.'

'You can't do that.'

'I can and I have. Who is the master of this house? Do you want me to run Flambards or not?'

'Yes, I do, but –'

'Or should we get back on the old terms – you can pay me to run it, and I'll live out! It's your decision, who is master here. If you want it changed you've only to say.'

'No, Dick, don't – please!'

'Or even the way it used to be – Mark Russell running the place and everyone scurrying to do *his* bidding! That is what Fowler got sacked for. That and preferring to play the fool with Clara instead of working. He hasn't been out in that stable when I've wanted him for over a week, nor showed his face at the farm to do the horses there.'

'But today he was doing *my* bidding, to go for the doctor. And Dorothy insisted somebody go. Mark was in a dreadful state this morning.'

'And who's fault was that? Mark *knows*, by now, God in heaven, what he can take and what he can't! But the consequences – has he ever cared a fig for what he brings on other people by the crazy way he carries on? First you, and now Dorothy, running round in circles day and night for –'

'He needed it! *You* saw how he was – you said yourself – you said how bad it was! Someone had to go today, even if it *was* his own fault. But you can't sack Fowler for that!'

'I can sack Fowler for running round after Mark Russell last night, fetching port for his guests when he should have been outside. The old man has forgotten what work is all about since the Russell canker has taken hold again here. I know Mark has had it rough, but it hasn't changed him. Nothing will change him. Work, responsibility – it means nothing to him. What is he planning to do now that he's on his feet again? Play the squire on Dorothy's money? Not work, that's for scum like me. Work, Christina, is what life is all about, and I shall never see it any different. It's all I know about, for better or for worse, and if the people I employ don't want to know about it they can go, for I'm not supporting any more passengers in this place. There's enough already.'

'Dick, when Mark goes – it's Mark that's causing all this trouble – everything will go back to normal then. Please leave Fowler until then! It would never have happened if Mark hadn't been here!'

'No, but the old fool prefers to serve Mark – perhaps Mark will give him a job! He's welcome. I know only too well what it's like to have that bastard as a master and not be able to answer back.'

'If you can remember that, you might also remember that when you got the sack here, Fowler cried. I went in the feed-room and he was standing there with tears in his eyes – I shall never forget it.'

'And now you're doing the same for him! A touching sight. When I got the sack here it was as well deserved as Fowler's getting it now. I didn't defend myself, did I? I did wrong and I got my deserts, the same as Fowler is getting his.'

'But, Dick, you know how it will be for Fowler – you went all through it yourself and you were a young man – what will happen to Fowler if you sack him? He's been here over fifty years! He doesn't know anything else and he's too old to get another job! You can't go through with it!'

'Who do you want as master here?' Dick's voice was vicious. 'It's your choice, Christina.'

'You, of course!' She heard her own voice come out like a cry for help, and knew it would go unheeded.

'You surprise me! I was pretty sure I was well down the list, third to be precise, after Major Russell and yourself. You say you want me? You're sure?'

'Yes.'

'Very well.'

'And Fowler?'

'Fowler will go.'

136

'*No!*' Christina screamed at Dick, beside herself with rage and frustration. 'No! No! You can't do that! I forbid you to do it! Flambards is mine, and I won't let you do it! You are as bad as old Russell – you are *worse*, because *you* should understand how it is for a servant! Will used to say – Will said –' Her voice broke off, the memory of Will getting beaten for his pains when he had tried to protect Dick as a boy overcoming her completely. 'Will would hate you for what you are doing.'

'Will was a worker. He would have understood.' Dick opened the door. His face was white; he spoke quietly. 'Fowler may stay. I shall go. You may run Flambards how you please.'

'No!' Christina started to sob hysterically. 'I want you! I want –'

'You want too much.'

Dick went out across the hall and made for the door. At the same moment Mark appeared at the top of the stairs, roused by Christina's screaming.

'What the devil's going on?'

Dick went out, slamming the door behind him. Mark pulled on his dressing-gown and sat down at the top of the stairs, swinging the tassel of his dressing-gown cord thoughtfully in his hand.

'Anything wrong, Christina?'

She was standing in the doorway, grasping the door-frame on either side and screaming. She screamed like a child, and heard herself screaming with a sense of amazement over and beyond the outrage that possessed her against Dick. She had never in her life lost control before; it was both terrifying and magnificent. Mary came out white-faced from the kitchen, looked at her, then at Mark, and retreated. Christina, exhausted, subsided into sobs. She leaned her arms up against the door-frame and buried her face in the crook of her elbows and wept.

Mark came slowly down the stairs.

'Is it all because of last night? My fault?'

Christina saw his face blurred by her own tears, not mocking but kindly. She wanted him to laugh and mock so that she could hate him, but he stood there looking fragile and remorseful. It was more than she could bear. She shut her eyes.

'You must go away,' she said, 'else Dick will never come back.'

'I'm sorry,' he said.

'Why don't you laugh?'

'I don't like to see you unhappy.'

'Go away,' she said. 'I hate you!'

'That's not true.'

'Don't,' he said. 'Don't, Christina.'

He came forward and put his arms round her and held her, resting his cheek against her bent head. She buried her face in the soft woollen collar of his dressing-gown and wept, clinging to him. The feel of him was both comfort and anguish. She wept for that too. He held her tightly, not moving. She heard him talking and knew there was someone else there too. She lifted her head. It was Dorothy. She heard Mark say, 'I don't know,' but he made no move to let her go, even while he was talking to Dorothy.

'What is it, Christina? Is it because of our party?' Dorothy asked.

Christina turned her head so that she could talk, laying it on Mark's shoulder. 'He's sacked Fowler. And when I said he couldn't he said I must decide who was boss here. I still said Fowler couldn't go, so Dick has gone.'

'What did he sack Fowler for?'

'For waiting on Mark instead of on him.'

'You see?' Dorothy said to Mark. 'It *is* you. It really is impossible for poor Dick, I don't blame him. All this is our doing. Listen, Christina, we'll go first thing in the morning.

If Mark was fit I'd say now, but in the circumstances I think it had better be in the morning. I'll pack tonight.'

'Do you think Dick will come back?'

'As soon as we've gone, things will be back to normal. Of course he will. It will blow over, Fowler and everything. I promise you.'

'Where will you go? The house isn't ready.'

'We'll stay at the Queen's Head, until we can move in. You can drive us over in the morning.'

Christina knew that Dorothy's decision was right. They went back into the sitting-room and sat round the fire, finding equilibrium. Christina felt exhausted, her head aching unmercifully, and Mark was still weak and subdued.

Dorothy went to pack, and Christina and Mark sat on, not speaking. There was nothing to say.

In the morning there was no sign of Dick, nor of Fowler. Christina went out to the stable and harnessed Pepper herself and brought him to the front door, and loaded the two suitcases Dorothy had put ready. Then Mark and Dorothy came out and Christina drove them to the Queen's Head, a hotel in the nearest town ten miles away.

'I hope it won't be for long.'

'No. I think we can have the house as soon as the solicitor is through. A week or so. And then when we move in, we won't let Mark near Dick unless everything is all right again.' Dorothy smiled encouragingly. 'It will be all right, Christina, I'm sure.'

She got down and went to see if there were two rooms. Mark turned to Christina and said, 'No one is going to keep me away from you for very long, Christina.' Christina turned her head away, not daring to say a word, and he leaned over and kissed her, and climbed down.

It seemed to Christina a very long, lonely drive home. She still had a bad headache and nothing she could think of made sense any more. There was no sign of Dick at Flambards, no one had seen him. Christina began to wonder if he had gone back to London. She looked in the wardrobe and found his coat still there, and his two suits; only his everyday working clothes were missing. She wanted him back desperately. The house was like a morgue with everyone gone. Clara had taken the children down to the village to visit Fowler, and Mary and Amy were sniffling and moping in the kitchen. Christina shut herself up with Marigold in the sitting-room and thought, 'If I'm really the mistress here, I can go and fetch Fowler back, and dismiss Clara, buy a horse and a motor-car, go gallivanting with Dorothy and – and . . .' And anything she liked . . . She lay back in the armchair and wondered why the prospect did nothing to warm her. Out of the confusion in her mind, only one thing stood out clearly, and that was Dick's face as he had stood, head back, against the door, the rain running down his cheeks. It might have been tears for all she knew. The damage they had inflicted on each other was dreadful. And she could not see, even now, how she could have changed it, given the circumstances.

'Dick will not come back,' she thought, 'unless I make the first move.'

He had a stubborn independence; she had seen it at work in the past. He did not take favours easily. She could not afford to be proud; it was Dick's pride now that mattered more. She went to Mary and asked her where Dick went.

'These Deakins – where do they live? Is that where he stays?'

'I reckon so, ma'am. He's always been welcome there, like a son you could say.'

'Do you think that's where he is now?'

'Yes, I do.'

'Does Clara go back in the evening?'

'No, ma'am. She lives in the village with her mother-in-law.'

Christina considered. She wanted to send a message, but did not dare take it herself.

'Amy, will you go there for me?'

'If you want, ma'am.'

'You can go early, now, and deliver a note for me. It's on your way home, isn't it? Not much out of the way?'

'No, ma'am. I'll call with pleasure.'

'Don't say anything. Just give them a note for Dick.'

She went back to the sitting-room and composed the message. There was no need to be devious, or hide her feelings. She wrote: 'Dorothy and Mark have gone and will not be coming back. Please come home, I do want you so. C.'

Amy went. Clara came home with the children and Christina dismissed her and busied herself with a game with Tom and Isobel, which somehow got to involve Marigold too, and the rearrangement of a lot of the sitting-room furniture into the Turkish army. This numbed her mind mercifully until the children went to bed. She enjoyed putting them to bed herself, and sat up reading stories until the nursery fire had fallen into embers and even Tom into the beginnings of sleep, and then she went downstairs and sat by the fire again, waiting. She waited all night until it was long past her own bedtime. It was windy outside and the house rattled and moaned to the draughts and the fire flared and crackled as she put more logs on, not wanting to go to her cold bed. If she thought of anybody, it was of Will, alone as she was alone, his friendly spirit shaking its head over the tangle she had made of her loves since he had left her. He had never been a one for tangles. 'I mean well,' she thought. 'I do my best.' But she was depressed by the utter failure of her attempts to integrate her nearest and dearest. Their perversity seemed wilful. Her own perversity was a complete mystery even to herself. Human nature had depths in which she could only flounder.

The fire at last died down, she having lost the will to nurture it. She lay in the chair and listened to the wind and the sound of the big clock ticking. Somewhere a door slammed.

She got up and went out into the hall and waited. He came through from the kitchen, weary and desperate, and said nothing, looking at her. She put out her hand.

'Say it's all right . . .' Half question, half request; nothing was certain any more.

'Yes,' he said.

She felt her hand taken in his cold, hard grip, crushed fervently. 'You fool,' he said. 'And me, too.'

'Yes.'

'It's all right then. It's all right.' And he carried her up the stairs as if she were five years old.

Chapter 8

'The fact is, I don't like Clara working here. I want to look after the children myself.'

It was necessary to talk it all out, in the aftermath of the storm, to set everything straight for the future. Fowler was reinstalled; there had been no trouble on that score.

'I shan't have anything to do at all,' Christina pointed out.

'You say that now,' Dick said, 'but I imagine you will want to go hunting when it starts again; you will want to go off with Dorothy sometimes, have a day in London perhaps. You want me to learn to behave according to the standards expected, so you've got to do the same, Christina. Everyone in your position has a nanny for the children. And if you have another child –'

Christina laughed, but Dick was serious. 'There is another side to it too,' he pointed out. 'Clara's side. She needs the job. So do thousands of working people now. And if people like you don't employ them now, who else is going to? She's got two children of her own to raise without any help. She needs the money.'

Christina did not like this argument, but knew it was right. She knew that Flambards in its heyday had had almost a dozen servants in the house and garden alone. She knew that Clara had a desperate future ahead of her to rear her family on the miserable widow's pension provided by the government.

'Well, yes . . . I know you're right. But –'

'It's a big house to run. There's plenty of work there.'

'And the farm?'

'The farm has never been a job for a woman, Christina.'

'I did it! I –'

'But you came to me and begged me to come and work for you.'

'I –' It was true. Christina could not bring herself to admit it.

'But you like workers,' she said. 'You told me. Your own wife wants to be a worker, and you won't let me.'

'I consider running the house your job. If you do it properly it's a full-time job.'

Christina knew that Dick was right, but the prospect was not as attractive to her as he seemed to think it should be. It was really quite easy to run the house. It ran by itself.

'I'm used to problems,' she said. 'Difficult things.'

'You ought to be glad to be without problems. It's the first time in your life. In mine too. You should be grateful.'

'Yes, I know.'

But Christina knew from past history that she rarely did the right and proper thing.

'Well then, I must have a decent horse to ride if I'm to live like a proper lady, if not a motor-car.'

It was her money, after all, she remembered Dorothy pointing out. But thought it not politic to say out loud.

'Mmm.' Dick gave her a shrewd look, which told her that he knew perfectly well the way her mind was working. 'A horse – I'll see what I can do. There is very little to be had that you could call a decent hunter.'

'And you too. You will want to hunt, when there's a pack again.'

'I'm not sure that –'

'Dick! You've got to have some fun! Life's not all work, every minute! You know you'd love to hunt properly, like a gentleman, instead of how you used to, as a groom, waiting

144

on. If I'm to be a lady, you've got to *try* to be a gentleman, otherwise it's not fair.'

Dick sighed. 'Yes, but it comes hard. I know I should, for you, and I don't want it ever said that you aren't living the life you would have lived if you hadn't married beneath you.'

'You're much too sensitive! I don't think about those things.'

'No. You're not in my position. I know they say I married you for the farm and your money.'

'I told you – they said that of Will. It would have been the same if it had been Mark. You mustn't be so prickly.'

'Neither Will nor Mark were beneath you, though.'

'Oh, stop being so old-fashioned! You won't let me come down and you won't come up. How are we ever going to get it right?'

Dick laughed. 'It's a daft thing to quarrel over!'

But the fact was that Christina found that time hung heavily. She had few chores to do; the organization of the house, after her years in the hotel trade before she married Will, she found very easy. She could not visit in the neighbourhood as she was not yet accepted without embarrassment and could not be bothered; and she had to be careful about not visiting Dorothy too often. She usually visited when she knew Mark was out somewhere, but it was difficult to know his plans in advance. Mark had no routine. He had bought a motor-car which was the talk of the neighbourhood, a monstrously smart and expensive Vauxhall 30/98 which was reputed to go at a speed of eighty miles an hour if it had the chance. Mark wanted to take it over to Brooklands with Fergus, but Dorothy said he was not fit enough.

Dick had never heard of Brooklands.

'Brooklands is a motor-racing track in Surrey, a banked concrete circuit nearly three miles round,' Christina told him earnestly, shocked that he was so ignorant. She had gone there with Will on the rare occasions he had ever taken time off from his aeroplanes.

'He's a madman,' Dick said. 'I thought he was bad enough on a horse.'

'Oh, no, he's mellowed, I think,' Christina said.

Having lived with Will, she was able to take motor-racing in her stride; it seemed by comparison to flying quite tame. She thought it perfectly suitable for a lady. Dick did not agree.

'He's only gone in for motoring because he can't ride properly yet,' Christina pointed out.

'Why has he bought those horses then?'

'You know what he's like! He's determined to ride. He does ride. And then afterwards he has to use the Vauxhall until he's recovered enough to have another go.'

'He ought to try side-saddle. It would be kinder on him for a bit.'

'What, a man?'

'Lots of men ride side-saddle. Who do you think breaks in the ladies' hunters? Not many ladies. I know lots of grooms who ride side-saddle a sight better than most ladies.'

'Lots of women ride astride now too. I would like to try that.'

A quick glance at Dick's face confirmed her guess that he did not like the idea. She did not press it. Dick was as conservative as Will had been progressive. She had come from one end of the spectrum to the other, and it was going to take a little while to find middle ground. She remembered, for the first time, what Aunt Grace had said just before she had got married.

She decided to challenge Dick. 'Look, I won't ride astride if you don't like it, but I do want a good horse. That's fair enough. You said ages ago you would find me one.'

'All right, I promise.'

Dick spoke defensively, knowing that what she said was

true. Christina had been sorely tempted to borrow one of Mark's. He had bought two geldings from Newmarket, ex-racehorses, and both spectacularly handsome. One was by Bayardo and one by Minoru, the King's Derby winner. They had been bound for the knacker's on account of their intractability, times being hard in the racing world and feed short, but Mark was not a man to be put off by such a detail. He could ride anything.

'Perhaps you can when you're fit,' Dorothy chastised him, when he showed them to Christina. 'A fall now is the last thing you can do with. You should have bought something more suitable.'

'She nags me,' Mark said to Christina. 'You hear? I've got to keep up with hounds, madam, and a racehorse is eminently suitable. Don't you agree, Christina?'

'Oh, yes.'

'If you had a horse to ride we could take Marigold and do a bit of hunting on our own. The place is stinking with foxes. She'd put one up, I bet. It would be great sport until we get a pack. Perhaps old Lucas would lend us Bellman, I'll ask him tonight. We're going there for dinner.'

Mark and Dorothy, having settled in at Dermot's, were now leading a busy social life. Dorothy was popular, being new, gorgeous, and of impeccable background, and now that the war was finished dinner parties and luncheons were coming back into favour. With the Vauxhall at their disposal, the young Russell couple were able to visit easily, and Dorothy enjoyed asking people back. Christina and Dick had not received a single invitation, save to Mark and Dorothy's which Dick had refused. When Mark mentioned the invitation to Lucas's in such a casual fashion, Christina felt a childlike envy of their gallivanting. There was no doubt that evenings by the fire with Dick were getting slightly monotonous, especially as he so often fell asleep.

Dorothy, perhaps sensing Christina's feelings, said cheerfully to Mark, '*I'm* going there for dinner, darling. You're just going to watch everyone else eat and drink, remember, and make conversation.'

Mark made a face. 'Old Mother Lucas will make me something special – she always does. Some people appreciate the sacrifices I made for my country, even if you don't.'

'I must go in and sort out what I'm going to wear. I don't feel at home in the stable yard like you two. Come in when you're through, Christina, and we'll have tea.'

'Yes, I will.'

Christina had ridden over on Pepper and put the horse in a spare loosebox. The stable yard was as she remembered it, save that the looseboxes had been cleared of old machinery and propped-up bits of engine, and were again housing horses. The Vauxhall was in the coach-house, covered with old curtains to keep the bird droppings off. Looking at the gorgeous son of Bayardo, a bright chestnut with a white stripe down his face called Ragtime, Christina felt infinitely jealous for this stable yard, far more than for the Lucases' dinner-party.

'Dick keeps promising to buy me a horse, but nothing happens! He says he can't find one suitable.'

'Use one of these. Let's go for a little spin. You can put Pepper's saddle on Ragtime here, and I'll take Tiptoe. Where's Maloney? I'll tell him to get them tacked up.'

He turned and bawled 'Maloney!' into the general direction of the garden, and a young man appeared at the double.

'Put our visitor's side-saddle on Ragtime, and tack 'em both up, there's a good man.'

Christina, not having had a chance to protest, was startled into a sharp memory of Mark ordering Dick about in just the same way. Maloney worked fast; servants always did exactly what Mark told them, and Christina wished she could work the same magic with hers.

'Maloney was my batman,' Mark said cheerfully. 'He came and found me when I got blown up, didn't you, you old devil? Wished he'd left me to rot since, I expect.'

'That's right, sir,' Maloney's face was dead-pan, sliding the side-saddle on to Ragtime's back.

'That horse – he's not going to kill me, I hope? I've not heard very good reports of its manners. Remember I'm a wife and mother these days, and slightly out of practice.'

'Nothing you can't handle, you'll find.'

Christina was slightly doubtful about what she was doing, with a pang of guilt in Dick's direction. And then she remembered she was only doing it because Dick had sold Pheasant, because Dick was so slow in buying her another horse, and it was perfectly in accord with being a lady: to ride out with one's neighbour on a fine February afternoon. Besides, she *wanted* to. The spark of excitement that stirred when Maloney led out the gleaming thoroughbred was something she had almost forgotten.

Mark saw it, and laughed. 'That's my girl! It's been a long time, Christina!'

She had forgotten what a real horse felt like, the elegant length of neck ahead of her and the fine, nervous ears, the mouth coming to hand at a touch. The air was cold, the frost still lying into the afternoon, and the fields stretched bare, not a sign of life save for the robin in the quickthorn. Their breath clouded the air. The horses moved like drilled soldiers, held in, marking time, pulling hard. Mark glanced at Christina, half doubtfully, half in challenge.

'You're not – you're not expecting, or anything delicate like that, are you?'

'No.'

'Good. I'm just being responsible – considerate, you understand. You're all right to go, in other words?'

'Yes!'

It only took the merest easing of the reins, and then the

stiff yellow grass was blurred beneath them and the cold whipped their faces, making eyes stream, breath freeze; the body revelled in the transferred power. Christina knew she was laughing out loud, seeing the hedges whip past, watching the stride alongside of Mark's horse, Tiptoe, fighting for his head, his great quarters bunching and stretching and his nostrils open and red with excitement, thinking he was back at Newmarket. There was a ditch and layered hedge ahead, neat and inviting, and Mark shouted at her, half pulling up, but she nodded her head and drove on, as strung up now as the horse beneath her, aware that she knew nothing about the horse's capabilities and not caring. Ragtime ducked for his mouth and his lean ears went forward; he gathered himself together and launched himself into space as if he would jump the whole field ahead as well. Christina went with him, and on, knowing she had no power now to stop the excited horse. She steered in a big circle to ease up, not afraid, as once she had been afraid long ago on Treasure, and Ragtime came back to her, tiring, the breath rippling in his nostrils, sweat riming his lovely neck. She took up the reins, talking softly, gratefully, to him and he fell into a long gliding trot, tail up, head up, smooth as silk, back to Tiptoe at the top of the field, whom Mark had pulled up after the jump. Remembering, coming back to her senses, Christina asked in alarm, 'Are you all right? Oh, heavens, I forgot –'

Mark was grinning, 'I'm not such a maniac as you!'

'Oh, since when? I haven't noticed, save you pulled up a minute or two before me. I couldn't, you see.'

The two horses fell in side by side, jiggling and pulling, but the fierce steam gone out of them. They had no manners at all. Marigold ran on ahead, casting backwards and forwards.

'If we take her into the covert over beyond the turnip field, she might find something,' Mark said.

'Well –' Christina was doubtful, knowing what might

happen. 'You're never good enough for hunting yet, surely?'

He shrugged. 'Let's go past Lucas's and see if we can pick up Bellman. And there was a young bitch he's got from Suffolk. He's all for my starting it up again, I was talking to him about it.'

It was crazy, but Christina was stirred up and wanted to do it as badly as Mark. She waited at the end of the ride while he went up to Lucas's, and felt that they were back ten years, as if nothing had happened in between. The riding with Mark had always been something special: they had shared times that were unforgettable, and had no part in the rest of their lives. It was going back with a vengeance, an instinct she had no will to overcome.

They took their motley trio of hounds into the nearest covert and rode down the clearings shouting encouragement to them. The two old hounds were full of excitement and the young bitch thought it was an amazing game, tangling with the horses, who were unused to anything but the heaths of Newmarket and shied at every other tree. They had a few false starts, tearing out into the open and doubling back again as fast, and Christina said the huntsman was no good and, in between the banter, and waiting for Bellman who seemed to have disappeared, she remembered what Dick had said about men riding side-saddle. Mark was obviously, if not in actual pain, riding with more stubbornness than pleasure, Christina could see from the way he sat.

'Why don't we swap over?' she asked. 'See if it works better for you. And I've always wanted to ride astride.'

'I don't mind trying. I can ride back like it, see if it feels easier.'

They changed horses. Mark pulled Christina's stirrups up for her and gave her a leg up, after she had flung the skirt of her habit over the front of the saddle, and then he mounted from a fallen tree-trunk, throwing his right leg over the pommel.

'God, it feels peculiar,' he said.

Christina was thinking exactly the same, the insecurity of the seat surprising her. There was no support at all.

'I think —'

At that moment Bellman owned to a line with a quite blood-tingling certainty in his familiar voice. Christina felt a stab of pure joy, nostalgia and longing go through her that put everything else out of her head.

'Mark!'

'Oh, Jesus!' he said, and put Ragtime into a gallop straight from standstill and headed him for the gate at the end of the ride. Tiptoe wheeled round in pursuit. Christina clutched frantically at a handful of mane and screamed, but she was still with him over the gate and all in one piece as the two horses belted hell-for-leather round the end of the covert. The three hounds had gone out on the other side, beyond the big hedge with a ditch in front of it. They could see them in the afternoon dusk, making straight as a die for a big wood called Sailor's Spinney on the far horizon. Mark turned to look at Christina, not taking a pull at all.

'Are you game?' he shouted.

'Yes! Yes!' she screamed, terrified out of her wits and loving the feel of it, as if she had awakened out of a sleep of years. If Mark felt anything like she did, seeing the big jump looming up and not knowing how on earth to sit it, he must be terrified too, but the two horses jumped without a check side by side, and they both managed to stay with them and set them speeding up the big field neck and neck. Christina had time to gather her wits together before a heavy fence came into her streaming vision. She got her weight forward and gathered Tiptoe anxiously together; he was tiring and a crazy jumper, inexperienced and wild. This time having two legs to use struck her as extraordinarily useful. Mark, judging from his expression, was finding out the reverse. Christina took a strong pull, frightened at the last minute, and Tiptoe seemed to decide that the jump was not worth lifting for, for he went straight through it with a crashing of rotted timber and a lurch that nearly put Christina over the side. Nothing daunted, his wild gallop did not slacken. Before she could regain her stirrups they were beside the spinney, ducking under the reaching branches and looking for a way in through the rails. The three hounds, having had a long start, were already in and running through from the sound of them.

'He'll go to ground here!' Mark shouted. 'There's a gate – look – up there!'

'It's padlocked!'

'You're *ageing*, Christina!' Mark taunted her, and put Ragtime at it from a cruel ninety-degree turn. It was the sort of riding that had once had Dick in despair, having to keep the horses fit, but Christina could only admire, and follow where he led, her animal in no way disposed to lose sight of his companion. The wood closed in on them, twigs and brambles clutching at coat and breeches and bare skin alike, hair disentangling, the horses stumbling with fright and weariness. Mark pulled up, not before time, and they sat listening. The only sound was of their own breathing, and the horses', and the distant shrieks of disturbed jays. Christina could feel her legs trembling. A warm trickle of blood ran down her cheek.

'It's dark,' she noticed.

'Well, we'll have to find 'em. They're lost in here. We can't go home without them.'

He started to bawl for the hounds, riding on, pushing his way through the undergrowth. Christina followed, not wanting to lose sight of him, but by now horribly aware of the situation she had got herself into: she was certainly going to be very late getting home and she was not going to look as if she had been out merely admiring the winter sunset. She ached all over, and her bare flesh was scored with bramble tears. Dick would be furious at her riding Mark's horses, although he need never know she was astride.

Unfortunately there were some village boys ferreting on the edge of the wood, and Mark called them to help round up the hounds. By the time they had been recovered, the boys had taken in the situation, recognized the riders, commented with interest on Mark's side-saddle experiment and become thoroughly cognizant of their afternoon's adventure. Mark tipped the boys handsomely and turned for home with the three hounds at his horses' heels.

'There'll be no hiding this little escapade after that,' Christina said soberly.

'What is there to hide?'

'Me, astride, on one of your horses.'

'Is it forbidden then?'

'Disapproved of, strongly.'

Mark turned to look at her in surprise. He was still riding side-saddle, using a long rein, and looking perfectly at home.

'Dick doesn't have the faith in your riding that I have. My horses are quite all right for those that can ride. They lack a few manners, that's all. They can gallop though, can't they?'

'They're wonderful! Just the sort I would like.'

'And you look good astride. Lots of women do it now. I suppose Dick wants you to look like a lady – he looks up to you, Christina. You're on a pedestal, as far as he's concerned. He'll never get out of his servant ways.'

'Don't speak like that!' To change the subject, she said: 'How's the side-saddle then? More comfortable?'

'Yes, by miles. I couldn't have carried on astride. It might be useful until I'm back in form.'

'Have you got one?'

'No. I'll keep yours.'

'I'll swap it for this horse.'

'Done.'

154

'Do you mean that?'

'I never say things I don't mean.'

Christina's feelings were so mixed, of weariness, elation, of fear of Dick's reaction, of a deep glow of satisfaction for the pure beauty of galloping such a horse through the winter fields, that she could think of no reply. She rode numbly, cold now, watching the flitching of the aristocratic ears to the murmur of their voices. The horse was a very dark liver-chestnut, whole-coloured save for a tiny star, and was nervous and volatile and exactly the sort of horse Dick had no use for. What had she done?

They rode in silence, and were in sight of the lights of Dermot's when Mark said suddenly, 'You know what I asked you – if you were – were expecting? Is there any reason why not? Do you want a child?'

Christina recalled her wits, to tackle this unexpected question.

'Yes, I think so.' She was always slightly relieved to find herself still 'free' – for that was the word that came to mind – each month, but Dick was always plainly disappointed. 'There's no reason. It will happen, I daresay.'

Mark said, 'You're not putting it off on purpose, like Dorothy?'

'No.'

'She says you are. She says all women want what she calls a bit of fun first.'

Christina was nervous of passing any comment, knowing the situation. She did not think it fair of Dorothy not to tell Mark the truth of her feelings, if they were so strong. She was probably frightened – with good reason – of his likely reaction.

'I expect she is a little afraid of the responsibility. It's no small thing, you know, to bring a child into the world.'

'Most people don't give a damn. I think she's unnatural, at her age. It's not as if she's seventeen.'

155

'Not all women want a child. It's not as natural as you think.'

'But I want one.'

'You might not always get what you want with Dorothy. You knew that when you married her.'

Mark half pulled up, frowning at her. 'But that's not a mere difference of opinion. That's the marriage itself.'

Christina realized she had gone too far. 'It's something between the two of you. Ask her how she feels, discuss it with her. It's not something you can dictate, even if it means so much to you.'

'But of course it does! And Dick, I reckon, is no different in that respect. Those feelings are the most natural in the world. Has Dorothy said anything to you about it? Do you know what it's all about?'

'No.' Christina felt justified in lying, as Dorothy had lied in telling Mark about her own failure to conceive.

Mark did not pursue it, to Christina's relief, but in the ensuing silence Christina sensed his genuine hurt. When they pulled up in the stable yard and he got down, Christina could see how much the ride had tired him. He was sharp with Maloney out of the same frustration with his own frailty that he had once directed at her, but Maloney accepted it with what Christina saw was understanding and sympathy. No doubt he had far bloodier memories than hers to put it all into perspective.

'Tiptoe is to go over to Flambards in the morning,' Mark said to him. 'Pepper had better go back tonight, in case he's needed. You take him when you've done these two, and I'll run Mrs Wright back in the car.'

'You're tired, Mark. I'll ride back.'

'I've got to go out tonight. I shall have to get the car out. It makes no difference.'

'You should stay at home. You do too much.'

'Yes, so Dorothy will tell me. But she will insist on my going out, because she wants to go.'

How badly we all treat each other, Christina thought wearily. And yet we all mean well. She curled up in the beautiful leather passenger seat, ducking down to keep out of the searing cold.

'Do you like him?' Mark asked, his humour restored. He drove as he rode, like a lunatic.

'Yes, he's a beauty.'

'You told Dick you'd like a car yet?'

'I've told him, yes.'

'If he doesn't agree to it, you can always come out in mine. I'll give you lessons.'

'I can drive. Will taught me.'

'Fergus is going to rent our carriage-house. Did Dorothy tell you? Set up a workshop, share the groom's cottage with Maloney. He wants to start a garage, repair cars, farm machinery and all that. He's a good mechanic, and thinks that is where the future lies, thinks it'll make him a living.'

'Will there be enough work out here? More in London, I should think.'

'It's coming pretty fast, and there's no competition down here as yet.' Mark changed down to turn into the Flambards drive. 'It suits him, a quiet place. He's very shy about his face, you know. He says it's dreadful to see people's expressions, before they recover and make them polite. If you live in a small community, it wouldn't be so bad, people would get to know you.'

'Yes, I can understand that.'

'He's a funny chap. Very serious, you know, underneath. Believes in hard work. Bit like Will.'

'Not like you!'

Mark laughed. 'I might come to it, in time. When I have a family to support.'

Christina felt a qualm at his words, but said nothing. She had more problems on her plate than he did at the moment, being late with Dick's supper, covered in scratches, and with the news to break to Dick about Tiptoe, which she could not believe would be taken with good grace.

It wasn't. Dick's face closed up with anger at the news, yet there was little he could justifiably say in protest, having failed to produce a horse himself.

'If it's one of those animals he got from Newmarket, they're neither of them fit for a woman to ride.'

'Well, I rode it this afternoon, and it went beautifully.'

Dick looked up from his dinner scornfully. 'Look at you! You were never in control, to get a face like that?'

'We were in Sailor's Spinney. A fox went away and we had Marigold with us, and Bellman – Mark borrowed him for the afternoon – and they lost it in the spinney, and we couldn't find them, and it was going dark. We had to ride about looking for them, and it's got terribly overgrown.'

'You obviously had a good day.'

'Yes, I did.' It was all very well being placating, but Christina refused to back down. She felt guilty about what she had done, but only because she knew Dick did not like it. She had done nothing she was ashamed of. 'It was generous of him, to give the horse to me.'

'Dorothy's horse. It was her money bought it.'

'Oh, Dick, stop it!' She had to bite back the argument that was on her lips, not wanting to quarrel. 'It's a beauty – by Minoru. Flambards has never had a Derby winner's son before! Please don't be cross about it!'

The fact that he was being unreasonable, and knew it, did not improve Dick's temper, but he said no more. They finished dinner and lit the lamps in the sitting-room, and Dick lay back in the armchair. Christina knew that he had been hedging all day; he was covered in more scratches and tears than she was. But his were nobly won in the course of duty, and hers were through frivolous play. She scowled at her sewing as she sat being a good housewife. She had done nothing that afternoon that she hadn't done dozens of times in the past; she could not change her nature to please Dick. He was not changing his one jot to accommodate her. If he had worked at it, they might have been at the Lucases' dinner-party tonight. He had made no effort at all to get to know his neighbouring landowners, although he talked with their men without thinking. It was no good his expecting to be accepted if he made not the slightest effort himself. One had to go half-way, make the right overtures. Not that she had ever hankered after the social round ... but being cut off from it altogether was different from not joining in through choice.

Right now, this moment, she thought, glaring at her haphazard darning of Dick's worn socks, she would rather be chatting away at the Lucases' dinner-table than sitting at home plying her needle. She could just see Dorothy charming all the old farmers into a jelly with her red hair piled high and her evening dress as low as would pass for respectability. She was a witty conversationalist and a sympathetic listener and always shone in company. Mark would like it, being proud of her. He had never been over-fond of dressing for dinner, but tonight he would have toed the line at her insistence; he found dinner-parties difficult, Christina knew, being sorely tempted by the freely flowing alcohol. Having to resist it made him bad-tempered, and keeping sober when everyone else was getting merry was hard, barely within his capabilities. But Dorothy, amid her witty conversation and sympathetic listening, watched him like a hawk, and was sharp with hosts who tried to tempt him. She had an imperious way with her that she could still use to good effect; Christina could remember being very nervous of her when she first knew her, intimidated by her undeniable strength of will and personality. She was well matched to Mark.

Dick had fallen asleep. Christina looked at the clock: it was only half-past eight. She put down her wretched darning and sighed. The exertions of her afternoon with the two Newmarket geldings came back to her with the twinges of her leg-muscles and the weariness of her shoulders. She lay back in the armchair, giving her mind to the feel of that lovely galloping excitement which she had gone without for so long. Dick could have shared it with her if he had wanted, if he had embraced a modicum of play in his mode of living, rather than hundred per cent work. He resented her joy because it had been with Mark, not him. Dick was a beautiful rider but did not ride for pleasure, only for transport. And again Christina found her mind going back to Mark with deep affection for what he had given her, not merely the actual horse, but the accord of the whole afternoon. They had been in tune, a duet, long practised; she had forgotten what pleasure she had had in the past riding with Mark, until it had happened again. Her mind kept going to him, she could not help it.

'Why are you smiling like that?'

Dick's voice came unexpectedly. Christina jerked up in surprise, and saw him contemplating her, not suspicious, but with affection. She was frightened of her feelings then. She stretched out to him, her hands clasping his knees.

'You must not try to change me!' she said. 'You know I always liked it – to ride like that. Not on a donkey. You can give it me too, if you don't want me to do it with Mark. But you can't change me, Dick. It's not fair.'

'You want to change me.'

'No! But you say life is for working – if you work all the time, and I'm not to have any part in the farm, we shall never come together! It was only like that this afternoon, because it couldn't be with you.'

'Like what this afternoon?' He picked her up on her words.

'Lovely! You know how I love it! And it's not fair for you to get cross. It's how I was when you first knew me – I haven't changed. Now I've got a horse you must get a good one too, and we can ride together, and go hunting next winter.'

'Who's being bossy now?'

'Oh, Dick, it matters!' It suddenly mattered terribly, far more than Dick knew. She needed help with her affections, for they were not totally under control.

He laughed then, and agreed, and she calmed down and realized how tired she was. Another five minutes and she too would be asleep in front of the fire.

The next morning Maloney rode over on Tiptoe and the whole of Flambards turned out to admire him.

'Some hunter!' Dick said, but not unkindly. 'Its legs will never stand it.'

'Then I shall have to have two, for when one breaks down. Do you want to try him, Dick? Go on, please! Take him in the home field and give him a canter and you will see why I like him so.'

'That's a command?'

'Yes. I think it is.'

'Go on, dad, make him go,' Tom said encouragingly.

Tiptoe was looking round his new quarters nervously, whinnying to Sweetbriar, while Moonshine banged about in his loosebox with excitement. Fowler was pursing his lips, muttering.

'They're nothing but trouble, that sort. Trust Mr Mark!'

Dick got up and let down the leathers a couple of holes. Tiptoe came together, the cold wind lifting his fine dark mane. He bunched his quarters and gave a couple of bucks while Dick was adjusting the tack. Dick did not budge in the saddle, but punished the horse with a quick crack behind with Maloney's stick. The horse bucked again. Dick took its head up sharply.

'These his normal tricks?' he asked Maloney.

'Well –' The groom scratched his nose thoughtfully.

'Hmm.'

Dick took him into the home meadow beyond the drive and they all moved across to watch him put the horse through its paces. Tiptoe went delicately, shying at every shadow, dancing over the winter grass. Dick gave him time to settle and then made him work, holding him and driving him into the bit, so that he trotted slowly but with great power, his hind legs lifting high, and then easing and lengthening so that he floated over the ground scarcely seeming to touch down at all. Dick rode with such grace and sympathy that he seemed to Christina to take on a new dimension; he had always had this ease on a horse, something instinctive, yet he did not appreciate it himself. It was crazy of him, she thought, not to want to do it, when he was capable of such art; it was perverse. She was seized with a determination she had forgotten she had. When Maloney was in the kitchen, having a cup of tea, the horse put away and Dick gone back to his hedging, Christina scribbled a message for the groom to take to Mark: 'Find a horse for Dick, PLEASE – I will pay for it, but be quick, and it must be a beauty, only the sort he likes.' She guessed that Mark would recognize the urgency in her note, if not entirely the reasoning that lay behind it, which even now she was not sure if she understood herself. It was to protect herself from Mark, she thought.

Five days later Maloney brought a horse over, a magnificent dark bay half-bred, with bone to match its blood, and quality in its fine head and bold, inquisitive eyes. It was a five-year-old, and a note came with it.

'For Dick, name of Ceasefire.'

'Who christened it?' Christine wondered, but not out loud.

It was too fortuitous to be coincidence. But Dick took the horse with good grace, full of admiration for Mark's choice.

162

'He only found it, he didn't pay for it,' Christina said. 'Now we can all ride together.'

But Dick said he had to finish the hedging, because it would be time for drilling before he was through, the weather going the way it was. And Ceasefire was turned out, save when he was wanted for transport, and Christina rode alone.

Chapter 9

Fergus came to live at Dermot's and brought with him a conglomeration of strange machinery, one or two bits and pieces recognizable as motor-cars, or parts of motor-cars. The only one which actually went was the one Christina called the Monstrous Mercedes, the pre-war, chain-driven, ninety-horse-power animal in which he had first visited Flambards. 'Unfortunately obsolete for what I want to do,' Fergus said.

'And what do you want to do?'

'Win a few sprints,' Fergus said.

'What is a sprint? A race?'

'Hill-climbs are what I prefer, yes.' And his eyes went reflectively to Mark's Vauxhall parked on the gravel, gleaming new and polished daily by Maloney as diligently as the thoroughbred Ragtime himself.

Christina followed his gaze. 'Would that win?'

'It would stand a very good chance, yes.'

Christina felt she was on very familiar ground, the pushing of engine power to its limits and the design of the efficient machine having been exactly what Will's short working life had been all about.

'Were you friendly with Will?'

'I met him, unfortunately only a month before he was killed. I was posted to his squadron when it was stationed near St Omer and when I flew with him I knew he was the sort of man I liked. It was obvious that he knew more about the machine he flew than any of the men on the ground, and that was my interest too, why I chose the R.F.C. But he wasn't an easy man to know, and time wasn't on our side. I was sorry.'

'You seem to think the same way. You know this is the place where he learned to fly? The man who lived here taught him.'

'Yes, so I understand.'

Christina felt at home with Fergus, for his interests, his manner of working were so like Will's. He lacked Will's flair and impetuosity, but he was reassuringly steady for a friend of Mark's. Christina sensed that he liked to hide an essential seriousness beneath a flippant surface. He did not talk much about what he was doing, but whenever Christina went over he was working, never sitting around. He had cars in for repair: Mr Masters became one of his first customers; he also worked long hours on the strange things he called his racing machines. They made an incredible din which Christina could occasionally hear from Flambards, and she found herself drawn to Dermot's by what Dorothy called 'the fun and games out there'. Dorothy too admitted that it was just like old times. 'It's what we were weaned on, isn't it, Christina? That frightful row and the smell of burning oil.'

Christina rode over on Tiptoe, and put him in his old loosebox and went to drink coffee with Dorothy in her kitchen amongst the buckets of whitewash and paint which were Dorothy's current preoccupations. She was transforming the whole house into a masterpiece of contemporary design, pale and spare and elegant, and – to Christina – incredibly impressive. Mark would drive his wife to the main line station for a day's foray in London, and meet her in the evening to collect an array of parcels from Harrods and Maples and Marshall and Snelgrove's. She made curtains indefatigably on her new sewing-machine, of fine, pale, plain materials, and lit her rooms with silver lamps in the guise of water nymphs and dancing maidens; she stripped paint from the doors and bleached the wood with solutions she mixed in the chaotic kitchen. She banned the two foxhounds Mark had brought back from a day's visit to an old hunting friend of his father's in Suffolk, and made Mark take his boots off to go into the sitting-room.

'It's like bloody Buckingham Palace,' Mark grumbled. 'I'll take dinner in the servants' quarters so I can be myself.'

'When the dining-room is ready we will have a dinner-party for you and Dick,' Dorothy said to Christina. 'I shall *insist* that he comes. And Fergus. It is compulsory. Just family.'

'I'll tell him,' Christina said, and described to Dick the transformations that were taking place. Flambards looked dowdy by contrast to her eyes, too homely and cluttered after the restrained ethereal schemes of Dorothy's rooms.

'It suits me,' Dick said. 'I don't like smart places.'

'You *will* come, though, when Dorothy invites you? It is her house-warming, just us and Fergus. You promise, Dick?'

'I'd rather not. It's not my way of life, admiring the furnishings.'

'Dick, you must.' Christina spoke abruptly, deadly serious. Dick noticed the change in her manner; he frowned.

'I shan't stop you going if you want to.'

'I cannot go without you, and Dorothy wants you particularly. Dick, I don't ask you to do much of this sort of thing, but this is different.'

'Their way of life isn't mine.'

'But a whole lot of their way of life *is* mine. And you married me and you have to come a little way to meet me, Dick. I don't ask you very much.'

He was silent.

'It is very important.'

Christina knew privately that it was far more important than Dick would have it. She was no social butterfly, but she knew now that she required more of her marriage than supervising the running of the house all day and watching Dick sleep by the fire after dinner every evening. Aunt Grace's forecast which she had dismissed so contemptuously kept coming to mind. She had married a sober and industrious young man, but she had not supposed that he eschewed pleasure so completely. She had lived amongst a lot of young and high-spirited people before Will had been killed, and now the war was over she longed to join in a little of the fun that was in the air again. Dorothy and Mark had had a night out in London with Jerry, visiting the Hammersmith Palais to hear the Original Dixieland Jazz Band, and they drove to Southend for thés-dansants and sat up late entertaining, and it was hard for Christina to be cut off so completely from such treats, and to hear all about them from Dorothy, knowing that she would have been included if Dick had agreed. They were always invited. 'Me dancing?' Dick seemed to find the idea worthy only of amused contempt.

'It's a social requirement for a person in your position – a big landowner in a small community. Even old Masters is capable of asking Mrs Lucas to do the Lancers. It's not a professional tango I'm asking, only a gesture, to join in.'

'Can you honestly see me asking Mrs Lucas to dance?'

'No, but it's surely not beyond the bounds of probability that you might at some time wish to ask Dorothy, your own sister-in-law, for a dance? At a party, or at Christmas – or have you decided never to attend parties?'

Christina tried to keep the bitterness out of her voice. She loved Dick dearly but she had not foreseen his stubborn disinclination to adapt to his new position. She realized now that he was too proud to risk being snubbed by people whom in fact he despised; he had no respect or admiration for the hereditary landowners, his own family having suffered gravely at their hands. The people he most admired were those who had pulled themselves up by their own dour determination, like the Deakins, like Will, like the local corn-merchant who had built up a business from nothing. He did not even respect himself, Christina sometimes suspected, for having accepted Flambards. But he had wanted her, and Flambards had been part of the deal. She was tempted to ask him this, but did not wholly want to know the truth. She only knew that she could no more go along with what he wanted, cutting herself off from the local community and directing all her energies into housekeeping, than he could find the heart to launch himself into the social calendar of their hidebound community.

'Please Dick, you have to make a bit of a compromise. Dorothy will be very hurt if you refuse her invitation.'

'I'll come if you insist.'

His attitude did not help her either in her hopeless desire to stop thinking about Mark. This was something she could not understand in herself, convinced that she was in love with Dick. When she was with Mark she could easily persuade herself that the attraction was a figment of her imagination, for she could look at him quite coolly and see him as the brother figure he had always been – no different – funny, infuriating, kind, cruel, overbearing according to the whim of the moment. She did not flirt with him. She could leave him without a backward glance. But when she was away from him she thought about him every time her mind was not consciously engaged in what she was doing. She thought about the colour of his eyes and the way he smiled, and the scar in his eyebrow that Dick had made, the way he still had, at unexpected moments, of revealing the legacy of his awful injuries, by the way he moved or a sudden look in the eyes – 'For let's face it,' Dorothy had said to Christina, 'he will never get over what's happened to him. There is no cure, only a coming to terms with the situation' – and she knew that such thoughts were the symptoms of being in love. But she could not accept that she was in love with Mark. The idea was completely unacceptable to her logic. But her instincts did not answer to logic.

She tried to reason that it was because he was Will's brother, and there had never been any doubt about her love for Will. Mark was out of the same mould and this love was a harking back, looking for her sweet Will. But when Will had been alive she had never acknowledged the comparison. She could discuss her problem with no one nor expect help from any quarter, least of all from Mark himself who made no attempt to hide the fact that he enjoyed her company, was always pleased to see her, and treated her with affectionate familiarity. Sisterly, Christina tried to tell herself, but knew that it was not. Like herself, Mark had areas of disagreement with his spouse that went very deep – Dorothy was both of independent means and an independent nature, and marriage was not going to change that. She refused to have a child and, even if she had not revealed to Mark that she was not ever going to change her mind on the subject, she had already hurt him irrevocably by her attitude.

'If I had known, I would not have married her,' he said to Christina, but Christina did not want the burden of such confidences and would not reply. It made her own position that much more difficult, provoking a reaction in similar vein: that if she had known how entrenched Dick's attitude was going to be to his working-class origins she might echo Mark's own sentiments. Perhaps, she thought, Mark and Dorothy had never truly been in love, pushed into marriage only by the prevailing wartime mood to seize a chance while it was there to be enjoyed. Mark had admitted at the time that he loved her more. She had supposed herself in love with Dick, but perhaps she had been in love with the idea of having a man at the head of her ready-made home and family, a man who had appeared to fit the role so exactly? Perhaps both Mark and herself had married dreams which had dissolved when exposed to the hard grind of reality. Certainly they had both married in haste. It also occurred to her that the basic reason for the dichotomy between Mark and Dorothy, Dorothy's failure to get with child, might have a bearing on her own predicament. She knew that Dick wanted her to have a child as badly as Mark wanted it for Dorothy, and if she became pregnant she might settle her unruly desires without any difficulty.

By the date of Dorothy's house-warming party she did in fact suspect that she was in that condition.

'I don't want to tell Dick until I'm sure,' she confided in Dorothy. 'I don't want to make a fool of myself. He wants it so badly.'

Dorothy made a face. 'I know it's lovely for you, and I'm pleased and all that, but the news will set Mark off. We have dreadful rows about it, you know. Sometimes I think I shall have to give in just for peace and quiet.'

'I can understand how he feels.'

'He says now I should have told him before we were married. But if you remember – who looked that far ahead? I'm pretty sure when he went back to France he didn't think he would come back alive. I know I didn't. The marriage was crazy anyway. It's no good now saying what we should or should not have discussed then. He'll just have to make the best of it.'

Christina did not reply, which Dorothy took as an inferred criticism, for she said, 'He's not easy to live with, you know.'

'I do know.'

'He wanted to marry you, didn't he?'

'Once, yes.'

'Did you –' Dorothy looked at Christina, and stopped. 'I sometimes think . . . I wonder –' She stopped again.

Christina knew she should swoop in swiftly with a cool,

soothing, placatory speech, but she could find no words to say. She stood there looking at Dorothy's troubled face and felt trampled and hopeless, and a lump came into her throat. It was no good telling lies; one did not treat a dear friend like that. Equally well it was useless to tell the truth, for she did not know what the truth was. She felt the tears coming into her eyes for pure despair at her stupidity.

Dorothy stepped forward and put her arms round her and held her, without saying anything. Her understanding made it worse, and Christina wept. Perhaps they both needed it, for it was better afterwards, a relief, without commitment.

'We are a mess, aren't we?' Dorothy said gently.

'We're not very clever.'

'I think –' Dorothy looked thoughtful, a glint in her eyes which Christina recognized. 'What do you say if – if we take a holiday? Just you and me, not the men. The children if you like, but not Mark and Dick. We'll go to France to the seaside and you can visit Will's grave. You said you wanted to. We've neither of us had a holiday for years, not even a honeymoon. So now we'll take a honeymoon, but without our husbands! What do you say?'

Christina looked at Dorothy in astonishment, and found herself responding with a surge of delight to the lovely, crazy idea.

'You and me and Tom and Isobel?'

'Wonderful! Do just as we please!'

'Oh, yes! And not Clara. Just the four of us.'

'We'll tell them tonight, over dinner. We'll get them well fed and well wined – Dick, at any rate – and then break the news. *Fait accompli*. No going back.'

'We could go to that beach where I landed with Will in the Blériot.'

'Hardelot? That's right close to where I was nursing. I know a little place where we can stay.'

171

'But will you want to go there? All those memories?'

'It will be interesting. It will be good, in fact, to take the children there and see it afresh, as a seaside place, how it should be. What I did there can never happen again, surely? It will be a looking forward, it will be good for me.'

Christina said reflectively, 'I can't imagine Dick ever wanting to take a holiday! He works until he's tired to death every night.'

'Not tonight,' Dorothy said firmly. 'If he falls asleep over dinner I shall be very annoyed.'

'Make sure he enjoys it, then perhaps he will want to go out more often.'

When he came in from work Dick was resigned to attending the dinner-party, if not actively looking forward to it. He had a bath and a shave and put his best suit on. 'Why are you going to church now?' Tom asked him. 'It's not Sunday.' Christina laughed. Mark and Dorothy joined them in the Russell pew on Sundays and they sat like a model family, the children between them. Afterwards Dick would pass the time of day amicably enough with the Deakins and some of his mother's old friends, but to the Lucases and the Masters he would accord a distant nod, no more. No doubt the sight of the four of them with the two contrarily conceived children was a constant reminder to the neighbourhood of Flambards' scandalous relationships but familiarity, Christina felt, in the end would breed boredom. Their story was stale now.

'You ought to have evening dress,' she said. 'The others will.'

'Yes, well, I shall be more comfortable. If it's not correct I needn't come?'

'No, you're not getting out of it like that!'

Christina had a beautiful new dress by Lucile that Dorothy had bought for herself in London and found too small: it was dashingly modern, of soft brown georgette draped to the figure, caught with a grey rose at the waist, the skirt narrow and ending just above the ankles. Dorothy's dress for the house-warming was of black satin, low at the front and even lower at the back, hung from her shoulders by narrow gold braid. She had given Christina a preview, and Christina thought Dick would disapprove and rather wished she might have chosen something less daring. Dorothy loved clothes and everything new, from jazz to the Russian ballet, from tennis parties to cocktails. Dick allowed her this, when the subject was discussed, for he admired her nursing record during the war, and said she needed her bit of fun now it was over, but he never suggested that Christina should join in the fun. Christina thought he would say her lovely dress showed too much leg, but when he saw her he made no criticism.

They drove over behind Pepper through the cold spring evening and Christina determined to buy a car. She would ask Fergus to advise her that evening, and he could teach her to mend punctures too, so that she was independent. Tyres were forever picking up horse-shoe nails and tyre-changing was a constant chore. She doubted whether Fowler could learn such tricks at his age.

Dermot's was all bright lights, the gramophone playing, fires burning in the new, modern grates. Mark and Dorothy were at the door to greet them, easy and welcoming, Mark on his very best behaviour, friendly and almost deferential to Dick. A maid took their coats, and Dorothy took Christina upstairs to the bedroom so that she could tidy her hair. Against her white walls Dorothy's black dress was startlingly simple and effective, and – by Flambards' standards – shockingly modern. Her face was powdered white and her lips coloured red, and she looked to Christina a whole generation apart, into a new age. Christina sat at the dressing-table and recognized the music from downstairs as the Scott Joplin rag they had played the night Sandy had been killed, his favourite, and she remembered herself at that period as bright and flamboyant as Dorothy was now. But looking at herself in the mirror she saw a sedate country lady dressed in brown, far more likely to be at home with the Blue Danube than Scott Joplin. The image upset her.

'Can I try your lipstick? Do you think it would suit me?'

'Of course! Look, I've got a selection. And the powder is in the bowl. Here –' She handed her a vast powder-puff. 'I'll show you.'

After five minutes of delicate, skilful work on Dorothy's part, Christina was much cheered by her new look.

'You don't think I look too fast?'

'Of course not! You should go to town more often, Christina – you will see everybody is using it – and the clothes! Some of the skirts are way above the ankles now, and nobody looks twice.'

'Dick will.'

But Dorothy just laughed. They went downstairs and into the sitting-room where Dick and Fergus were standing in front of the fire talking and Mark was pouring drinks at the sideboard. Christina went to greet Fergus, who looked uncommonly clean and correct, and was talking to Dick about tractors. Christina saw Dick's look of shocked surprise at her new appearance. He made no remark, but when she went back to Mark to choose her drink, Mark kissed her tenderly on the cheek, brother-in-law fashion, and said, 'Darling, you look gorgeous!' The look in his eyes was not brotherly at all. She did not dare stay near him, aware that it was Mark she had wanted to impress more than Dick, and confused yet again by her hopeless instincts.

Dorothy then lit a Turkish cigarette and stood by the hearth with the men smoking, and Christina saw Dick watching her as if hypnotized, shocked and admiring, and no doubt wishing himself safely at home by his own fireside.

At this thought Christina was more than ever distressed by her disloyalty. She drank her glass of sherry quickly, hoping to forget herself in pure conviviality, and was glad to be distracted by the noisy arrival of Jerry and a girl-friend called Jean, as white-faced, red-lipped and bare-backed as Dorothy, although by no means as elegant. Christina went to Dick's side then to support him against this preponderance of fast friends, and they went in to dinner. Dorothy insisted on having Dick beside her, and Christina found herself next to Mark, whose job was to pour the wine without taking any himself, a task which made him progressively more withdrawn as the dinner progressed, in marked contrast to the rest of the party. What he ate was not much of an improvement on what he had eaten when at Flambards, and Christina found her old compassion engaged in a way that frightened her.

Fergus and Jerry when slightly drunk were great company and the evening digressed into an explosion of music and dancing, helped on by Jerry's cornet accompaniments and Jean's demonstration of the shimmy. Christina, joining in to try to cover up her disastrous inclinations, was aware numbly of Dick's disapproval and Mark's brooding contemplation of her antics from the sidelines, and was infinitely relieved when Dorothy, always a tactful hostess, called for a waltz to be played and went to Dick and said, 'I knew you were going to ask me, Dick, so here I am,' with such sweetness that he could not help but soften and oblige. Mark was at Christina's side instantly.

'Please, Christina, will you dance with me?'

She danced with him, not daring to speak, gazing bleakly over his shoulder. He bent his head down to hers and whispered, 'Please, Christina, will you love me?'

'No,' she whispered back.

'You do.'

'How can I?' Her voice sounded agonized, although she had intended tartness. 'Why don't you learn?'

'I don't want to learn,' he said, and danced then in silence, holding her closely. He tried to dance her into another room but she pulled herself away adamantly, close to tears. She saw Fergus watching, his half-a-face registering intense interest. He came over and held out his arms and said, 'Can you bear to take a turn with Uncle Fergus? Always ready to come to the aid of a distressed gentlewoman.'

'Is it so obvious?' Christina asked in despair.

'Forgive me.' He was genuinely put out by his tactlessness and made to repair the damage as he took her in his arms. 'Mark finds parties difficult, naturally. Being hungry and stone-cold sober is not conducive to having a whale of a time. The inhibitions need to be softened for all of us. I, for example, would not dare to ask you to come into my arms if I were not fairly inebriated. Do you mind?'

'Why should I?'

'You are kind. Perhaps the drink is speaking in you too.'

'Not at all. I feel very sober indeed.'

'You do not find me repulsive?'

'Fergus!'

She hugged him, as much dismayed by what lay buried in his consciousness as in her own. Did they all have such hidden agonies to be revealed only under the party influence?

'I never notice now. I did when I first met you, I admit.' It was the truth; she did not have to invent.

'You are very sweet, you do me good.' They danced in mutual accord, Christina keeping her eyes down, not wanting to see anyone else, holding on to her own equilibrium in this interlude with Fergus. Fergus was a comfort, wiser than the rest of them, a man to be trusted. She felt closer to him by what he had revealed; other people's frailties, when one was obsessed by one's own, could only reassure.

They left at midnight, Maloney bringing Pepper to the door.

'You really will have to get motorized, Dick,' Mark said, seeing them down the steps. 'Christina can afford it.'

'If Dorothy can, I daresay,' Dick said.

Christina huddled down into her fur collar, realizing that nothing was changed. She caught Dorothy's glance, rolling her eyes, and giggled.

'Thank you for a lovely evening!'

Dick touched Pepper with the whip before Mark could kiss Christina good-bye, and almost before they were out of earshot he said, 'Thank goodness that's done with. You won't catch me going through that sort of rigmarole again.'

'Why not? *I* enjoyed it.'

'By the look of you, I didn't get that impression.'

'Everyone was nice to you, weren't they? What didn't you like?'

'All that carry-on – what did they call it? The shimmy? And the tango – it's not my style. And you painting your face, for heaven's sake! You're lucky I didn't tell you to take it off.'

'And you're lucky you didn't too! I'm your wife, not your daughter.'

Christina was too tired and upset to stop herself from fighting back, having foreseen what would happen on the journey home.

Dick said, 'I'm glad you admit it. I could have sworn you were Mark's, at times.'

'For better or for worse, I'm married to you. And I'm carrying your child, and when you are so petty and old-fashioned I wish I wasn't. God help it if it grows up like you!'

As soon as she had said this Christina was appalled at herself, but it was too late to change anything. Dick drove on without a word. She saw his face in the moonlight, set and pale, a small muscle twitching in the curve of his jaw. She was sorry, and wanted to say she was sorry, but Dick was as cold as the moonscape itself, and there was no putting it right.

Chapter 10

Christina lay in the sand-dunes watching Dorothy and the children on the shoreline picking up shells. They moved slowly, bent over, concentrating, Isobel's white pinafore shining against the tawny sands, blowing up to reveal frilly drawers and fat brown legs furred with sand, feet bare and dimpled through the pools. Christina felt possessive of the children, loving their company without Clara. They loved the sun-baked, pine-scented estuary of the Canche with its racing tide flooding and ebbing over the miles and miles of sand night and morning, the hours spent wandering and collecting bucketsful of seawrack and crab-shell and popping seaweed and bleached white sticks, laughing at Dorothy's capers, picking bunches of heather and sea-lavender and frail blue harebells. Christina was fat and lazy with child, and nursing every carefree minute of her magic holiday. The release of being freed from the tangles of her emotional home-life for a fortnight was bliss.

'And not only for you. For me too,' Dorothy confided, and behind them across the warm heaths and hills of the Pas de Calais the tangled debris of the war lay like the mess of their own marriages, somehow to be tidied by time. Christina knew she was in France to visit Will's grave, that she must look at the horror behind them and remember how Mark, how Dick was wounded there, along with God knew how many more hundred thousands, be awed and agonized by all that had happened, pray on her knees that it would never happen again. But all she did was lie on the beach in the hot sun and laugh. Dorothy was such perfect company and the children so funny and happy, the bulge in her stomach moved with its own life and made her feel blissfully contented: pregnancy suited her both mentally and physically. She was like an animal, she thought, lying in the sun enjoying the feel of its own body coming to fruition. She wanted it to go on for ever. She did not want to go back to the agonies of trying not to love Mark, and of realizing that she had nothing in common at all with her husband.

When she confided in Dorothy about her doubts towards Dick, Dorothy said, 'I'm afraid I'm a bad influence on you. If Mark and I were in another part of the country and not distressing you with our fast ways, you would have settled down with Dick far more easily.'

Christina spent a lot of time trying to work out if this were true. Up to a point perhaps it was, but not entirely. How Dorothy and Mark lived was how she had lived too before she had been widowed. She had fallen into the trap Aunt Grace had been astute enough to foresee.

'Having Dick's child makes you happy, so it can't be too bad,' Dorothy said.

'No, and it makes him happy too. It makes us all happy.'

'It doesn't make Mark happy.'

Wrapped up in her own problems, Christina sometimes forgot Dorothy's. For Dorothy too the holiday was a lovely respite from insoluble difficulties. With Christina's pregnancy, Mark had become more bitter about her attitude towards the same subject. Dorothy, although appreciating his disappointment, would not change her mind.

'I don't see how, if he decides he wants one, you can do much about it,' Christina said.

'I know a thing or two, Christina darling.' From the life she had led, Christina had always suspected it. 'I was a nurse, you know, and I number several doctors among my friends. Mark is not – inconvenienced.'

It was a rockier basis for marriage, Christina thought, than mere boredom.

Opening a picnic hamper on the dunes and handing the children bottles of ginger beer and hunks of warm French bread and squashy tomatoes, Christina could not help feeling, watching Tom, that Mark was virtually of the party, so like were father and son. Tom must be a constant reminder to Dick of Mark, as he was to her. But the similarity brought her great joy, which she doubted applied to Dick.

'This child, Harry, is going to be blond and blue-eyed and a real chip off the old block,' Christina said to Dorothy. 'We shall all dote on him and live happily ever after.'

'Amen to that. Would that we all could!' Dorothy's smile was wry and disbelieving.

The fortnight slipped away in a daze of pure delight, all the more precious for the feeling of release being constrained into the short time, the date of return irrevocably fixed. It was a dire reflection on the state of her marriage, Christina realized, that this interlude was as sweet as it was. She guessed that the visit to Will's grave would provoke difficult emotions, both about the past and the present, and she purposely put it off until the day before they were leaving for home, not wanting to upset the animal delight of their days. Dorothy hired a motor to take them up to Béthune and to the village near-by where the grave was, and then on to Boulogne in the evening, where they could stay the night ready to take the boat in the morning. They packed up their suitcases, and knew that the unreality was over.

'Perhaps we want too much,' Christina said, as they sat on their last evening in the garden of the small pension where they had been staying. 'We're rich, we're healthy, we're privileged in every way. Our husbands don't beat us. They are kind, we have everything we need. What's wrong?'

'What's wrong is that you're in love with my husband and he with you, and I love only myself.'

Christina, after the moment's pause to absorb the shock, said, 'What I do like about you, Dorothy, is that you do believe in calling a spade a spade. No beating about the bush. A straight right to the jaw. I'm afraid it's something it would be better not to discuss, only that you know I would never do anything to harm you.'

'No. I'm afraid there is no future in it for any of us. You asked why we aren't happy.'

'Silly question.'

'Life is silly.'

Driving up to the erstwhile front line confirmed this conviction. The shattered landscape appalled, yet the sun shone, the birds sang, the stupid poppies flourished in the cratered ground. The driver took them out of their way to show them the more resolute of the stretches of line, the more desolate places, the most shattered villages, the largest cemeteries. They wanted to stop him, but it seemed right merely to know what their future was built on. It seemed terrible, then, not to be happy, to be so wayward as to see this as an irrelevance. Yet if Will had still been alive, Christina thought, she would be happy now.

His grave was in a peaceful, untouched village, in a part of the churchyard separate from the ornate memorials of the large French families, under some walnut trees. The grass was mown, the line of five stark wooden crosses soldierly in the shade of a stone wall. Captain William E. Russell, D.S.O., R.F.C.

'Hullo, William,' Christina said.

He was as close then as he had ever been. She sat with her back to the wall and shut her eyes. Dorothy said she would take the children for a walk for an hour or so but Christina did not see her go. She saw herself sitting on the dry grass, smelling its hay smell and feeling the scratchiness through her stockings, seeing the close-growing daisies and the old coltsfoot stalks which had withstood the mower, and she saw Will beside her, no different, no older, reasonable, well disposed, not even in uniform, but in the summer white shirt and oil-stained breeches of his early flying days. He was sucking a grass stalk and his dark eyes were staring into space. She could talk to him quite rationally.

'Why did you leave me, Will? I'm in a mess without you.'

He shook his head.

'I seem to do all the wrong things. Love the wrong people, marry the wrong people . . .'

'You always married the wrong people. I was the wrong people too. Didn't Aunt Grace tell you about me, as well? I didn't make you happy.'

'I was frightened you were going to be killed, and I was right. You were.'

'You never tried to change me, that was the best thing. Now you think you can change Dick and you can't. That's your trouble.'

'And Mark?'

'You know you will never change Mark. At least you have your eyes wide open there.'

'What shall I do?'

And he laughed. She saw him quite clearly, as if he had no care in the world, no aeroplanes to build, no money to earn, no stunts to practise, no wife to support. As if he had just made love to her. As if he had some sublime aeroplane in the sky which need never come to earth. As indeed he had, she thought, opening her eyes – no cares, no life, no being, no substance.

'Will!'

She was lying on the hot grass beside his meaningless wooden cross, his bones hidden from her sight, his spirit beyond her waking reach. She was obsessed with her present

tangled desires and had come to Will's ghost to be consoled;
but there was no consolation there. No wonder he laughed!
When Dorothy came back she found Christina stony-faced,
anxious to leave.

'I did love him so, Dorothy! It none of it makes sense. I
am not even loyal to him, let alone Dick.'

'Oh, hush! He was a lovely person, but he's gone. You did
the right thing. And you've got little fatty here, hasn't she,
Isobel?' Dorothy bent down and took a bunch of wild
flowers from Isobel's sticky hands. 'Who are these for then?
Who did we pick them for?'

'For daddy.' Isobel laughed, pleased with her coaching.

'That's right. We've even got a jam jar of water to put
them in, haven't we?'

'The man in the shop gave it us,' Tom said. 'We told him
what it was for, and he gave us sweets, and his wife cried.'

'They said they went to the funeral,' Dorothy said. 'The
whole village did. And they look after the graves. They said
if you would like to call –'

'No.' Christina wanted to get away. 'They are kind, but –'

She could not bear to hear about the funeral. The dispassionate grave was enough.

'They kept kissing us,' Tom complained, wiping his face.
'It was horrid.'

'Daddy's at home,' Isobel said. 'Not here.'

'This is your other one,' Tom said prosaically. 'Like my
other one is Uncle Mark.'

Christina and Dorothy exchanged glances and started to
smile.

'You're very well off for daddies, the pair of you, do
you know that? Now back to the motor-car! We're going
home.'

Christina brushed the grass off her skirt and set off down
the churchyard path, feeling the heaviness of the child. She

was glad it was done, and it was all right now, back with the children, and aware of her blessings. The coming child was eternal comfort, as Isobel had been before it.

The holiday had done her good.

Chapter 11

'Uncle Fergus is dealing in tractors,' Tom said. 'He says he's going to sell you one, dad. He says it does the job of a pair of horses in a quarter of the time.'

Dick smiled. 'Yes, but look what it does to the land! Our clay, pans it down hard as cement.'

'Masters has bought an Overtime,' Christina said. 'He says he wouldn't be without it, and his land is the same as ours.'

'His crops are no better.'

'Perhaps he doesn't have to work so hard.'

'I like work, in case you haven't noticed.'

'You're a glutton, my dear. And I'm getting lazier every day.' Christina yawned, smoothing her apron over her large stomach.

'It's that Harry,' Dick said. 'You've good excuse.'

'I've nothing to do.'

'As it should be. You rest up while you've got the chance. He'll have you run off your feet in a month or two.'

'We can bring your lunch out today. Where are you ploughing?'

'Over the Chase. It'll be easier for me to slip into Deakin's and have it with Sim. It's a long walk for you.'

'As you wish.'

Dick was in for breakfast, having been at work since five. The day stretched ahead for Christina: riding was forbidden; Clara was taking the children to the village shopping. Amy had the house polished and shining, Mary had the dinner in hand and was going to bake all afternoon, Fowler had been working in the garden and the beds were all raked and smooth, the roses dead-headed, the lawn scythed short.

'What shall I do?' Christina asked Marigold when Dick had departed. Marigold, like herself, was occupied with breeding, but her young were already born and ready to leave her. Christina lay on the floor, amusing herself with the puppies, enjoying the autumn sunshine falling in through the long terrace windows. The dog was all the company she had. 'I am becoming a vegetable,' she told Marigold. 'Really there is no reason why I should not ride. Ceasefire isn't dangerous.' But Dick would not allow it.

'I shall go over and see Dorothy.'

She had resolved to avoid Mark, forget him, love Dick and be an exemplary wife. But it was not easy because she longed to be over at Dermot's as much to see what was going on as to see Mark. Fergus had completed the renovation of one of his pieces of machinery which was now revealed as a chain-driven Bugatti racing car of pre-war vintage. Motor-racing had come back with the cessation of war as one of the compensating excitements for the demobilized male, should he have the money and the skill to participate. Mark had the money and Fergus had the skill, and Mark underwrote Fergus's engineering business in exchange for driving the cars in competition.

'Not that there are many competitions around just yet, but they are coming,' they explained to Christina. There had been a speed trials meeting at Westcliff in the summer which they had attended as spectators. A Vauxhall like Mark's had put up the fastest time of the day at over sixty miles an hour, and Mark had driven since then in the style of the racing driver – 'to get in the practice'. Much of the interest was in hill-climbs rather than flat-racing, a more hair-raising and flamboyant style of competition that appealed to the two men at Dermot's, and the Bugatti was in the process of being tuned for the events that were scheduled for the following year. Mark had earmarked the local gradients and took it for work-outs over the most testing courses he could find. Christina, used to a similar euphoria on the experimental airfield, found that the crackle of the unsilenced exhaust, the scream of tyres and the smell of burning oil and rubber was remarkably engaging after the hypnotic mechanical rhythm of the Flambards reaper, the day-long creak of harness, the eternal to-ing and fro-ing of the dairy herd to graze, to be milked, to graze. She had been weaned on excitement, and now found it hard not to be attracted back to it.

'If it wasn't for you, Harry,' she remarked to the bulge in her stomach, 'who knows that I wouldn't have a Bugatti of my own by now?'

Pregnancy had a soporific effect. Because she had failed to fight for her rights, there was no car yet at Flambards. Dick used Ceasefire or Pepper and the trap and saw no reason to change his ways, and Christina hadn't the energy to put up a fight.

'When Fergus finds the right car,' she thought, 'I will buy it.'

He had cars in for repair all the time, but mostly boring Fords or ex-army Crossleys, and Christina wanted something more classy.

'I want a Tiptoe of a car,' she thought, and asked Fowler to put Pepper to so that she could drive over to Dermot's. Tiptoe was at grass with Sweetbriar and Moonshine. Dick had taken Ceasefire over to the farm to start work again and would not be back till late. He quite often took his lunch to the Deakins' when he was on the village side of Flambards. Christina knew he was happy there, as she was happy at Dermot's. They had separated out in a strange way. Christina, because she asked Dick to come to Dermot's and was cross when he refused, had visited the Deakins' to see if it would work for her, and it was disastrous. Nell had been obviously flustered, Rosie resentful, and Simeon silent as the grave. Dick had tried to cover up the awkwardness, just as she had tried hard at times to include Dick into the company of Mark and Dorothy (and she remembered some of the strains). Afterwards Dick had asked her belligerently why she had come.

'Because I want the same of you with my friends. I was testing it, to see how difficult it was.'

'And what conclusion did you come to?'

'That it is very difficult.'

'Yes.'

Perhaps, she thought, it would have worked if they could have met new people altogether, so that there were no pasts to consider, but there were no new people in the neighbourhood, and Dick never left home to meet anybody else, save for the market.

She drove over to Dermot's. It was October, a day of mellow sunshine, the air still and sharp, the late leaves hanging yellow and fragile and spent. Christina loved the autumn, and the feel of her baby, and the thought of seeing Mark. She could reconcile these things, there being no other way. The pregnancy had taken precedence. The seed sown, the sower was less important than the seed. Christina loved the strange self-revelation of pregnancy, her independence, her total concern for her own being because of what it was carrying. She could feel little resentment for the things she had fretted about earlier.

Dorothy and Fergus laughed at her, teasing her for her complacency, but Mark never laughed. He concentrated on the cars.

'It keeps him occupied,' Dorothy said tartly.

She went up to London more often than she used to, borrowing Mark's Vauxhall for the day.

When Christina drove into the yard she found Fergus and

Mark delving into the bowels of the Bugatti, Maloney searching through the tool-box just as she had once done for Will. Maloney came to take Pepper, but Christina said to him, 'He can stand for a minute – I'm not staying. I'm driving over to Coleshill rectory to see about getting a tutor for Tom.'

Mark said, 'Poor little devil! Remember what we went through with the curate?'

'More like what *he* went through with us,' Christina said.

'If you wait a few minutes I'll drive you over.'

'What in?' Fergus inquired. 'Dorothy's taken the Vauxhall.'

'Oh, blast, I'd forgotten. No good, Christina. We've got to test drive the Bugatti, so I'll follow you over in that, and try it on the Rectory hill.'

The Bugatti was a single-seater. The other racing-car in Fergus's care was a new Straker-Squire which a friend of his had crashed and was hoping Fergus could make as new. It had seats for two and Christina had been promised driving lessons in it when it was ready, but as yet it sat forlornly without its wheels in the coach-house. The friend, apparently, was more badly crashed than the car and was planning to go back to animal horse-power.

Mark came over to Christina wiping his hands on a cloth and Christina said, 'You're getting more like Will every day.'

He laughed. 'I only do as I'm told. I'm the labourer. I wish I knew as much as Will.'

'You're getting very modest in your old age. It becomes you.'

'You think I'm mellowing?'

Christina considered. 'I would say – yes. You are slightly nicer to people than you used to be.'

'Servants, you mean? Maloney, for example? Well, I owe my life to Maloney so I have to be nice to him. Isn't that so, Maloney?'

'Quite so, sir.'

'Before we go, Christina, I've something to show you. Get down a minute. You'll like it.'

Christina got down, wondering what lay behind Maloney's non-committal exterior, what strange relationships were thrown up by the war. She wondered if Mark had been a good officer or a bad one, if Maloney had taken the job because he wanted to, or because there was no other. However unfair Mark was, she imagined he had always been ready to go first in any skirmish, being one of nature's thrusters, which Dick put fairly high in his estimation of officer qualities.

She followed Mark out into the orchard behind the stable yard where there was a row of outbuildings which had once been pigsties. They now housed no less than ten foxhounds, which came up to the new wire fences at Mark's approach with a great howling of excitement and fervour.

'What do you think? Lucas got them for me, from a friend in Suffolk. We're going to take them out pretty soon, see what they can do. The place is over-run with foxes, you know, so we should see some good sport. Pity you'll be out of the running for a bit.'

'You haven't wasted any time!'

'I've tried to get Dorothy riding, but she doesn't want to – says she can't see the point when there's a car. She's got a blank spot about some things. Her urban upbringing, I suppose. She wants us to go back to London, can you believe?'

'Yes, I can.'

'But she knows she'll never budge me from here. She'll have to make the best of it – and poor old Dick. I'm keeping nicely out of his hair lately, you must admit. Get him to come out hunting, Christina – it'll do him the world of good, get him out of his shell. We're going to have a Hunt Ball again too, we thought. Get it all moving again, have some fun. Dorothy's going to ask Jerry to bring his band.'

'That'll stir up the old fogies! Can you see them – old Mrs Lucas and the Badstocks doing the shimmy! What a shame I shall have to miss it!'

'Oh, no. Jerry plays quite respectable old stuff when required. He's a pro, after all.'

The subject was academic, as far as Christina was concerned, knowing that the social round was not for her this coming winter, but she was pleased about the hounds and thought that Mark would make far better sport with them than old Lucas. Even if he didn't actually work for a living, he seemed to be occupying his time fully enough.

'He's calling them all after cars, did you know?' Fergus told her. 'There's Rolls and Talbot, Nash, Morgan, Bugatti, Sunbeam, Lagonda ... isn't that right, Mark? When a fox goes away there'll be a man with a starting-flag to signal the field –'

'Stuff it, Fergus! If they go half as fast we'll be laughing. You going to come and see what the Bug will do?'

'No. I've got this Ford lorry to do before the day's out.'

Christina left them talking and set off for the Rectory with Pepper. She was perfectly content, bowling along the lanes in the afternoon sunshine. When Mark came up behind her in the Bugatti there was no room to overtake between the high hedges, but he insisted on blowing his hooter and shouting insults over the racket of his engine.

'Get that pre-historic contraption out of my way! Shouldn't be allowed on the road.'

The lane widened out but Christina kept purposefully to the middle, laughing now as Mark started to weave about behind her. He came very close, so that she could see his face, half amused, half exasperated.

'You've been exceeding the speed limit, to catch me up,' she shouted. 'I shall report you!'

'I shall report you for obstruction, woman!'

She drew over slightly, and he came alongside, and stayed with her.

'You're a hard one to chase, but I shall never give up, Christina!'

'Idiot! Keep in your place!'

Christina gave Pepper a belt with the end of the reins as Mark dropped back a little, intending to take the road again and keep Mark behind her, but Pepper seemed to have taken aversion to the loud motor-car so close and was already quickening of his own accord. He was so used to the cars that it had never occurred to Christina that he might take fright, but she could feel now that he had decided that he did not like it. Mark, seeing what was happening, throttled down immediately and dropped back, but the lane at this point started to run downhill and Pepper, cantering now, felt the weight of the trap come down behind him and quickened still more.

Christina sat still, putting all her weight on the reins, not particularly frightened, more annoyed.

'Pepper, you idiot, you'll do us a damage if you don't come to! Steady on, my love. You're not a Bugatti!'

But Pepper was galloping now with dogged purpose, the bit hard between his teeth. Christina did not like it, but still thought if she concentrated on steering they would weather the approaching bend, not too sharp, and run out of steam on the ensuing uphill, but at the crucial moment a boy on a bicycle appeared round the bend, which prevented her from taking it in a wide sweep. Having to keep to her own side of the road, she then had no room, at the pace she was going, to get round. Pepper went straight through the hedge and ditch on the far side and took the trap with him.

Christina was aware of flying through the air and actually thinking that things were not too bad: she was going to land in soft grass and was unlikely to break anything. A few yards further on and she would have a hit a tree. The crump of landing winded her and she lay gasping like a stranded fish, even then not totally convinced that this was disaster, but more a bit of luck for missing the tree. It was only when she saw Mark's face coming and going in a strange way in her vision, and saw the horror in his eyes, that she realized that it was no mean accident.

'Am – am I all right?'

'Oh, Christina, how should I know? Are you? You look all right. God almighty, I was terrified! How do you feel?'

She had never seen him so concerned, his goggles pushed up, his hair standing on end as he crouched over her, kneeling in the grass. She moved experimentally but nothing hurt. She rolled over on to her side, and a great searing pain like a labour pain contracted her, agonizingly. She gasped with it, and cried out.

·'Oh no! Mark!'

He cradled her in his arms, wild with fear.

'Christina, don't! It's all right! Please, please be all right!'

She lay against him, terrified for what the pain meant, but it did not come again. She felt very sick and frightened, and Mark went on holding her, talking soothing words, rubbish, comforting her. She tried to move again, and this time the pain did not come. She felt overwhelmingly relieved.

'Is – Pepper all right?'

'The boys are seeing to him. Yes, he's on his feet.'

The boy on the bicycle had been joined by one who had been making a bonfire of hedge clippings. Christina could smell the autumn smell of the fire and see the sky pale and cloudless over her head. She was frightened to move, feeling now as if something was wrong with her, although there was no more pain. Mark was needed to sort out Pepper and the trap but she did not want him to leave her.

'I'll drive you home if the horse is all right. You should

get home, Christina. Lie still, don't move. If Pepper's no good, the boys will have to get help.'

He left her and she lay still, suspended in her little cocoon of fear for the pain coming back. It can't, it can't, she told herself over and over, not that pain. I'm not ready. I don't want it yet. It must be all right. After what seemed a very long time Mark came to her, and picked her up very gently in his arms. Nothing happened. She held on to him, still frightened.

The boys were holding Pepper, awed and excited. Mark got into the trap and laid her on the seat, putting the cushions behind her head. One of the boys handed him the reins.

'Stay and look after the car until someone comes,' Mark told him. 'Don't leave it. Here's something for you.'

He handed the boys some money. Pepper moved off back the way he had come, apparently none the worse for his adventure. Encouraged, Christina said, 'I think I'm all right.' Very gingerly she moved herself again, and sat up, and nothing happened. She pulled herself more upright, cautiously. She felt sick, but her body was quiet.

'What do I look like?'

'Not too good. A bit green.'

'I don't think it meant anything, that pain.'

'I hope to God you're right.'

'I don't think Dick ought to know what happened. We were stupid, what we did. If he knew – he'll make such a fuss.'

'We'll have to tell him something.'

'Yes, but not about the Bugatti, and larking about.'

'Well, if it saves trouble . . .'

'We could say you came along and found me stuck in the hedge. I'll say I was going too fast and the bicycle came round the bend and made me swerve. That's the truth, after all.'

'If it makes it easier for you.'

'He will fuss so anyway. And if he knew . . . I never thought – it was stupid.'

'It's always easy to say that afterwards.'

They made a steady pace home, both subdued. Christina hoped it was her imagination, how she felt, but she did feel very strange. She tried not to show it for Mark's sake. He was not laughing it off, as he had always laughed off such escapades in the past, and she knew it was because of the child.

'You just say you found me like that,' Christina told him. 'You never saw what happened. Then I can make up the rest of the story.'

'Very well.'

'I think I'd better go to bed, to be on the safe side.'

'Yes, and perhaps Dr Porter should come.'

'Oh, no, that's silly. I'm all right. I'm only being careful.'

Mary and Amy made a big fuss, and Clara cooked her some special broth and Christina lay in her bed feeling a fraud, feeling unaccountably nervous, and rather sick. Dick came home and came upstairs in a panic when he heard the news.

'I'm only being careful, Dick, coming to bed. I'm quite all right.'

'How do we know if the baby is all right? Can you feel him how you did before? How do we know?'

'Of course it's all right.'

But she wasn't sure at all.

'I'll send for Dr Porter.'

'No, don't. If you send for anybody, send for Dorothy.'

But Dorothy came without being sent for, having heard the news at home.

'I've never seen Mark in such a sweat.'

'What did he tell you?'

'He told me he found you lying in the field and the trap

turned over in the hedge. He was taking the Bugatti to do a test on Rectory hill.'

No one need know at all, Christina thought, comforted by Mark's caution.

At ten o'clock that night, she had another pain. Dorothy was still there, for which Christina was eternally grateful. Dick came up and walked up and down and fidgeted with the curtains and said they should send for Dr Porter.

'We can if necessary,' Dorothy said shortly. 'I can fetch him in the car. It's outside. I can be back with him in twenty minutes.'

'Do you think the baby is coming?'

'It might be. Even so, a seven months baby is common enough. You don't have to worry.'

'Will you stay?' Christina asked her.

'I wouldn't dream of leaving you now, darling, you know that. Just get some rest now, and I'll see that everything is all right.'

But it was beyond Dorothy's power to make everything come right. Christina was in labour for two days. Dr Porter came, and sent for another doctor from the town, a young man who was supposed to know everything, but Christina was unaware of whose faces were whose, as the hours passed and the pains wracked her to no avail. She kept thinking she was still lying in the field and that Mark was holding her. She said, 'Mark, don't leave me. Don't leave me,' and Dorothy held her hands still and said grimly, 'Be quiet, Christina. Don't talk! For God's sake don't talk!' Christina did not know Dorothy was there, nor Dick, nor the smart young doctor whose ideas were not working out. She was in the field, lying in the grass, and could smell the woodsmoke from the boy's bonfire.

'Don't let it catch the hedge. The leaves are very dry,' she said, remembering past fires at Flambards, the home farm burning, and Tizzy pretending he had not been there with his matches.

'He didn't mean it,' she said. 'It was a misunderstanding.'

She thought the fire was going to reach out to her; she could hear the crackling of it in the leaves, and screamed out, 'Take me away! Take me home!' but her body would not move. It felt so heavy, a dead weight engulfing her soul which she knew was trying to get out, and could not. Its struggles exhausted her. Everything it tried to do was in vain.

'I am useless,' she said to Dorothy, seeing her suddenly quite plain. 'Everything has gone wrong.'

Dorothy was crying.

'Don't cry,' she said to her, and nothing seemed to matter very much any more, not even her soul. She slept for twenty-four hours. When she woke up she knew she was in bed at Flambards, that it was afternoon, a fine afternoon. Mary was sitting by the fire knitting.

'Why aren't you working?' Christina asked her.

'Oh, lawks, ma'am!' Mary nearly jumped out of her chair with fright. She dropped her knitting and came running up to the bed, her wrinkled face working with emotion, a gabble of words making no sense.

'Don't you worry, my dear, don't you worry about a thing! I'll fetch Mr Wright now – he'll be up in a jiffy!'

Christina did not know what she had to worry about. She felt incredibly weak, scarcely able to turn her head on the pillow. She could not remember why she was in bed.

Dick came up and sat on the bed. He looked terrible.

'Whatever's wrong? What's happened?'

'The baby is dead.'

'What baby?'

'Christina!' Dick's face was suffused with anger, blotchy, almost unrecognizable. He got hold of Christina's wrists in a grip which made her weep. 'You stupid bitch! You killed him! Our baby – *my* son! Because you are so stupid –'

He broke off, flinging his grip off her.

'You and that brother-in-law of yours . . .' The anger died as it had come. 'I didn't mean to hurt you, Christina. I don't really care. It doesn't matter any more.'

'What are you saying?' Christina asked, the life suddenly frightened back into her. 'What do you mean? The baby is dead –'

'You bore a son, and it was dead. They've taken it away.'

'The child? Our son? Harry, you mean?'

'Yes.'

It wasn't what she had wanted to wake up to, the dread she had experienced lying in the grass in Mark's arms made into reality. She remembered everything now. The peace was shattered. She knew now why Dick looked as he did. She reached out to him with an agonizing sense of loss. It was Will all over again, the living person snatched away, worse this time because there was Dick to suffer too, not just herself. He took her hands because she needed him. He sat beside her while she wept, but he did not comfort her. He kept saying, 'It doesn't matter, Christina. It doesn't matter.' But it only emphasized how much it did, as much to him as to her, and his cold grief was almost a worse torment than the loss of the child, because she knew the truth of it, that what he had said first was true.

When she was quiet, he said he would fetch Dorothy. He left her, and Dorothy came up with a pot of tea and some teacups. Mary had gone away. The fire flickered cheerfully in the grate and the autumn sun poured in through the windows.

'There, my sweet, you're lucky you didn't go the same way, so don't take it too hard. I've told Dick he should count his blessings.'

'I'm no blessing to Dick.'

'Perhaps not. But we're all as God made us. It was touch and go for you, Christina, and the other thing to me is of no consequence.'

'It was a boy, he said.'

'A lovely boy, yes, with blue eyes and fair hair the image of Dick. Here, drink a cup of tea and you'll feel better.'

'You are hard, Dorothy!'

'I must tell you, my dear, that when you were having your pains you called upon Mark not to leave you. Dick heard you. It's not the first time I've heard such home truths uttered under the influence of pain or anaesthetic, but normally it goes no further than the nurse or doctor. This time I'm afraid it definitely fell on the wrong ears.'

Christina was appalled, beyond words.

'I'm telling you the worst straight away, to get it over, because no one else will tell you that, save perhaps Dick himself. And now you are warned. And when things are so bad, Christina, they can only get better, so don't despair. The human condition is amazingly resilient. Have a cup of tea, and try to think about getting better. Nothing is truly any different than it was before, if you stop and consider it.'

Dorothy's strength was valuable to Christina, trying not to sink into the slough of self-pity. She felt as if she had undergone an amputation, the sense of loss so terrible for the child she had not so much as set eyes on. Yet she was sorrier for Dick, for what she had done to Dick was unforgiveable.

Dick went to the Deakins' after he had seen his baby boy wrapped in a shroud and taken away by Dr Porter. After the dreadful hours of labour and hearing Christina calling for Mark, he could not bear to stay in the house a minute longer. He wanted the comfort of his own people, his familiar place, like a rat to its bolt-hole, a child to its mother. Striding over the stubble, along the edges of the new plough

200

where he had been working and dreaming of the boy who would take the farm over when he was past it, he cursed his dependence on Flambards and its people. Everything had gone sour on him, and now there was not even his son to invest in. Tom, his adoptive son, was growing up so painfully like his father that Dick could no longer find joy in his company, although he knew his feelings were unfair to the child. He had staked everything on this new boy, stupidly, sentimentally, unthinkingly. He thought the new child would make Christina into the domestic creature she seemed to have no will to be; he had dreamed of watching her nurse by the fireside, of seeing her lean over the cot at night-time with her hair loose like an engraving his mother had once treasured and had framed on her bedroom wall. What a fool he was!

His bitter disappointment was more his own fault than anyone else's; it was himself he was angry with. It had not been Christina's fault that she had lost the child; her fault perhaps that now he cared more for the lost baby than her suffering. After she had cried out for Mark he had wanted her to suffer. Dorothy had told him that she was hallucinating about the accident, because it was Mark that had helped her and brought her home and comforted her, but there was no proof to satisfy him. He would never know the truth of it, as he had never known all along, from the moment Mark had come back from the hospital and Christina had nursed him with such abrasive fervour, with such a strange, nervous devotion to his needs, as if his pain hurt her more than she would have him know. He believed that she had probably never given in to her feelings for Mark, but he could not believe any longer that they did not exist.

The baby had been going to make everything come right, but now the whole business was beyond repair.

Nell was in the kitchen, scrubbing the table, Sim was down the bottom of the garden, digging.

'How is it then?' she asked him, knowing what had happened.

'A dead child.'

'Oh, Dick, my dear boy, my poor boy!' She came and put her great soapy arms round him and hugged him. She was a big woman, and he felt her strength like mother earth, understanding everything. Perhaps she even understood Christina. She said, 'And poor little girl – how is she? Did she have a bad time?'

'She'll be all right, the doctor says.'

'The waste, and the disappointment! We've been through it too, I know how it feels. Sit down, lad. You look tired to death! What a long time it's been – Clara told us she'd started with pains, so I was expecting to hear some news. I thought it might be all right, she was so big. Was it your boy?'

'Yes, a lovely baby.'

It was a relief already, telling Nell. It was like coming home after a long hard day at school, back to the relief of one's own hearth and the mother figure. Perhaps I've never grown up properly, he thought, that I cannot take these things in my stride. Grown men did not grieve for a life that had never existed. But he would not tell her about Christina calling for Mark.

'You can stay awhile? Or will you have to hurry back?'

'They said she would sleep for a long time. Mrs Russell is there.'

'You look quite done in. I'll make you some tea, get some colour back into your cheeks. It will not seem so bad after a little while, Dick – you'll never believe it now, but that's so.'

He took Sim's chair by the fire and for the first time – it felt for days – felt a semblance of comfort come back to him, for Nell's solidity, for the values he was always conscious of under this roof. The feeling he had of coming home was to do with the Deakin philosophy, which was as plain and honest as the earth floor under his feet. They owed nothing; they were four-square and proud by the endeavour of several decades; they were independent and enduring. They were everything that he would have liked to be, and could have been, if he had not sold himself to Flambards. He always felt right in this setting, and a stranger in his own home. The feeling was very strong now, and he sat enjoying it as a balm for his loss.

He made no effort to talk, and when Sim came in the story was briefly told, and Nell made a meal. Sim rolled Dick a cigarette, and brought him a glass of beer from the outhouse, and it grew dark as they sat there.

'I'm keeping you up. I'll be getting along,' Dick said, when the drink and the smoke was finished. 'I shouldn't be away, I suppose.'

'You'll feel better, a bit of a break, and the walk. It'll seem easier, you see, as the days go by.'

He went out and down the grass walk to the lane, feeling the sharp air on his warmed body, the crispness of an early frost. As he got to the bottom, Rosie came up the other way from the village, half-running, with an air of excitement. When she saw Dick she stopped suddenly, surprised.

'Dick! I've just heard what happened! Bobby Dale saw it and he was telling me – about Major Russell trying to overtake and Mrs Wright not letting him! I thought it was just the trap getting a wheel in the ditch and turning over in the hedge – I never knew it was so bad! Is she all right? Ma said she had gone into labour.'

'She's all right, yes.'

He stood quite still, feeling himself jerked back into the irresponsible patterns of the Flambards community, caught like a fish on a hook, the shock of it scattering his newly garnered scraps of comfort. He made an effort not to let it show. Even if he had been hoodwinked from start to finish, there was no need to reveal just how badly. Rosie took his silence for acquiescence in the ways of the world, for she prattled on sympathetically.

'He said they were having a race, and Mrs Wright pulled over so Major Russell couldn't come by, and they were shouting at each other and laughing, and weaving about all over the place. Major Russell was in that racing-car, you see – no wonder the horse got frightened! And then they came to the hill and Mrs Wright couldn't stop. He said he knew she wasn't going to get round the bend. He could see it all from where he was working. And Major Russell was that upset, he said, beside himself, almost in tears, he said, and her moaning in the grass! It was a terrible thing, Dick – I never knew. I'm so terribly sorry!'

She could not know the effect of her words on Dick, and he did not reveal them, using a self-control he did not know himself capable of. He heard Rosie say, 'Can I walk with you as far as the wood? I've got some snares to look at – the ones you said I could set there. They've done well.'

'Yes,' he said blankly.

'I got two last night. Do you want one? – they're yours, after all.'

'No. I get enough in the home wood.'

They walked together up the lane and into the field of stubble, shining silver under the high half-moon and the green-fired stars, the air still and cold and the stalks crunching underfoot. Rosie walked like a boy, and handled her snares like a boy. Dick had no need to help her. She had no sentiment, cutting the strangled but still alive and feebly kicking young buck out of the wire and dispatching it with a sharp blow on the back of the neck. Dick stood looking down dispassionately on the spread of her blonde hair in the moonlight, the same colour as his own, the same colour as his boy's, and was moved with an unholy passion, seeing plainly the path he should have taken, and the path he had taken, diverging like two cart-tracks making for different gateways. They said that the moon affected people. When she stood up, he put out his arms and turned her round to face him, holding her shoulders. She was surprised, half-laughing, then she saw his face and stopped laughing. He pulled her to him and kissed her on the lips, and she stood like a statue, holding up her face to him. She could not believe what had happened. He dared not stay, frightened by the strangeness of his feelings. He turned away from her and started walking quickly back to Flambards along the side of the wood, not knowing whether he was driven by anger, by love or by madness, or a combination of all three. But it was anger that prevailed, and did not leave him, even after several days.

Mark was driving the Vauxhall over to Flambards with Dorothy to visit Christina.

'You are a fool,' Dorothy said to him. 'What do you think Dick is going to say to you, now that he knows the truth?'

'How does he know what happened? We didn't tell him.'

'I don't know. He's heard it from somewhere, and he also heard Christina call out for you when she was in labour. He's hardly going to embrace you like a brother when you arrive on the doorstep, under the circumstances.'

'I can't keep away just for those reasons. I won't deny what happened. I'm sorry – we just didn't see any danger at the time. It was a lark. We've never done anything to be ashamed of. I will apologize profusely to Dick – what more can I do?'

'I think it would be wiser to keep away.'

'Better to have it out and have done. I'm not going to skulk about in sackcloth and ashes.'

Dorothy laughed. 'Don't say I didn't warn you!'

Mary looked surprised when she answered the door and saw Mark, but ushered him in with her usual fond indulgence for 'the proper master', as she still referred to him.

'She's a lot better, ma'am,' she said to Dorothy. 'Taking a nice bite of food now.'

'Is Mr Wright in?' Dorothy asked, hoping he was not.

'Yes, ma'am, he is. Shall I tell him you've called?'

'Yes,' Mark said. 'Do that. Tell him I would like to visit Mrs Wright.'

'You are a fool,' Dorothy said anxiously, as Mary departed. 'What do you think he feels about it? You could have just stayed away, until it was past history. It's called tact. You wouldn't know.'

'No. I'm not like that. I've come to apologize.'

'I'll be surprised if you get the chance.'

Dorothy's guess was accurate. Dick came out of the small study, walking fast, hunched up, visibly restraining himself. His face was coloured up and his eyes positively blazed. Dorothy, amazed by the piercing blue of the gaze that flashed upon them, had time to start saying, 'Dick, please, we've come –'

Dick said to Mark, 'You bastard, I'm going to kill you for what you've done!'

'I'm sorry. I –'

'You can never be sorry enough,' Dick said, and hit him a vicious blow to the head.

Dorothy stepped back abruptly and Mary came hurrying back, shouting out, 'Stop that, you two boys! Stop it, I say! You're grown men now.' To Dorothy she said, 'Oh, my dear God, we've had all this before! Are they never going to learn sense?'

'No,' Dorothy said.

Dorothy was professionally worried for Mark, terrified that Dick might hit him low down where he was in no state to take punishment, but Mark seemed to be making very little effort to defend himself and Dick had a clear field for his wild swings to the face that he obviously wanted to pulp.

Mark avoided a few of them by ducking, but Dick's ardour required satisfaction and Mark was aware of it. Backing off momentarily, watching Dick eyeing distance and opportunity, he said wryly, 'I've got my white flag up – don't you understand?' and received a blow which proved quite clearly that Dick was not interested. Mark staggered back and fell against the hall table and a great vase of late dahlias and yellow leaves that Dorothy had arranged herself the day before. They went down with a crash on the stone flags, shattering and scattering, and Dick followed up with his fists still going. The broken pieces of pottery added to the carnage. Dorothy stood looking on at the melée, the great gaudy flowers mixed with blood and autumn leaves, the thrashing arms and legs and foul language, still clinically worried by the fact that one blow from Dick in the wrong place could kill Mark and wondering if Dick knew it too.

'Please stop,' she said. 'It's so silly.'

Mark still hadn't the strength to put up a fight, even had he had the inclination, and Dick's satisfaction was dissipated by the unevenness of it. Mark lay still with a yellow dahlia in his hair and bright blood flowering from his nose and mouth, his arms crossed over his midriff, watching to see if there was any more to come. Dick sat back and waited, wiping a hand across his face and leaving a swathe of red.

'You're not worth it,' he said.

'I was apologizing.'

Dick shrugged, backing off.

'What did you expect me to do? Shake hands on it? Get up. I'm not swine enough to hurt you any more, in your condition, but I would dearly like to.'

'I came to say I'm sorry, I would not have hurt Christina for the world.'

'I daresay.'

'That apart, I've never offended you, Dick.'

'Only by being.'

'I can't help that.'

Dorothy pulled a handkerchief out of Mark's pocket and thrust it in his face. 'Go and get cleaned up. I must go and tell Christina what's happening, then I'll come and see to you.'

Christina's inquiries as to the noise were issuing urgently from her bedroom door and Dorothy hurried upstairs. Mark got up and sat groggily on the hall settle.

'You throw a fair punch. I should have guessed. You box in the army?'

'Yes, I did.'

Dick was thrown by Mark's humility, and when Mark went to the kitchen to bathe his face – telling Mary somewhat sharply that he didn't need any help – Dick followed, and sat scowling on the table while Mark drew some water from the range and took it across to the sink. He studied his face in Fowler's shaving mirror and said, 'I deserve far worse, you don't have to tell me. It was only a bit of fun I was having with Christina. If I could have foreseen the consequences ... well, I didn't think, did I? I couldn't be more sorry about the baby, believe me.'

'I wanted that boy.'

Mark started to wipe the blood off his face with the dishcloth. 'At least your wife is willing to bear you one, which is more than I can say for mine.'

Dick, not expecting Mark's confidences, looked up suspiciously.

'She won't for a bit, the doctor says. Not for two years at least.'

'Two years is nothing. Mine's a life-sentence.'

'Why do you tell me this?'

'Because you resent me, and yet you have two things which I haven't got, and which I would have above everything else: your health, and a wife who will bear you children. I shall never have either.'

'I can't feel sorry for you.'

'I'm not asking you to. I'm saying stop being sorry for yourself – I don't mean about the child – that's understandable – but think about everything you've got here. Enjoy it, for God's sake! You've got it all on a plate: this lovely place and Christina into the bargain. A man can't ask for more.'

Dick knew that it was true that he did not enjoy it; he felt unable to argue with Mark, for Mark was only speaking the truth. But Dick knew that for himself enjoyment must be earnèd. He was in debt all round.

'I'll tell you what –' Mark had done his best with the dishcloth but his face was undoubtedly a mess, cut in several places and swelling fast – 'you've pasted me twice in our lifetimes, and if ever there comes a third time – and I've a feeling in my bones that there will – believe me, Dick, I'm going to win. It's owing to me.' He washed the dishcloth out in the bowl and hung it up. 'And now, with your permission, I should like to visit Christina, which is what I came for.'

'She will want to see you, I daresay.'

Dick felt that his victory was hollow, and followed Mark upstairs, not wanting to miss Christina's reaction to seeing him again, in his battered condition. But Christina was flippant and cool, considered their behaviour reprehensible and obviously preferred Dorothy's company to either of theirs. She looked far worse than Mark, with her white, hollow cheeks and dark shadows under her eyes, and the underlying grief which she found hard to mask, and Dick quite soon asked Mark to come downstairs for a drink. It seemed the best thing in the circumstances.

And, remembering the confidences Mark had revealed in the kitchen, and seeing his bleak face as he stood at the sitting-room window looking out on the autumn glory of

Flambards' home covert which he had once owned, Dick acknowledged the truth in his unexpected lecture, and for the first time in his life felt a faint affection, and stir of pity for Mark Russell.

Chapter 12

Christina recovered from her miscarriage, but remained in low spirits, having no inclination to ride or gad about. She preferred to sit by the fire reading to the children or sewing, not wanting to think, to participate. She was how Dick wanted her, she thought, domesticated and acquiescent, but Dick did not seem to feature very much in her life any more. Having moved to sleep in the spare room while she was ill, he made no move to come back to her when she was better.

'Why not?' she asked him.

He shrugged. 'It's better this way, if you're not to get pregnant again. The doctor said you're not to.'

'But –' It seemed to Christina a sweepingly final way of dealing with the problem, eschewing all the many minor companionships of lying in bed with one's husband which she had always found almost as desirable as making love itself. Marriage was for being friends, after all, but Dick did not seem particularly friendly any more.

'What's wrong?'

'I bore you, I think.'

'No, I never said so.'

Dick, having experienced the analogy of the two cart-tracks in his life, the one he had chosen and the one he should have chosen, was obsessed by this vision, and had a great hankering to get himself on the right track. He felt that he had to be alone to see things properly. He could not go on the way he was going. He wanted his self-respect back. He had always been content with his own company and it suited him now to withdraw, to take stock, to recover.

'It's not for ever,' he said. He would not explain more.

Christina was not used to being rejected, and felt more lonely than she would have thought possible. She was deeply hurt, suspecting that it was because she had cried for Mark in her delirium, but Dick seemed to have less rancour towards Mark since the incident than he did before, which she could not reconcile.

Dorothy's visits grew more infrequent, and Christina knew that her doldrums were not good company.

'It's time you were snapping out of it,' Dorothy told her. 'You have mourned long enough, Christina. You are getting beastly rustic, you know, with your darning and your petit point. Will wouldn't recognize you.'

'It's cold outside. I like it here.'

'Mark takes those hounds out three times a week. Why don't you join in that lark? Quite a lot of people go – it's what you used to like, isn't it?'

'Yes, I did. Have you learned to ride?'

'No. It's not for me. I'm an urban girl, remember.'

She went up to London frequently, rarely with Mark, and quite often stayed the night. With her father, she said. Christina no longer felt close to her, as she had during the fortnight in France, feeling that there was a part of her now that was alienated from the life at Flambards and Dermot's. Christina could not bring herself to ask any questions, sensing that she herself was guilty of causing the alienation by coming between her and Mark.

'We're determined you shall come to the Hunt Ball, you know. You're perfectly fit now.'

'Who with, for heaven's sake?'

'Won't Dick –?'

'No, not a chance.'

'I shall find someone to take you.'

'Don't be silly.'

'Dick seems to be more obsessed with work than ever. Is he ever home?'

'He's getting the old farm rebuilt, the one Tizzy – Tom – set on fire, and mending all the barns and stables down there. He's there all hours, most evenings too. It has to be done, I suppose.'

She thought he was doing it to keep away from Flambards. She could not tell Dorothy the real situation; it was too hurtful.

'Really, I'm worried about you. What about those driving lessons in the Straker-Squire? It's on the road now. Life is passing you by, Christina. I shall have a word with Fergus.'

Christina laughed. 'I tell you, I like sewing!'

'It's a bad sign. I thought you only do it to impress Dick. But when he's not here, there's no point.'

'He's never here.'

'That's what Mark says about me. I think perhaps our marriages are what people now term casualties of war. But it's no good brooding on what might have been; best get on with it, Christina. You need to get out and about. I shall do something about it.'

The next day Christina was cutting out some white cotton to make Isobel a new pinafore when she heard a scrunch of wheels outside on the gravel and through the window saw Fergus arriving in the Straker-Squire, now looking very jaunty in bright new paint. She went on cutting out the pinafore, and presently Amy came to the door with a visiting card on the salver which lived on the hall table for the purpose but had never been used for it to Christina's knowledge since she had lived there. She took the card and read it.

> *Fergus Ashley-Clark*
> *Repairs to Motor-Cars and Farm Machinery*
> *at Competitive Rates*

'Please show him in.'

Fergus came, rather hesitantly.

'I hear you might not be able to spare time from your domestic duties . . .'

'Well, five minutes perhaps.' Christina smiled.

'That's not long enough for a test-drive.'

Christina looked up in surprise. 'A test-drive?'

'That little fellow out there needs a new owner. Charlie has given up. We want to keep it in the family. It's too nice to let go, you see.'

'This is a trick of Dorothy's!'

'Not at all. I haven't said a word to Dorothy.'

'She has to you, I'm sure!'

'She said you're wasting your time sewing.'

Christina dropped her scissors and went to the window. The little blue car gleamed in the winter sunlight, low to the ground between its wide-set racing wheels, long low bonnet and racing stern, one passenger seat and nowhere to put any shopping, no hood, only an excuse for a wind-shield. Its brass radiator winked at her through the window. She looked at it for a long time.

'Very well. I'll go and get dressed.'

'That's a girl!'

She knew she was being manoeuvred, and was wary, but there was a spark stirring inside her that she had not felt for a long time. It was three months since she had lost the baby. She had scarcely been out.

In her wardrobe she had Will's old leather flying coat which she now pulled out, to go with a rather smarter motoring hat and veil and woollen scarf and gloves. Fergus wore flying gear with helmet and goggles, his old R.F.C. issue. They went outside and she went to the passenger door, but Fergus insisted she sit in the driving seat.

'You can only learn by doing. You used to drive with Will?'

'Yes, but not in a thing like this.'

'You'll like this,' Fergus said.

She did. She had been frightened of flying, but motoring was far more predictable; one did not have to go fast merely to avoid crashing. She loved the feeling of contained power, and the raucous noise, the sense of lightness and manoeuvrability at her fingertips. Changing gear was difficult, but Fergus was a steady teacher, not hurrying her. The morning flew; by the time Christina had stopped asking questions and was changing gear without nasty noises, it was lunchtime and they were some ten miles from home.

'There's a nice road-house a mile from here,' Fergus said. 'Why don't we stop there for lunch? It'll thaw us out.'

Christina felt positively excited at the thought. She always ate in the kitchen with the servants and the children, not even bothering to have her place set in the dining-room any more, nor even in her sitting-room. They talked about the chores, and which curtains needed washing, and which carpets switching round. Fergus was surprised at her glee in agreeing to the suggestion.

'I haven't done this sort of thing for years – not since Will . . . I've forgotten.'

'Well, if you have a little motor like this at your disposal, country life need not be at all constricting, my dear Mrs Wright.'

'No, my dear Mr Ashley-Clark, especially if it's not actually raining. This is a ridiculous car for me.'

'But I have a feeling you might buy it?'

'So have I.'

She tried to tidy herself up somewhat before entering the hotel, but Fergus assured her that ladies were now received in such places in all states of dishevelment. 'It's quite the fashion.' It was a new place, very much out to entice the passing motorist, and the waiter took her leather jacket as if it were mink, and escorted them to a table in the window.

215

A large fire burned in the hearth which soon brought the life back to Christina's nose and fingers. She could gaze out on her little car – which was attracting a good deal of attention – and sip the cocktail Fergus ordered with a delicious sense of daring.

'How fast I am! And I don't mean the car – I mean drinking at lunchtime with a gentleman friend. My Aunt Grace wouldn't like it, Fergus, but I think it's lovely. I've been getting into a dreadful rut lately. You were very kind to call today. Was it under Dorothy's instructions?'

'Not entirely. She reported that you were low, and only interested in sewing, but she didn't suggest the cure. That was my idea.'

'She could have come too, in the Bugatti!'

'She's gone to London.'

'She's always going to London. What does she do there?'

'I wouldn't dream of inquiring, I'm much too much of a gentleman. I think she enjoys herself – she goes to the theatre, and eats out with friends, and dances.'

'She always liked a gay life,' Christina said sadly. She wanted desperately to ask how Mark felt about Dorothy's gay life, but knew she could not. If Dick had rejected her, Dorothy seemed equally to have rejected Mark, yet there could be no mutual comfort for Mark and herself in this unsatisfactory situation. The three loves of her life seemed doomed in all directions.

'The war is a lot to blame,' Fergus said. 'People react in different ways, come out of such experiences as different people, quite often. It's not an easy time.'

'Did it change you?' Having asked the question, looking into the grotesque face opposite, she realized as soon as the words were out that they were hardly appropriate. 'I'm sorry – what a stupid thing to say! I don't think of your face any more, you see – you can take it as a compliment, if you like, that I just see you as – as Fergus. Not as –'

'As a hideously disfigured creature whom strangers find hard to speak to without their stomachs turning over?'

'I don't think it's as bad as that.'

'I'm a connoisseur at reading people's reactions. It's not encouraging. To come into a place like this – it's only having you with me, you see, that I've got the nerve. It's as much a treat for me as it is for you, not having done it for so long. It's impossible alone.'

Christina was surprised, never having noticed Fergus show any sort of diffidence about his condition. He seemed to her more in command of his emotions than anyone she had ever met.

'I would never have guessed. You seem so sure of yourself.'

'Good! Because I'm not. Sometimes I'm nearly as sick with nerves at meeting people as they feel on looking me in the face.'

'Oh, Fergus, truly – people accept it! They know what it is. It's worse than most scars because it's on your face, but there are men with legs and arms off wherever you look. Even Mark, if that had been his face – imagine ...' Her voice trailed away. It wasn't easy to give comfort in the circumstances, seeing how the unaffected side of Fergus's face was so sensitive in reflecting his feelings: he had never, she thought, been an insensitive boy, but an intelligent, finely tuned character, as highly charged as his little racing cars.

'What did you do before the war?'

'I went to school, I went to university. I was reading classics. I got my degree and then war was declared and that was it.'

'What about the classics now?'

'What about them? They seem singularly inappropriate to the world about me at the moment. I prefer to be a humble mechanic, a working man.'

'Were you going to be a teacher?'

'I had applied for a few jobs, yes.'

'Is it because of your face, that you don't want to teach now?'

'I've asked myself that, and I think I can truly say that it isn't. Boys, after all, like wounded soldiers and would thoroughly enjoy introducing me to mater and pater on Open Day and seeing their reaction. I daresay I could get used to it. But the war brought me down to earth, both literally and metaphorically. Classics don't seem frightfully important any more. Engines do, and the farm machinery side seems to me interesting. With luck, it might have a future. The racing is the fun bit. It goes with having lunch with you.'

'If I'm to learn to drive properly, we might have to do this again.'

'We might indeed! Do you want to race in hill-climbs? Ladies do, you know. And your little car is eminently suitable.'

'And beat Mark in the Bugatti?'

'It *is* possible.'

'Or will you race the Bugatti?'

'Indeed not. Mark puts the money up – he's entitled to the fun. Until I can make the business pay, that is – I look at it in the nature of a loan, and a base to get started from, but Mark has not attached any strings. He's very casual. I shall make sure his generosity is rewarded, eventually.'

'You do sound like Will. He was forever working hard to pay off debts. He used to get so cross when Dorothy said he should go out and have a bit of fun. He couldn't bear owing money. He even paid Mark the money he lost by losing the point-to-point – which was William's fault for crashing his plane on the finishing line just when Mark was all in line to win.'

'Funnily enough, Will told me that story. He said I should

218

meet his brother and ask him if it's true, because no one ever believed him when he said he had won a point-to-point in an aeroplane. Strange, isn't it, how things work out? Shall we have a bottle of champagne, and drink to it?'

'What a very good idea!'

Christina bought the Straker-Squire, and had driving lessons with Fergus for several weeks afterwards. Dick never inquired, and Mark was out hunting four days out of seven and not often in evidence. Dr Porter told Christina she was not able to ride until the spring, so there was no point in hankering for what she was missing: the Straker-Squire compensated nicely. Fergus took her to some hills and taught her the techniques of racing climbing, and had her practising starts.

'A good start is half the battle won,' he told her. 'That and changing gear at exactly the right moment. You'll be streets ahead of Mark, because he doesn't bother with the finesse of the game.'

Fergus was punctilious about detail; he was incapable of doing anything in a slap-dash fashion. Sometimes Christina found him too demanding to be fun, but realized that she stood a good chance of becoming a competitive driver with him to guide her. If she wanted to ... and she wasn't sure exactly where this new occupation was leading. It had certainly done the job of getting her out of her rut but it had not done anything to cure the ills of her marriage. The second anniversary of the wedding came and went without Christina so much as setting eyes on Dick all day.

Fergus took her to lunch in the road-house where they were now regular diners.

'Because it's your wedding anniversary.'

'Thank you very much. I do appreciate it.'

Fergus told the waiter that it was Christina's wedding anniversary, and the waiter brought a bottle of champagne so that they might toast their 'obviously very happy wedding'. Fergus acknowledged this pleasantry with a cordial reply, and poured the waiter a glass. The waiter drank and wished them very many more happy years.

When he had gone away, Christina said, 'My life is a dreadful mess. I can't go on like this for ever.'

Fergus did not reply. Christina saw that he looked painfully wary and did not press for her confidences, but she was aware of a great need to talk to someone, to find some sort of a way through the impasse. She could not find one on her own. Fergus never gossiped, but she thought that he missed very little, and she had come to value his opinion on almost everything, from the state of the country to the nature of the Straker-Squire's misfiring. His one grey eye, regarding her over the rim of the champagne glass, was wise, guarded, kindly.

'What are you going to do about it then?'

'What can I do?'

'What is your problem exactly?'

'That I am in love with Mark, that Dick is not in love with me, and why should he be under the circumstances? But I need to live with someone, and Dick won't come to me any more.'

'I cannot cure those things.'

'Say something to make it better then. I just need to feel a little more optimistic about it all, a gleam of light somewhere to cheer me up, not a cure. I agree that a cure is asking too much.'

'Mark is in love with you. Dick, I think, has another woman. That might not make you feel better, but it will stop you feeling guilty.'

Christina thought for a moment she was going to pass out. The whole dining-room spun round several times, and Fergus had to pour her a glass of water.

'Please don't faint on our wedding anniversary! Whatever shall I say to the waiter? You did ask, Christina.'

'How do you know?'

'In my job I meet a lot of people around the village. They talk to me while I'm mending their punctures. They say Dick works very late in the farmhouse.'

'But he does, Fergus! That's true. Dick would never do a thing like – I can't believe it . . .'

'Perhaps I overstate my case. He has interests, say, on the other side of Flambards. I believe this is true, both from what I've heard and what seems reasonable. A man doesn't leave his wife for bricklaying alone, Christina, not even a natural worker like Dick. People only make broad hints, you understand. They mention no names, they know I am involved in the family and they say just enough to see if I will be drawn out. But I take care not to be, so I never learn any more. But if you are guilt-ridden, which I believe to be the case – about Mark, and losing Dick his baby – you needn't be. That is the reason I tell you. After the shock, it will make you feel better.'

Christina did not speak for a long time. She ate her dinner without noticing, drank the champagne, felt rather cold in spite of the usual fire. Fergus did not prompt her. His eye, clear and sympathetic, regarded her at intervals in a doctorly fashion. She did not know who Dick could be interested in, unless it was Rosie Deakin, and that did not seem possible, considering in what regard Dick held the Deakin family. A married man could not compromise a young girl in that fashion and still be friends with her parents. But if what Fergus said was true . . . it was also true that she felt a weight lifting off her which in fact she had never been aware of, the hint of a gigantic feeling of freedom and a new self-confidence.

At the end of the dessert course, she said, 'It is true that I feel very guilty towards Dick.'

'I think you probably do, having changed his life to such a degree, and then seeing that he did not like it.'

'I never expected him to be grateful!'

'No. But I think you expected to be more of a partner in the enterprise, not just the good wife in the kitchen. That is how Dick has been brought up to think of women. You had such emancipated treatment first time round, with Will, you were dreadfully spoilt by it. You took it for granted.'

'I suppose I did.'

'You have very little in common, you and Dick. You're being very unfair to yourself to take all the blame.'

'But loving Mark, being unfaithful in spirit – I have tried and tried to think that I don't love him, not seeing him hardly at all now, on purpose, and for Dorothy's sake, too, but it doesn't make any difference. If Will had lived it would never have happened!'

'Of course not. That is why Dorothy calls your two marriages casualties of war.'

'She said that to me. I often feel I am guilty of breaking hers up too.'

'No, she has done that. You're a great one for taking blame! No wonder you took to vegetating like a maiden aunt! I think we have cleared away a lot of cobwebs over this lunch – all these skeletons we've taken out of the cupboard and dusted down. You will feel much better when you've thought about it, even if there are still no solutions. Solutions have a habit of creeping up on you over the years; they seem to happen, rather than get invented.'

'You're very comforting. You make me feel very selfish, all this trouble on my behalf – and what comfort have you got yourself? You never complain.'

'I've got my comforts. I've got a lady-friend up my sleeve, you'd be surprised. I do all my courting in the dark. I am very circumspect. I always approach her from the left. So far she hasn't noticed how ugly I am.'

'Are you telling the truth, or are you joking?'

'No, it's true. She needs me. Her car is always getting punctures.'

'Is that when you meet?'

'That's right. She gets so many punctures I suspect she likes my company.'

'I thought Dorothy and I were the only ladies with cars round here. Who is she?'

'She's a professional lady, very quiet and funny. I shall say no more, only enough for you not to feel sorry for me. One day I hope you will meet. I'm not joking.'

'I do hope it will work out for you. You deserve somebody nice. I feel so grateful to you. I think *you* should drive home – my head is going round so. I have such a lot to think about.'

'One more thing then: this Hunt Ball. Will you come with me? It's in two weeks' time.'

'Do you mean that, or are you being polite?'

'Mark and Dorothy are going, naturally. They want you to come too. Everybody knows you won't come with Dick, but to come with me, a friend of the family, will cause no scandal. Would you like to?'

'Would *you* like to? You don't like crowds.'

'For you I will go with pleasure.'

'You are a gentleman, Fergus. I do appreciate it. Yes, I think I would like to go to the Hunt Ball very much.'

'And then, in the spring, your first hill-climb? To take your mind off your troubles? It's certainly no good staying at home sewing, under the circumstances, Christina.'

'And I might even fit in a little gentle hunting before the season closes, who knows? I'm sure I'm strong enough now.'

'I would say that's an entirely therapeutic programme, eminently suitable for a wronged woman, with nothing on her conscience.'

'Very nicely put. What a very strange wedding anniversary

223

this has been, Fergus! Thank you for it. It was just what I needed.'

The waiter brought her leather coat and held it for her.

'I hope madam will continue to be very happy.'

'Madam is looking forward to the future with interest and optimism, which is more than she was when she came in.'

'Indeed?'

The waiter was puzzled. As they went out Fergus said, 'I don't think we should go there any more. It's served its purpose. You are now a fully fledged driver, ready for your first race. You don't need any more lessons.'

'Thank you, Fergus. I can't thank you enough.'

And she kissed him on the dreadful cheek, slowly and gratefully, and knew from the look in his eye that some of the therapy was working for him too.

Chapter 13

Dick had been repairing the home farm gradually ever since he had come to Flambards. It lay on the far side of the Flambards acres, more than a mile from the house, but close to the village and not far from the Deakins. The farm horses were kept there, and the farm machinery, and Dick did all his travelling to and fro on Ceasefire, who had his own loose-box at both ends. The farmhouse and the old stables had been burnt down, but Dick had made new stables out of the barns that had stood apart and not been affected, and had cleared out the gutted cottage and put a new roof on it. Because it was close to the village it had the electricity laid on – unlike Flambards – and Dick was able to work there through the winter evenings, off-loading his discontent into laying new floors both upstairs and downstairs, tiring himself so effectively that he sometimes dozed off on his ride home. After the death of the baby Harry, this work had an entirely satisfying nature to it which Dick found necessary; it was tiring, constructive and rewarding, and kept his mind occupied, away from the miseries. He felt that this place was his own. This was a myth, but one he could conveniently forget. In all essence it was his, the work of his hands, the sort of place that suited him, without frills and servants' quarters, a farmhouse for a working man where Sim and Nell would be at home visiting. He tried not to think of Christina at all, for his mind was in complete confusion as to his feelings towards Christina. He told himself that this hard work was in fact for her; she owned the place, he was repairing it for the estate; he worked his fingers to the bone for her. He was entirely honest in his dealings with the estate, entering everything up in the books in the Flambards study. It was like the old days when she had employed him, before they were married. He had been happy then.

After the night he had kissed Rosie, he knew he would never go back to Christina. How it would work out between the two of them he could not foresee, but he knew that she loved Mark, although she tried not to, and that he no longer loved her. It was honest to stay away. He was sorry for her, seeing how sombre she had become and all the spirit gone out of her. If she would bring her sewing down to the farmhouse and work in the kitchen with him and shop in the village and cook him meals and take beer out to the men he would have warmed to her again, he thought – just the two of them together. But too much came between in the big house, all the claptrap of servants and masters, and saying the right things in the right places, and holding one's end up: he had never felt right anywhere, neither in the sitting-room with Christina nor in the kitchen with Fowler. And never feeling right undermined the self-confidence which he knew was desperately important to a man. All his life he had held on to his self-confidence by his fingernails, through poverty and injustice in his youth, through the squalor and injustice of the army and the equal squalor of living on his disablement pension after he had been wounded. The best time of his life had been when he had come back to Flambards to work, and been paid for it, before he made the mistake of marrying Christina. He supposed that that was the state he was harking back to now, setting up the farmhouse as a den of his own to work the farm from, to acknowledge Christina as an employer, but not as a wife.

His failure with Christina was something he could not bear to dwell on, the dream of his lifetime dissolving in less than two years. Dreams were never meant to be acted out in the flesh. The Deakins had told him it was a dangerous thing to do, marry Christina, and he understood that her old Aunt Grace had said exactly the same to her. They had married on the strength of their adolescent dream-love, and the fact that it had been convenient – convenient for Flambards. The old place had a lot to answer for, in the way it had dominated its inmates: none of them had been happy there except Mark, and he was the one who had actually had to sell it, yet they had all put it first in their lives, arranging their affairs to keep the place going. Even he now – in spite of all that had happened – he wanted to make Flambards into a good farm. He did not want to go away.

But it seemed an idle dream to build a life away from Flambards without a woman to share his bed with him, and much of the carpentry in the farmhouse was routine enough to allow his mind to wander as he worked. It wandered quite a lot on women, perhaps sparked off by the kiss he had bestowed on Rosie. He had since apologized to her, but she had coloured up fearsomely and stammered that she had been pleased, not at all offended, which had made him nervous of her since. It was true that Rosie was a lovely girl, but he knew that what he wanted of a woman was in no way to be asked of Rosie. He was a married man and could not offend Nell and Sim by making advances to Rosie when he was only free to offer a clandestine relationship. He knew he was wrong in thinking along these lines with any woman, but his instincts compelled him. The villagers were few of them as clean-living as they would have it appear and young men were now in short supply; he could have had a casual coupling every night of the week if he had so desired, without difficulty, but that was not in his nature. He wanted a good woman friend whom one day he might be free to marry, if things were ever tidied up between Christina and himself. He had made one bad mistake, and the next time he would make sure it was right.

The woman was there under his nose and had been for a long time, but it was only when his mind started to work along these lines that he actually opened his eyes and saw her. And he saw her nearly every day, when she brought the children up to the village and they all stopped off to greet him: Clara, Rosie's older sister. During the months of January and February, when he was working on the house full-time, waiting for the land to come dry enough to plough, she came up with his lunch, put up by Mary or Christina every morning. Tom and Isobel loved to play in the half-built interior amongst the wood-shavings and the bricks, and Dick usually had a fire going in the range with the odd timber and an old kettle there he could brew up on. Clara would sit on the wooden chair that Dick used as a sawbench; she generally had a bit of tatting in her pocket that she would pull out, working industriously, and she would tell him about her life in Canada and about her children, young Jim and young Clara, whom she was just managing to care for on her wages. Dick could remember the boy she had married, Jim Munrow, whose yen had always been to emigrate to Canada. An uncle had paid for the young couple to go, but as soon as war had broken out Jim had come back and volunteered. He had been killed in the battle of the Somme. Clara had returned home and gone to live with Jim's mother in the village. Now she looked after Tom and Isobel for her living, calm and firm with them in a way Dick approved of. Dick could see Nell in her, the rock-like quality that made her so desirable to him; she was quiet-spoken, shy like Rosie, but with the strength and humour that her younger sister lacked. Dick did not speak about Christina to her. He knew that she knew what the situation was; a servant in a house knew everything. He was perfectly well aware that everyone knew he no longer slept with Christina, but he felt that it was probably rather harder for Christina to know that everyone knew, than it was for himself. The more he saw of Clara, the more he knew that there would be no change in that direction.

As it grew towards spring and the ground warmed and it was time to start ploughing again, Dick knew that work on the house would have to be put off.

He told Clara, 'You can still bring my dinner out, but it won't be so cosy any more. I'll be out in the fields.'

'Summer is coming,' Clara said.

They were in the kitchen, which was now finished, the window glass replaced, a new sink installed, a new door, the walls whitewashed. The door gave on to a railed front garden, trampled and spoilt from the fire, and beyond was a duckpond where the mallard ducks were nesting. Tom and Isobel were feeding them crusts they had brought from Flambards especially.

'If you've finished tramping in and out, I could make the garden nice for you. I'm a good gardener,' Clara said.

Knowing that, with the ploughing starting, a new pattern was going to develop in the relationship, Dick did not want to lose the intimacy they had built up in the confines of the house.

'When are you starting ploughing?' Clara asked him.

'Tomorrow.'

He was standing close to her in the doorway, watching the children. He knew he could not let the moment go, for it might not happen again. He put his hand up and let it rest on her shoulder. She turned and looked at him very directly, not pulling away. She had heavy, dark blonde hair which she pinned up rather untidily so that long tendrils fell down on her neck; her eyes were grey-blue, hiding nothing, faint wrinkles growing from the corners of her eyelids already. She had had a hard and not very happy life and her face showed it; Dick had an overwhelming desire to kiss away the melancholy the face showed in response.

'Clara.' He pulled her away from the doorway, out of the

view of the children. She came with him and stood smiling. He still had his arm round her neck.

'What do you want?'

'You know what I want.' He stroked her warm nape and touched the heavy coil of her hair, then drew her to him and kissed her on the mouth. He had meant it to be a gentle, suggestive kiss, but she returned the suggestion with such ardour that he was taken by surprise. He had been expecting Rosie's innocence, had forgotten that Clara was a woman who had been married for eight years and widowed for four.

She pulled away of her own accord, and stood there laughing at him. There was a glorious look on her face; he was astonished by her, thinking her suddenly the most beautiful and desirable woman he had ever set eyes on. The gesture had not turned out at all how he expected. He felt as if his new floor had fallen away from under him.

'What do you want?' she said again. 'Do you mean it?'

'Yes, I mean it all right. Oh, Clara, you are lovely!'

She put her hand out and laid a finger on his lips. She was still smiling. 'We cannot do this when I am with the children. If you want, I will come to you here in the evenings.'

He could not believe what was happening.

'Tonight?'

'If you like. Before you are too tired out with ploughing.' And she laughed.

Chapter 14

Christina was getting ready for the Hunt Ball. She had her Lucile dress on and was busy applying the make-up that Dorothy had supplied her with. Mary had done her hair and was tut-tutting at the red lips. The others were going to call for her en route in the Vauxhall – with the hood up, Dorothy had stipulated, in spite of Mark's groans. 'We want our beautiful coiffures all in one piece when we arrive! No argument.'

'I'm your M.F.H.! You can't give orders to me.'

'I can, darling. I do.'

Christina knew that Fergus was in fact regarding the evening with dread, using it as proof to himself that he could surmount his craven fear of exposing his disfigurement to a crowd of inquisitive acquaintances. She was going to show the same crowd that she was no longer in mourning for child nor for husband. Neither of their motives for going were exactly ones to guarantee enjoyment, but as Dorothy and Mark were going solely in order to enjoy themselves, she thought they were the ones more likely to suffer disappointment. Christina foresaw an interesting evening, somewhat unpredictable. Jerry and his Rootin' Tooters were coming to play, having been severely primed as to what was suitable for the occasion. She had a sixth sense that they might forget after several pints of beer.

When she was ready and Mary had gone downstairs, Christina went out on to the landing, feeling ridiculously nostalgic for the evening long ago when she had waited in just the same place, dressed for the Hunt Ball, for Will. She had thought he would not come, but he had. Compared with then, her love so clear and simple, she felt hopelessly at sea with her present affections. She scarcely saw Dick at all; he had started ploughing with the coming of spring. She had never said anything to him about Fergus's news, not at all sure if it was true, and feeling that if it was, it was more her fault than his. She thought far more about Mark than about Dick.

While she was looking out of the window, Dick came up the stairs behind her. She turned round. He stopped on the top step and looked at her for what seemed a very long time.

'Where are you going?'

'To the Hunt Ball.'

'Who with?'

'Fergus is taking me.'

He seemed in no way put out. He looked very well these days, his face having lost the haggard cast she associated with his bad temper. His hair was damp with the evening air: it was a clear, cold evening, a late blackbird calling in the garden and a mist coming up over the home fields so that the trees stood out in the dusk above it. Far away at the bottom of the drive she could see the lights of Mark's Vauxhall coming from Dermot's. She felt unaccountably sad, remembering the night Will came, and the lights of Mr Dermot's Rolls-Royce.

Dick said, gently, 'I am sorry I can't take you. I hope you enjoy yourself.'

'Yes, I will.'

Again unaccountably, she felt tears rising up behind her eyeballs in a hopeless, most untimely manner. Dick was looking at her in a way she could not fathom. She shook her head hopelessly.

He came up to her and said, 'You don't need that stuff to make you beautiful, Christina.'

'No. You're probably right.'

'I'm terribly sorry,' he said, 'at how it's worked out. I never meant to make you unhappy.'

'It wasn't you,' Christina said.

The tears rolled over the top and down through the white face-powder. She could feel the warm marks they inscribed as they dropped off on to Lucile's chiffon frills. Dick pulled out a handkerchief and very carefully dabbed at her cheeks.

'A good soil needs no top-dressing,' he said.

'I shall enjoy myself, all the same.'

'Yes, you do that.'

'I never meant to make you unhappy either.'

'I know you didn't. I am sorry I can't make it come right for you.'

And he kissed her very gently on the cheek, his lips cold as ice from the evening, and went to his bedroom. Christina heard the Vauxhall hooting, snatched up her fur wrap and ran downstairs, sobbing. She ran out into the drive. Dorothy was in the back seat and opened the door for her; Christina got in and sat there howling uncontrollably.

Dorothy put her arm round her and said comfortingly, 'There's nothing wrong that we don't already know about? Just the same old things?'

'Yes – nothing – I'm all right! Do go on. Dick – Dick – just kissed me –'

'God almighty!' Mark opened the throttle with a roar and set off down the drive with a great spraying of gravel in all directions. 'I don't understand women,' he said to Fergus. 'They cry when you don't kiss 'em and they cry when you do.'

'It's the timing that has to be right,' Fergus said. 'We tend to get the timing wrong.'

'Well, Christina's timing is all wrong at the moment. She can't go in at the door in this condition.'

'I shall be all right by the time – we get there.'

She snuggled down against the fur shoulder, with Dorothy's arm still round her.

'I did want that baby so,' she sniffed to Dorothy. 'It would have been all right with Dick if –'

'Don't cry for Dick,' Dorothy said to her. 'It's all for the best, in the end. It will work out.'

'I – I'm terribly sorry.'

'Don't be silly.'

'The children are what matter, after all.'

Dorothy said nothing, and Christina remembered too late, wrapped up in her few minutes of hysteria, and knew that Mark had heard too, and that she was making a mess of the evening before it had even started. She made a great effort to pull herself together, bitterly ashamed of herself. She sat up straight and pulled her collar up round her ears.

'It's all right now. I'm quite all right. I'm sorry I was so stupid.'

Badstocks had memories enough to make her cry, apart from anything else, for it was where Will had proposed to her and they had eloped the same evening in Mr Dermot's Rolls-Royce. If she did not pull herself together now she was never going to get through the evening at all. She despaired of herself, thinking of how well she had been doing lately with Fergus's help, and not to ruin it in front of both Mark and Fergus together ...

She had not foreseen the effect her presence would have on the country society she had not mixed with for so long. When she went in at the door on Fergus's arm – having tidied up her face in the driving mirror with the loan of Mark's torch – she was surprised by the look of astonishment on the faces of her hosts, Colonel and Mrs Badstock and the Lucases. After the first shock, both the old ladies kissed her warmly, as if welcoming her back to the fold, and neither inquired after Dick. Christina remembered that the moment was a bad one for Fergus, and held him tightly by the arm as she introduced him.

'Ah, we know of you, of course,' they cooed, looking him unflinchingly in the face with the beautiful coolness of their county manners. 'How lovely to meet you!'

Fergus whispered to Christina as they passed on into the hall, 'I'm trade, of course, but I have indisputably suffered to free this country from the thrall of the Boche.'

Christina giggled, her spirits having rocketed. Although they mocked, it was warming to be made welcome after so wilfully flouting all the rules of this tight community. Christina wondered what would have been the welcome if she had been on Dick's arm, instead of Fergus's. Far more guarded, she was sure, and crucifying for Dick. Even if Dick had desired it, it would have taken him years to penetrate this far country, and he would only have done it by being humble and respectful: he had known it was impossible, given his temperament, long before she had begun to see it.

What a fool I've been, she thought, going upstairs to leave her coat and tidy her hair ... why could one only learn by what actually happened, instead of being able to think ahead? Everything was plain in hindsight, even to the result of her lark with the Bugatti. She wondered what was looming on her horizon now, that she was going to blindly walk into and then live to regret.

She repaired her face properly at Mrs Badstock's dressing-table, where Dorothy joined her.

'Fergus and Mark have discovered Jerry and the band. It's like a reunion of the old regiment down there. I hope they are all going to remember where they are as the evening progresses.'

'Mark will have to behave himself now he's the M.F.H. It's his ball, after all. You must keep him in order, Dorothy.'

'We tend to go our own ways these days,' Dorothy said, rather dismissively. 'I try to stop him drinking mainly to save

235

myself being up the rest of the night afterwards looking after him. I really can't stand by his side and talk to these old diehards about the chase into the bargain. I want to have some fun!'

Looking at her, as provocatively dressed as usual, bright and tough and irreverent, Christina guessed she would succeed. Somewhere along the line she and Dorothy were parting company. Christina had a feeling that Dorothy would for ever be questing for something new, something different, and would not know or care for contentment as she herself wanted it. Equally, she felt that this opinion was disloyal, for no one could have a more magnanimous friend than Dorothy.

They went down. Christina found that a lot of people wanted to talk to her; they were sorry about her losing the child, they reminisced about Will, they talked of Mark and Fergus, but no one mentioned Dick. Christina began to wonder if Dick existed at all. They were unfailingly kind to Fergus.

'Having scars that show is really an advantage, you see,' Christina pointed out. 'You have had quite the wrong attitude to it all this time. If Mark were to bare his midriff, they would all fall over themselves to be his friend.'

'He seems to do rather well for himself without,' Fergus said drily, nodding his head in Mark's direction, where he was chatting up the distinctly more giddy element among the county females.

'He gives them good sport, you understand.'

'I can see it, yes.'

'Out hunting, I mean.'

'Of course.'

Christina laughed. Jerry's band played very good music, increasingly hotter as the evening progressed, dropping the selection from 'The Maid of the Mountains' for the Barnyard Blues and the Skeleton Jangle. As Christina danced and

236

ate and drank and the atmosphere grew less formal and altogether more uninhibited, she felt herself harking back more and more to the same ball when she had had to make the choice between Mark and Will. Everything, save the fact that Will was now dead, was just the same, as if no time, no war had intervened: the people were all the same, the place was unchanged; she knew that if she went out into the conservatory it would be full of the Colonel's camellias in the selfsame pots, and in the library where Will had proposed to her a dog would be asleep in front of the fire – if not the same dog, a son or daughter of the one which had slumbered at her feet then. Mark had said that same far-distant night to her, in the conservatory with the camellias, that he would fight a war to ensure that none of this changed. He had said he would die for it. He had been drunk at the time, but he had been true to his words. He had very nearly died for it, and it was the same.

She went to Mark then, upset by the futility of her thinking, because he was the focal point in her stupid life whether she would have it or not, and she wanted the comfort of being with him. She had avoided his company for so long, by the use of her iron willpower, and now she was tired. Her iron willpower was bending. She no longer owed her loyalty to Dick; he had proved that to her tonight. He no longer cared for her and Dorothy no longer cared for Mark. She was hurting no one.

Mark was talking to Colonel Badstock. He was wearing hunting evening dress, the same startling red and white and black he had been wearing the very first time she had ever set eyes on him, so strange to her then after her grey urban upbringing in Battersea, and now, it seemed, so well matched to the person; Mark never had been a one for shades of grey. Christina knew she had her eyes wide open. Mark turned to her, and excused himself from the Colonel immediately.

'Will you have this waltz with me, Christina?'

'Yes.'

Jerry was resting; the music was undemanding and romantic. Mark made two revolutions of the room in silence and then stopped and drew away from her. They were standing by the doorway into the hall, unnoticed in the throng. Mark took her hand and led her out and across to the library. The door was open. It was a small, cosy room where a black Labrador dozed in front of the embers of a fire, and the chairs were worn and comfortable. Mark kicked the door behind him, the last log fell in the fireplace and broke into flame, and Christina saw Mark's face touched with the flickering light, the dark eyes pinpointed scarlet like a fox in the darkness. Danger signs all the way, she thought.

'Mark, dear Mark –'

It was no good hiding it any more. He came to her and took her in his arms and kissed her as she had dreamed of it for so long, and she knew that what she was doing was disastrous, even worse than marrying Dick, but the knowledge had no power to spoil anything at all. It was so lovely to give in and to say to him all the things she had never even said to herself, rambling and tumbling between his kisses, and his mouth moving down her throat, his head dropping down so that she could put her face into his soft hair, hold him against her breast.

'Darling Mark, I do love you so.'

'Twelve years it has taken you to get round to it,' he murmured. 'You are incredibly *slow*, Christina.' And he lifted up his head and kissed her again on the mouth, so that she all but lost her senses. His eyes had the flames reflected in them still; she felt she was going to go up in flames herself, and pulled away violently.

'No!'

'You want me to,' he said. 'You know you do.'

'Yes, of course! But – oh, Mark! You know as well as I do –'

Someone had to face facts, come back to earth, make sense of what they were doing. She could not bear to lose hold of him; he picked her up in his arms and sat down in one of the armchairs in front of the fire and she lay with her arms round his neck, her cheek pressed against his.

'This is where Will proposed to me,' she said. 'In this room. There is no future for us, Mark, because of Will. But I can't go on pretending I don't love you, because I do. I can't help it. It is all wrong but I am tired of always doing the proper thing. Just sometimes I want to be able to tell you, like now, and have you kiss me. That's all there is. You're married to Dorothy and I'm married to Dick.'

'But Dorothy, I think, has other lovers than me, and rumour has it that Dick now goes his own way.'

'He hasn't slept with me since the child was born. In that sense I am free – he doesn't love me any more.'

'I can never understand why you married him.'

'I know you can't. It seemed right at the time.'

'I never understood why you married Will either, when you could have had me. You're very bad at decisions.'

'No, Will was lovely, much nicer than you! – much kinder, more gentle. I did love him. But you – oh, Mark, I have tried so hard not to love you! Giving in – now – doesn't make any difference. We can't do anything about loving each other –'

He started to kiss her again, but she pulled away, and stood up. 'We must go back. You're the Master – they'll be wondering where you are. I shall have to go upstairs and do my hair. I think I should go home.'

'I'll take you home.'

'No. I came with Fergus and I shall go home with Fergus.'

'Will had the right idea, driving away into the night with you. Poor young bastard! To lose you, and everything. He didn't deserve it. I can't believe we have no future at all, Christina, but God knows, being content with kisses isn't much of one. I suppose that's how it will have to be, I admit, but –'

He broke off, and Christina saw the look on his face, and knew that she had indulged herself at Mark's expense. She pulled her handkerchief out and gently wiped the lipstick marks off his face.

'I shall come hunting with you tomorrow. I am not going to sit at home regretting things any longer.'

'No. It's best. Things will work out somehow.' He kissed her very gently on the end of her nose. 'I adore you,' he said. 'You have made me very happy tonight.'

He went back to the dancing, not looking happy at all, and Christina went to Fergus and asked him to drive her home.

Christina left a note out for Dick, saying, 'Please leave me Ceasefire today. You can take Pepper or Tiptoe.'

She half expected him not to comply, but when she went out to the stables she found Ceasefire there and Tiptoe missing. She had not ridden for so long that it seemed unwise to take her first outing with hounds on Tiptoe, who was as unfit as she was. Ceasefire was fit and steady, and was reputed to carry a side-saddle without any trouble. It was a day of strong wind and a spattering of rain and Christina had no regrets for what had happened. As from today, she decided, I regret nothing. I shall do what I please. I have no obligation to Dick, nor to anybody else save Tom and Isobel, who are impeccably cared for. I can look anybody in the eye for I am acting with complete honesty. She had sat and mulled over her mistakes for so long that to ride out and forget her troubles in physical action was an antidote whose efficacy she had forgotten. As soon as she was aboard and heading for the meet over the muddy tracks she felt scoured of her gloom and when she reached the rendezvous, a modest public house happily called 'The Fox and Hounds' some three miles from Flambards, and saw the same old faces imbibing the mulled ale that was being handed, she felt as if the last five years had never happened. Even Mark, arriving on his crazy thoroughbred, Ragtime, already in a muck sweat of excitement, was a huntsman with a job to do, not the doomed love of the earlier mood – how much more plainly the physical life saw the path ahead! . . . the problems not as traps and snares and ambushes, but as plain fences to be overcome by strength of character. She had to laugh at her new outlook, the optimism bubbling, just because Ceasefire felt like a lion beneath her and the wind was tossing the rooks up over the bare elms like scraps of cloth to caw and claw their way back to their rackety nests. Old Lucas and Mr Allington, even smart Amy Masters who had once chased Mark and was now engaged to a munition mogul, greeted her as if she had come out of hibernation.

'Ride up with me,' Mark said to her. 'Like you used to. You can be honorary joint-master today.'

His red coat flared against the dark woods. Christina kept with him as if it were her purpose in life, never letting him out of her sight, although Ragtime had the legs of Ceasefire and the nervous energy of his rider. Christina had heard it said that no one knew how the two of them survived their wild days out hunting: the thoroughbred weed bred for a six-furlong sprint and its master who by all the evidence had been robbed of his stamina for life in Flanders. He took no food or drink all day and rode home like a white ghost through the dusk, as exhausted as the horse, yet the two of them turned up three days later fit to go again. Mark had always been hard on his horses and now was as hard on himself. Christina saw that he drove himself by the same willpower she had been crediting herself with last night. The riding hurt him but he completely disregarded what he did not want to acknowledge. Drawing another covert after killing their first fox, he cursed the weary Ragtime for the weakness of his own body.

'You are crazy,' Christina said, pushing up through the thickets at his side. 'Three-quarters of them have gone home now. You will kill yourself if you always ride like this.'

'If you lecture me I shall demote you back to the field. I'm not changing my ways for you.'

And they were away, the mud flying again, the horses recharged by the wild cries of the hounds, the rain slashing their faces. She understood him then, in her own excitement, the horses quivering on the banks of a running ditch and her own exuberance brooking no hesitation, Ceasefire taking off like a volcano erupting and the branches rattling her bowler, snagging her veil ... into a wood and blindly down the quagmire rides after Mark's red coat, down banks of deep slithering leafmould, crouched to avoid the low branches, to a gravelly stream where the leading hound had bowled over the quarry. Mark was off his horse and wading into the mêlée of excited hounds. Christina sat and watched the great swirling of animals in the stream, Mark bending over talking to them as he took the dead fox ... 'Well done, Lagonda, good fellow. Down. Mercedes, let go, you fool!' He came back with the brush, dripping wet, and leaned against Ceasefire, holding it up to her, out of breath, laughing. His face was pale, streaked with mud and blood, the black cap torn with dead leaves caught in the button like a decoration.

'From one – joint-master – to another –'

He put his arms round her waist and she bent down and kissed his cold wet face. Ceasefire moved off to drink at the stream and Mark staggered after her saying, 'Have you no control of your beast, madam?' Christina flung her leg over the pommel and slipped off into his arms and he kissed her again and said, 'This is the best day's hunting I've had this season and quite the nicest quarry I've ever caught.'

They separated as the crashing and swearing in the trees

above them heralded the arrival of the rest of the field, all in much the same state of exhaustion and dishevelment. Mark caught Ragtime up, but hadn't the strength to mount again. He loosened the girths instead and they all rested their horses and took out their hipflasks. Old Lucas toasted Christina's return to the hunting-field and Mark said, 'She's a very fast lady. I could scarcely keep up.'

They rode home, and the last bit Christina and Mark did alone together, the pack of hounds padding silently around their horses' legs, and they in silence too. Christina, looking at him, hoped that Dorothy would be home to look after him, but he said she was in London.

'She went back with Jerry.'

They would be alone by their respective hearths, but there was nothing to be done about it.

They kissed good-bye, the horses tired enough to stand still at last, although it wasn't very easy and made them laugh, and Christina did the last mile to Flambards through the dusk, the rain having stopped and the sun slanting belatedly through the trees on the horizon, casting an uncanny greenish-gold light over the sodden fields. The wind was cold, and a star was shining in the east even while the strange sunlight lasted.

'The weather will have put a stop to your ploughing,' Christina said to Dick over supper. 'What did you do today?'

'I did a bit more down the farm. I've started to put a new roof on the stables, so we can use the threshing barn again next winter.'

'Ceasefire went beautifully. He's wasted as a hack.'

'You bought him, not me. I'll ride whatever's at home. Tiptoe got me there and back without any trouble. But you use Ceasefire if you want, he's safer for you.'

'It was lovely, hunting again. Are you never going to give it a try?'

'Who'll do the work, while I'm gallivanting?'

'One day a week off? The farm will hardly suffer ...'

'It goes too deep, Christina. I'll bring you a second horse, if you like, touch my forelock to the gaffers like I used to do.'

'Why can't you be a gaffer too? Get Fowler to bring *you* a second horse – not that anyone's got second horses any more. It's not like it used to be. Not even a huntsman. Mark hunts them himself.'

'He'll give good sport, I daresay. He was always a thruster.'

'You'd enjoy it, Dick. Life's not all work.'

'Mostly it is.'

'Are you going back to the farm after supper?'

'For a couple of hours.'

She wanted to ask him then who he met in the evenings, but she dared not.

'Do you see much of the Deakins these days?'

'I call in, yes, same as I always have done. Nothing's any different.'

'And Rosie?'

'Rosie's well enough. She's not much to say for herself. She's going into service, if she can find somewhere.'

'Is it hard, to find somewhere?'

'You know it is. The unemployment is something dreadful. I've men come and ask me for a job every day of the week.'

'In the summer, we can take –'

'It's steady work they want. They mostly have wives and children to support – they're not boys out of school, but men back from France.'

Christina, weary, felt depressed by the realities, just when she had managed to slough off her own self-pity. Dick made her feel that fun was wicked, whereas Mark made fun of everything he threw himself into. Even the car business was a lark at Dermot's, the customers in and out at all hours and stopping for a chat in the same way that they passed time in the forge over a new set of horse-shoes. Whenever Christina went over there would be a farmer or a chauffeur sitting on an oil-drum exchanging the time of day, chatting to Fergus's legs sticking out from underneath an old Ford, or to Mark who rested up after hunting days lying on an old sofa in the workshop, desultorily cutting out rubber strips for mending punctures or writing out bills for Fergus in his execrable hand. Fergus had also set up an agency to sell tractors, a British Austin model and also the American Overtime, which he or Mark, bizarrely dressed in British army great-coat and flying helmet, took out on demonstrations when required.

Christina commented on the fact that Mark appeared to be working, if spasmodically, and Fergus said, 'He's a fright-fully good salesman, not nearly so pedantic as me. Bowls them over with enthusiasm. He believes it all himself, you see – doesn't know about the snags, because he doesn't really understand engines. But the farmers don't either. They call the controls the reins. And his being a Master of Foxhounds seems to help – they think they can trust him, for some reason. It's an amazing combination.'

'It's all done by charm,' Mark said.

'We're actually making money,' Fergus said.

'And racing the cars is going to make us famous. People will flock here, to find the secret of our success.'

The first hill-climb was looming up and as Christina had rashly committed herself to entering she was nervous about it. Unlike the hunting field, it was strange terrain, and a whole lot of different people. Motor-racing took on con-veniently when hunting left off. Christina was not sorry to have Mark occupied with something that was surely less demanding than hunting. His days on the sofa worried her, but Dorothy said, 'What can you expect? He'll never grow old – he might as well enjoy himself. That's what he chooses.' Their relationship had grown abrasive and uncertain, with periods of gloom and bickering alternating with careless high spirits. Dorothy's long absences seemed not to be resented; rather they made the partnership more tenable, the days apart restoring equanimity. Whether she knew of Christina's acknowledgement of her feelings to Mark, Christina had no way of knowing, but her friendship was unwavering.

Christina practised on the hill-climb, which was part of a public road some fifteen miles from home, and learned where to change gear and how to start as best she could, and how fast she dared take the two fearsome bends on the way up. The spring weather made the surface very bad, and as a good number of the intending competitors practised as arduously as she did it grew rapidly worse, and one's plans less and less predictable according to new ruts and bared, slippery patches.

Dick was invited to the meeting, out of courtesy.

'It's not serious, you understand – just a bit of fun. Everyone takes the family and picnics and the children, to enjoy themselves. We're taking Tom and Isobel – they'll love it. Clara can have the day off. Dorothy's coming, and Jerry and Jean are coming down, and Fergus, of course. He has a lady-friend who he is persuading to come – we've none of us met her yet. He's very secretive about her – all we know is that she gets a lot of punctures.'

'I'd far rather you wouldn't make an exhibition of yourself.'

'It's hardly that, Dick. It's nearly all amateurs the same as me, and I'm not the only woman, you know. I suppose it's altogether too frivolous for you?'

'Yes, probably.'

'It's work for Fergus and Mark.'

'Well, perhaps.'

'But you won't come?'

'No. I'm drilling now the weather's fair.'

Christina tried not to show her exasperation, although she wasn't sorry, or surprised, about the answer. There was no doubt he was an exemplary farmer and as that was what she had always wanted for Flambards how could she complain?

Dorothy made the arrangements. 'Mark and Fergus can take the two racing-cars over, and Christina and I will bring the children in the Vauxhall, and the picnic. We'll just have to keep our fingers crossed for the weather.'

'Wouldn't you like to enter the Straker-Squire instead of me?' Christina asked Fergus.

'My dear girl, certainly not! I wouldn't deny you the pleasure!'

The Saturday dawned blustery and bright, warm and summery one moment and piercing cold the next. Mark rode out to exercise the hounds, which he always enjoyed, Fergus made last-minute adjustments to the racing cars and Dorothy and Christina packed the Vauxhall with all the things they would need. By the time Mark was ready, Fergus had already set off, and Mark settled down happily in the Bugatti to catch him up, but a leak in the radiator upset his plans. He knew he would have to stop for more water, and decided to get it at Flambards home farm, knowing there was a tap in the kitchen if the door was open, and one in the stable yard if not. He turned in at the drive, accelerated up to the newly renovated farmhouse and round to the back door. Seeing someone in the window he got out and walked up the path. The door opened abruptly and Dick stood there. Mark saw a figure move across the room behind him and disappear silently into another room, and was so intrigued by the sight that he forgot for a moment what he had come for.

'What do you want?'

Dick did not look at all accommodating, but addressed him as if he was a complete stranger. Under the circumstances Mark was not surprised, more amused.

He smiled. 'Sorry if I'm disturbing you. A jugful of water, if it's convenient.'

Dick fetched him one without a word. Mark made much of having to wait for the sizzling water to cool before he removed the radiator cap, and engaged Dick in amiable conversation, to which Dick replied curtly.

'Your drilling would be done by now if you'd bought one of our tractors. It's not too wet for you today, is it? You're late starting.'

'I'm just having a bite of breakfast.'

The jug needed a refill and Mark stared interestedly at the places set for two on the table while Dick went to the tap. He made sure that Dick had noticed where he was looking before he went back to the car.

The incident afforded him a good deal of pleasure, but as he drove fast down the narrow lanes, listening to the satisfying crackle of his exhaust and the beautiful note of the highly-tuned engine, the pleasure gradually changed to resentment. None of the rest of them – least of all Christina – had ever made themselves out to be perfect, far from it, only too well aware of the shortcomings in their relationships which could be blamed on nothing but the failings of their characters. They all of them, himself included, were depressed at times by their inadequacies. But Dick, who always appeared to Mark to pride himself on his honest ways and be impatient with their frippery concerns, seemed to be having it both ways: Christina's generous patronage in his job, and another lady's patronage for his home comforts. Who the lady was Mark wasn't sure, but there had been no doubt about her presence. Dick's treatment of Christina angered Mark. Even if it was to his own advantage, he felt deeply indignant at the deceit he had uncovered. When the day was over he decided he would do something to have it out with Dick – exactly how he could work out later.

The venue for the hill-climb was swarming with spectators. The practice runs were already under way, and the revving engines in the paddock crackled fiercely, gusting on the wind. Spectator cars crowded the grass slopes, quite a few of them already stuck in the mud, and the roped-off road was lined thickly with people, especially on the bends, where groups of marshals struggled to stop spectators crossing.

'It's like a point-to-point,' Christina said to Mark, gazing at the scene from the parked Vauxhall. 'Just like old times, save the noise is different. I feel quite at home.'

'It's nothing like a point-to-point at all, idiot woman. It's like a hill-climb.'

'Dad, Uncle Mark, take me in the Bugatti,' Tom begged. 'Please give me a ride!'

'I'll take you down to the paddock.'

'Me too!' Isobel shrieked. 'And me! It's not fair!'

'You can come with me, Isobel,' Christina said. 'There's more room in my car. Fergus is getting our times and numbers. He said he'd see us down there. Do be careful with Tom.' Tom had to sit on Mark's lap in a very cramped space. Seeing the two of them together, both with the same expressions of contained excitement, their faces so close together, Christina was moved with a great wrench of longing for her family to be sorted out happily; the suspicion that the tangle was all of her own making provoked her into a wild, frustrated acceleration down to the paddock, overtaking Mark on the way. Isobel sat shrieking with enjoyment, and when Christina turned to her to lift her out – for the car had nothing so civilized as doors – she realized it was the first time the child had ridden in it. Clara had taken charge so thoroughly that Christina only saw the children in the house at meal-times and in the evening.

She hugged Isobel. 'Did you enjoy that?'

'Yes. I want to go up the hill.'

'No darling, you can't. But I'll take you for a ride tomorrow, a proper ride.'

Mark roared up beside them. Tom appeared to be steering, but they managed to avoid disaster, parked the cars amongst their fellow contestants and went to find Fergus.

Christina had not expected the meeting to be so well attended and now felt very anxious. In spite of having been led to believe it was just a bit of fun, she noticed that it was not exactly high spirits that characterized the demeanour of the competitors as they waited one by one at the start, but rather an extremely tense and nervous anticipation. Each car went off from a standstill when its signal was given with an excruciating burst of throttle, a screaming of tyres and a devastating shower of mud, grit and filth from the spinning wheels. The noise was ear-splitting at close quarters, both from the starting competitor and the one coming up behind, dabbing at the throttle to approach the start in a wild series of jerks, braking and leaping forward again to get into concert pitch. Christina had practised all this herself but in cold blood. Now she felt she was being drawn into some sort of gladiatorial arena with her little blue car, and she knew she must do well, for her car was a thoroughbred, not like some of the hopefuls. Fergus was a professional, and was not expecting her to fail.

'Let her go first,' he said to Mark. 'We'll see her off, and she'll feel better when she's done her first run.'

It was all suddenly very much in earnest, the picnic forgotten. Dorothy took charge of the children, and Christina got down behind her steering-wheel in the queue of motley machines, tucking her hair up firmly into a tight woollen cap and hoping the elastic of her goggles would keep the structure proof against the coming hazards. She felt better, sinking into anonymity, for in spite of her protestations to Dick there were very few women driving – only one other that she could see.

Fergus and Mark took up station one on either side of the car, after Fergus had tinkered under the bonnet for a few minutes, putting in new plugs. They pushed it up the queue, and as the cars in front went off to meet varying degrees of success or disaster Fergus pointed out to Christina the lessons to be learned.

'For the first bend, change down by that bit of hawthorn – the one where that woman in the pink dress is standing. She might move, but the bush won't. Don't leave it too late because you'll want both hands on the wheel for the bend in case she goes into a slide. Go into the middle of the bend – the ground is better. The inside is getting really torn up. Watch this one now – he'll do it properly – it's Archie Frazer-Nash – look at that – gear-change exactly right ... oh, that's very nice! That's lovely! Did you see his line through the bend? – that's what you want, Christina ...'

The fiendish crackle of the extraordinary little G.N. blasted on a gust of wind from the top of the hill like the noise of machine-gun fire, along with roars and shrieks from the crowd. Christina was afraid of going off the bend into the crowd ... she was afraid of the whole business now she had only two cars in front of her ...

Fergus went to start the engine, and the sudden throaty unsilenced racket stopped their conversation. Christina clenched her sweaty hands on the wheel. There was a Talbot just about to go, and a ten-horse Morgan in front of her, and the noise was deafening. Christina screwed up her face, feeling for a moment that she was back with Will in one of his equally rackety aeroplanes, but it was Mark's face close beside hers and his arm round her shoulders momentarily: 'It's only the practice, remember! Don't be scared.'

She was scared, she could not conceal it. She knew now that her eyes were charged with the same demoniacal light she had noticed in the starters before her, and her body braced with the same agonizing concentration. The Morgan went off like an explosive – a stench of burning rubber, the ears scorched, her car splattered with a shower of filth. The starter was looking at her, the marshal taking her number. The crowd pressed round and she looked at Fergus bending down beside her. He beckoned her on. She let off the brake and put in the clutch, her foot on the throttle and the car sprung beneath her like a startled race-horse – God almighty, what had Fergus been doing to it! She was nearly through the start in her mere approach, braking wildly in a great scrunching of flying cinders and muck. The marshal bent down and mouthed something to her – she had no idea what – she nodded, remembered to look at the starter, mud-streaked and grim, looking up the hill for clearance with the flag upraised. Panic – suppose I stall! Christina thought, agonized again – all those grinning, grimacing faces pressed round and the black scar of the road clear ahead of her, heavily fringed with the undisciplined crowd ... the flag dropped. And Christina found that she had anticipated it to the split second, the car at full throttle, the brake off in a flash, and the shattering, magnificent roar was the sound of her own car as it leapt at the road. She had never started like that in all her practices, the adrenalin never having been roused as it was now, opening out to get the fastest speed possible on the easiest part of the route, the white faces spinning past, idiot spectators who would never know the bliss of – God almighty! a sticky patch and the tail of the Straker-Squire took hold with a sickening swing out to the far curve, exactly where she had planned not to go ... she wrenched at the wheel, but the dear car was in hand ... the bend was looming up, a great wall of spectators in a bank ahead of her, the most terrifying sight of the day so far. She looked for the hawthorn bush, saw nothing, a pink frock – pray God the woman had not moved! Christina stamped on the clutch and moved the gear-lever adroitly. The car was too far out to the right because the skid had upset her line, but it was on good ground and she knew she was going to miss that dreadful, innocent bank of picnickers as she hauled the wheel round again. The slope steepened and the car lost speed rapidly. Change gear again – don't leave it too late! But no, it was right; the power strained the poor little car up into the second curve of the wide S, shuddering and gallant, wheels slithering and spinning in the soft patches and the flying stones clattering on the metalwork. It was work now, the climb galling her poor car and only her skill to see it safely through: perhaps cleverer, this, than the first flying straight, to nurse it through the second leg until the slope slackened a fraction and the speed picked up again, and then to slam it round the second bend, much sharper this time, the ground even worse. Several cars had come to grief here, and had been pushed off into the field, mostly lacking sheer power to see them through, but the Straker-Squire was not lacking in guts and ploughed round in a spray of mud and dirt. Christina was half blinded and could judge the road best by its flanking ribbons of spectators, but she was over the brow now and coasting, realizing she had no idea where the finish was, never having troubled to find out. She spared a hand to wipe at her goggles, and saw by various waving marshals that she had already passed it and was about to drive on into far country instead of into the finishing paddock. She braked, turned where she was beckoned and came to a standstill on quiet, smooth grass. She switched off the engine and pushed up her goggles. A beautiful serene view of the country scene blessed her eyes, clear to the distant silver gleam of the river Thames from her perch on the hill-top, the cold wind bringing with it the delicious scent of flowering hawthorn and homely cow-pats, the family groups dotted about eating out of their baskets like photographs in women's magazines. Christina slumped back, feeling trembly and exhausted and magnificent all at once, deeply satisfied that she had not let Fergus down. Nothing else seemed to matter very much. She had not been stupid; she had kept in control all the way and probably made quite a reasonable time.

She guessed that Mark would follow her up fairly quickly in the Bugatti and strained her eyes on the start, driving her car to a good view point. She was not mistaken. She recognized the sound of the Bugatti's engine as it broke into life, and saw it vibrating on the starting-line with Fergus in anxious attendance. Mark was a wild and careless driver and she had some anxious moments as he went into the bends in hair-raising fashion, but he managed to hold the road and took the second bend as neatly as Captain Frazer-Nash himself, opening up along the home stretch with a roar which brought several of the picnicking parties to their feet. Once more she was reminded of the point-to-point before the war. Mark was a born competitor, having neither nerves nor caution. He skidded up beside her and turned off the engine, pushed up his goggles grinning.

'Good, eh? Bet I beat you. Fergus has really got them going, hasn't he? She's never felt so good. Did you enjoy it?'

'I think so. I'm not sure.' She wasn't now. She wished that had been the real thing, and the ordeal over.

'I got up at least.' Which was more than could be said for many of the entrants, losing power on the bends, stuck in the mud and often having to go down in reverse to find a less severe gradient to try and get started again.

They drove down with all the others during a lull in the proceedings, and the crowd cheered and clapped. Fergus was pleased and full of congratulations, the children excited and whirling about, wanting more rides, wanting something to eat. Jerry and Jean had arrived with two more friends, and they all went back to the Vauxhall to have their picnic before racing proper started. But Christina found she had very little appetite. She sat on the spread rugs in her leather coat, watching Mark and Jerry playing with the children, wondering what she was doing in such a situation. To take her mind off emotional problems? ... it seemed extreme and crazy, and reminded her strongly of her days with Will, when their love was rarely given precedence over new warp wires for the Blériot or magneto trouble with Emma. Perhaps if her day's racing could be sweetly terminated by an evening at Flambards with Mark – and a night too – it would make more sense of what she was doing. And she realized that whatever she did with her days, it would have little relevance, for the one thing she wanted for her happiness was not available to her. She was ashamed then of her feelings, watching the children, who should have been enough, conscious of her privileges and friends and comforts which were all lavishly hers, more than she ever deserved.

'You're not nervous, are you?' Fergus asked gently, mistaking her silence.

'No.' She smiled at him, switching her thoughts. He was watching a very stately, old-fashioned de Dion advancing up the hill towards them in low gear, driven by a lady swathed in veils. He stood up.

'Excuse me,' he said. 'This is my lady-friend, whom I told you about.'

Christina jerked to attention, terrified of what the veils would reveal. She had an instinctive lurch of protective possessiveness for Fergus, that this lady should be worthy of his kindness, his humour and his courage. To please her, she would have to be a paragon of matching talents.

Fergus was more discerning than Christina had given him credit for. He did not make hasty and unwise decisions, but trod his path thoughtfully, intelligently. The relationship was still nicely formal, even distant, but full of an underlying regard which was quite clear on both sides. Christina, hypnotized by the unveiling, was astonished to see not a bright, painted flapper but an undoubted lady of considerably advanced years – the early thirties, Christina would have guessed, a good ten years older than herself. Her hair was already greying at the temples, which perhaps gave an older first impression; her skin was clear and unwrinkled, her eyes grey and serene, her dress slightly severe. They all got to their feet, for she was that sort of a person, and the lady climbed down and shook hands with each of them in turn.

'Helen, Miss Helen Portman,' Fergus said.

Helen, it transpired, was the headmistress of a convent school in Southend. Mark was plainly thrown by this information, but Christina was enchanted. One could hardly ask for a steadier recommendation; she would surely harbour no deceit, she would not flirt or connive or want Fergus for the wrong reasons; she would desire him for his heart of gold, which was exactly the relationship Christina had decided he needed. No one, to be honest, was going to fall for his looks. Helen was steady and respectable, but that she was not stuffy was obvious by her genuine interest in the proceedings. As they went about preparing for the climb proper, Christina began to think she might quite easily be persuaded into making an attempt with the de Dion.

'I never knew Fergus did all this – he never told me! I shall be ashamed to ask him to do my punctures in future! He is so modest.'

'Yes, it's true. He does all the work, but is perfectly happy to forego the excitement. He never wants the limelight.'

Christina, as Fergus bent to start up her engine again, would have been glad to forego the excitement herself at that moment. But when she was back in the line for the start again, Mark right behind her, she forgot her qualms in the midst of the spine-tingling din, the tense concentration required to get the Straker-Squire just right at the required moment, juddering on the hand-brake, foot poised, eye on the flag ... this time it was in earnest. The car went off with as fulsome a screech of burning rubber as Captain Archie himself, and Christina had no care for the spectators this time, only the exact right line for going into the bend and the absolutely right hairsbreadth fraction of a second to choose for the gear change, smooth and losing no impetus, the white faces spinning, looming and receding and the spray of dirt blinding her. She had to take a hand off to wipe her goggles and the car swerved and bumped and for a moment she panicked, not knowing where to steer, but then she saw the black scar of the road curving away ahead, cutting through the smooth green hillside, and she put her foot hard down on the floor so that the crackle of her acceleration split the afternoon like gunfire. The car rocketed up the gradient, much too fast into the bend. She had to brake hard, lost control ... felt the back end swing round with a sickening volition all its own and found she was looking downhill instead of up, giddy into a great sea of faces and gesticulations, people running in all directions and the car apparently going back the way she had come. She slammed on the brakes and groped for reverse. It went backwards with more power, and power was what she needed now. The wheels spun and a shower of dirt fountained off the road. The car lurched and ground into the verge, the wheels finding virgin grass and biting in. Sods and turf mashed up behind her; she changed into forward and went back into the bend in the right direction, grinding out into the second leg of the hair-pin, heading for the finish. The little car gathered speed valiantly, but Christina knew that this time her exuberance had been her undoing. First time up had been beginner's luck. The crowd cheered her back into action, but she had lost her chance. Killed no one, however, and felt that she had not come out of an unpleasant spin too badly. At least no one had had to manhandle her back into action, and she had completed the course. She coasted into the finish, half annoyed, half relieved, again in the same state of trembling reaction.

'How stupid it is!' she thought, switching off and slumping like a rag doll. 'What is it all about? What am I doing this crazy thing for?'

And then Mark came up, even more reckless but by sheer

injustice not getting into any trouble at all. He roared in to meet her, sprang out and crossed to her car, grinning. She felt very close to bursting into tears.

'What's the matter? Did you get frightened? I didn't see exactly what you were up to, only you went into a spin.'

'I love you,' she said.

He leaned over and took her face in his great muddy gloves and pressed it to his own, his lips as cold and gritty as hers, tasting of oil and the sweat of fright.

'Number seventy-two, you came up in fifty-five flat. That's not bad. You're the Bugatti, aren't you?'

'Yes, that's right.' Mark removed his face for a second. 'What's the best time so far?'

'Fifty-two forty, so you've nothing to be ashamed of.'

'No fear.'

Mark kissed Christina again, but she turned away, not knowing whether to laugh or cry.

They drove down in calvacade, back to exuberant Fergus and his friends and the leaping children, the remains of the picnic, the lovely hot flasks of coffee. Christina was hungry now, wanting to stave off her trembling weakness. She did not know whether it was physical or emotional or both. Dorothy had a pair of binoculars, she noticed for the first time with a pang, but Dorothy bore no grudges.

'Fancy letting Mark beat you! Really, Christina.'

'I did it on purpose, so as not to upset him.'

'Of course, I knew it! It's best to keep him sweet. He can be quite violent when crossed.'

'He was spoilt as a child.'

'Thrashed regularly once a week. Both you girls would have been much improved by it. I'm sure Miss Portman beats her girls to keep them in their place.'

'Morning and afternoon. It works wonders.'

Christina warmed to Miss Portman, dry and intelligent. She was probably the best thing that had happened that day.

They all packed up to go home. Fergus wanted to stay till the end and kept the Bugatti; Dorothy took the children in the Vauxhall and Mark decided that he and Christina would go together in the Straker-Squire. Dorothy seemed agreeable so Christina did not argue. Mark drove it, and Christina settled down in the passenger seat with a rug over her, feeling very tired. Mark was in no hurry and when they were alone on the road he put his arm round her and Christina huddled against him.

'There is something we have to do on the way home,' he said. 'You won't like it but it is necessary.'

'Like medicine.'

'Exactly.'

'What is it?'

'I'm not sure yet, but I thought it wise to warn you.'

'As long as I'm with you, darling ...' Christina was too tired to care.

It was only when Mark drove into the chase that led to the Flambards home farm that she sat up and took notice.

Chapter 15

Mark stopped out of earshot of the house and sat for a moment staring at the light that shone out of the window.

'Is this my medicine?' Christina whispered. 'I don't want it.'

'No. But I told you it's necessary.'

He got out of the car and held a hand out to her. She climbed out and they walked round the side path together, still holding hands. Christina's mind was a blank. It was necessary, Mark said. So it was, she supposed. She was surprised to see how much work Dick had done on the house, for she had not visited it for months. She could see the new roof in the dusk, and the new window-frames. The light was on in the back kitchen, and they could see two figures sitting at the table, laughing. They were at supper, the cooking pots still on the range in a homely manner, a jug of ale between them.

'Clara!' Christina said.

It seemed so obvious, so right – why ever hadn't she guessed? They were happy and Dick was quite different with her, relaxed and talking eagerly, animated as she had not seen for months. In fact he never had been like that with her. She looked on silently, very chastened, indignant but not angry. She felt sorry, but who for she had no idea. It should be for herself, but it wasn't. She supposed it was for the dream they had had of being happily married, which had not worked.

'Can we go now?'

'Certainly not,' Mark said. 'You must face facts, Christina. Don't be such a coward.'

'Why?'

'It's like brushing the dust under the carpet, your way. It must all be sorted out properly. You want to know where you are.'

'It's quite obvious where I am, I would have thought.'

'I'm not having it, then. I'm not having you treated like this.'

And he moved forward swiftly. Christina had no choice but to follow, scenting disaster. Like going over the top, she thought; Mark had never been one to shirk issues. He knocked loudly on the door, opened it and went in. She followed. Dick stood up angrily but Clara did not move. She looked at Christina and a deep colour came into her cheeks.

Dick said to Mark, 'You didn't have to do it this way!'

Mark started to unbutton his coat. 'I told you there was going to be a third time.'

Christina did not see exactly what was going to happen until Dick quite deliberately pushed the table out of the way. Mark took off his goggles and motoring helmet and dropped them on the floor with his coat. Clara stood up then, looking scared.

Christina cried out, 'You're not going to – no, you can't! Clara, stop them!'

She went for Mark but he pushed her to one side with considerable force and closed with Dick before she recovered herself. She heard the thuds of connecting fists and backed up against the window out of the way, realizing instantly that this was no token fight. The two of them were grappling in earnest, threshing about the small room to the detriment of furniture and table things, already grunting and gasping. Clara saved the ale-jug, and Christina nipped in and gathered up the plates and stew-pan before Dick fell backwards over the table and Mark followed him up with such force that one of the legs gave way. They both went down on the floor in a tangle of arms and legs and splintering wood, punching wildly.

'They'd be better at it outside,' Clara said, very practical. 'It'll be easier on them – the grass – than these stone flags.'

As they both staggered to their feet she closed in and shouted at them, 'Get outside!' and shoved them bodily towards the door. They neither of them seemed to be aware of their surroundings and staggered out in a close embrace, directed by the hard-muscled Clara, her shoulder to the nearest back. Christina stood admiringly, as anxious as Clara that no one should get hurt, but not at all optimistic. Both the men were tired, Dick having been ploughing all day by the evidence, but there was no doubt about their intentions. It was far more than a sporting contest. The scores to be settled went back a lifetime. She followed Clara to the door, cold and sick at what was happening, scared for Mark's permanent, essential weakness. She did not know how he expected to stand up to Dick for long, for Dick had the strength of an ox. But right on one's side was perhaps more advantage than she had imagined, for Dick was by no means getting the upper hand. The two of them sparred the whole length of the newly dug garden, brutally over the cabbage seedlings and broad beans and hard up against the fence. The ducks in the reeds beyond, settled for the night, flew up with loud squawks of alarm; the top rail of the fence cracked and the two men went over, half into the pond. The cold water stopped them momentarily. Dick got to his feet and waded out on to the hard stones of the farm path and turned round and waited for Mark to come after him. He had his head down, weaving slightly, fists clenched in the very manner of an old sporting print, Christina thought, and his face was bloody and cut about. Christina hoped Mark would be satisfied and call it a day; Dick was marked enough to content him, but it was a forlorn hope. She might have guessed ... Mark straightened up, his hands clutching his stomach, paused for breath momentarily, then followed up with the same headlong fervour with which he had earlier driven his Bugatti into the hairpin bend. Dick, watching and ducking adroitly, was driven back towards the stable yard. He stumbled over a stone, half fell against the stable wall and Mark threw several punches which connected. Dick then ducked and Mark's fist drove into the wooden boards. He let out a gasp of pain, leaned for a moment against the wall, stopped in his tracks, and Dick turned round and banged his head against the boards with his fist. Mark slithered down in a heap and Dick went down on top of him, turning him over and bringing a knee up to hold him across the chest. Mark wriggled out of the way like an eel, terrified for his vulnerable midriff. He flung up his feet and kicked Dick full in the face.

'Oh, ma'am, they're being very foolish,' Clara said anxiously. 'They're both going to get hurt something terrible like this.'

'What can we do?'

'Perhaps if we get some sticks – a spade or something –'

They looked round hopefully, despairingly. There was a pitchfork stuck in one of the haystacks, hardly a suitable implement for the job. Clara pulled it out, hesitated.

'No – not that,' Christina said. Her eyes went round the dusking yards. There was a tap set in the wall and a long length of hose disappeared from it to the troughs in the stockyard.

'What's the water pressure like? Nice and strong? It might do the trick.'

She started pulling it in, coiling it at her feet. Mark and Dick were back up the path and in the garden again, slugging it out amongst the raspberry canes, reeling with exhaustion.

'There's no way they're going to finish until they drop.

263

Turn the tap on hard, Clara. We'll see if this will do it.'

The pressure came through the hose like something live, as Clara opened the tap to its limit. Christina picked up the end of it and hauled it after her towards the grovelling figures, going in close. She turned it full in Dick's face and had the satisfaction of seeing him fall back, his flailing hands coming up to cover his face. As Mark followed up the advantage she then turned it on him and screamed at him, 'Stop it! Stop it! It's not to help you, you fool! It's to stop you!'

Mark came at her then, snatching the hose out of her hands. She had never seen his face so wild, suddenly scoured of the mud and blood that streaked it and gleaming in the dusk, the drops of water flying off as he shook his head. He was like a mad bull, pulling the hose off her and turning it for a moment full in her face so that she spun back, all her breath taken, blinded by the force. When she opened her eyes again he was straddled over Dick and holding the hose full in Dick's face. Dick threshed about but Mark was kneeling on him and with every fresh flailing Mark was able to follow him with the hose. Dick started to choke, his arms dropping back, his body falling limp. Mark got hold of him by the hair and forced his head back. Christina flung herself on Mark, beating at him wildly and screaming to Clara, 'Turn it off! Turn it off!'

Mark threw her off and she fell into the mud and the raspberries. She thought he was going to follow up with the hose after her and stayed where she was, her head buried in her arms, but suddenly the fierce hissing of water stopped, and the only sound was the dreadful gasping from Dick. Christina lifted her head up and saw Mark get hold of the hose and swing the brass nozzle with furious intent, still straddled over Dick's inert figure.

'Mark!' she screamed and launched herself at the vicious arm, not with her hands but with her whole body, terrified of the damage it would do. She fell across Mark and knocked him over, landing heavily on top of him. He lay still then beneath her. She lifted herself up, her hair sliding loose in a great wet tangle over her shoulder into Mark's face. Mark brought his hand up and held it, and said softly, 'I've done for the bastard this time. I said I would.'

'You were going to kill him –'

'I would gladly.'

Christina lifted herself on her hands and knees and turned to Dick. Clara was bending over him, pulling him over on to his side. He was still gasping and choking, his swollen face blue-white and ghastly in the near-darkness.

'Mark, get up. Help us,' Christina said.

They turned Dick on to his stomach and beat him frantically on the back. He started to cough and sneeze, and then he got up on his elbows, gasping and struggling for air. They rubbed his back, and gradually he started to breathe more easily. Christina turned back to Mark, feeling as exhausted as if she had fought Dick herself – had, in effect, for she was in much the same state, covered in mud and dripping wet. Mark, although not half drowned like Dick, was not, as victor, in much better trim, his face badly cut and bleeding, his fist the same, and his old injuries obviously making themselves felt. It was difficult for him to straighten up; he gasped and groaned, and Christina put her arms round him for him to lean on her shoulder and said, 'You fool, you idiot ... what good does it all do? You have half killed yourself ...'

The four of them staggered back to the kitchen. If the men had not been in such a bad state, Christina supposed there was a funny side to it, but she found that she was trembling with shock, and distressed by the damage. In the electric light, they both looked terrible, white-faced and completely exhausted, splashed all over with mud and blood. Clara got a bowl of water and a towel, but Christina said, 'I'm going to take Mark home in the car. He should be in bed with his injuries, and it would be the best place for Dick. I'll come back for Dick – or someone will. It's no good staying here. Dorothy is at home and she will patch them up. It's best, Clara.'

'Very well, ma'am. I'm sure you're right.'

'I'll go and fetch the car.'

She drove it to the back door, and the two of them helped Mark into the passenger seat. Christina knew that he was suffering more from his old trouble than he was from what Dick had done to him, and she was anxious to get him to bed. She drove back to the road and down the familiar lanes to Flambards, Mark huddled beside her, groaning at intervals, and muttering, 'I smashed him, Christina. I'm not sorry – it's what the bastard needed – has needed for years.'

'Don't be so ridiculous! Smashed yourself, I'd say. You are crazy! Look at your hand! You'll be laid up for weeks.'

'I won though.'

'I grant you that. I hope it gives you pleasure!'

'Yes, it does. It really does, the swine.'

Their arrival at Flambards, where Dorothy, Fergus, Helen, Jerry and Jean were having a civilized aperitif before dinner in the sitting-room, caused consternation. Christina could scarcely slip in quietly, her own appearance being bizarre enough, and she was glad enough for Fergus to come out and help Mark who was scarcely able to lift himself out of the car. Dorothy took one look at him and went upstairs to run the bath.

'He is a maniac!' she raged. 'A complete and utter maniac! Why ever didn't you stop them?' she appealed to Christina.

'I did! I did! How do you think I got in this state myself?' Christina was close to tears. 'I'll go back and get Dick. He's just as bad – worse, if anything –'

'Fergus will go! You can't go out again in that state!'

Christina was not sorry to have the whole business taken

out of her hands. She changed into dry clothes and went down to the big fire where she was plied with much sympathy and strong drink. Fergus and Dorothy coped efficiently with the protagonists upstairs and Helen, surprisingly, put the children to bed in the midst of the upheaval and organized the dinner to the table. Christina found herself being treated with the utmost concern and kindness, and when all her guests had gone except Dorothy, she was calm enough to go and sit with her by the fire, lie back in the armchair and consider the extraordinary events of the day. Strangely, she remembered the night Dorothy had had leave from France, when they had sat together in the same place and conjectured on the likely problems of their two marriages. Through it all, the fact that their friendship had not wavered struck her as the most surprising – and comforting – feature of their sorry relationships.

'You are going to have to divorce Dick,' Dorothy said. 'You know that?'

'I suppose so.'

'And if it would help you, I would get a divorce from Mark.'

'It won't though.'

'No, I know. But I shall leave him sooner or later, and go back to London – he knows I shall.'

'Is that because of me?'

'No. Acting true to form, it is for my own good reasons, my own selfish desires, to see more of a certain gentleman I am in love with.'

'Does Mark know?'

'He has a very good idea.'

Christina felt, but did not say, 'Poor Mark,' and Dorothy surprised her by phrasing the identical regret, adding, 'He didn't deserve what's happened to him – marrying someone more selfish than himself. Will you look after him for me?'

'You know I will,' Christina said bleakly.

But friendship, in that context, was thin consolation, and when Christina said good night and went upstairs, her large empty bed stood forlorn in the moonlight, a life-sentence, and she knew that nothing that had happened that day had made any difference to anything that mattered. Dick, Fergus, Dorothy, Jerry . . . they could all take the lovers of their choice, but she, having made her mistake, must abide by the rules.

And when she climbed into bed and pulled the eiderdown over her head it was the baby, Harry, that she had lost that she felt the saddest for, and if she had wept it would have been for him. But she did not weep.

When Christina went down to breakfast the next day she was aware of a new attitude in herself. She had woken fearfully, remembering the horrors of the day before and the truths she must now come to terms with, but the biggest truth of all, as she lay in bed in the cold spring dawn looking at the sky out of the window, seemed to lie in the fact that she was on her own again, whether she liked it or not: she was once more the mistress of Flambards and no one, not even Dick, was going to tell her what to do. She got out of bed and padded to the window, and saw the first of the new leaves like a green veil over the covert, the sky washed-out and colourless and cold; there was a pheasant on the lawn, arrogant and flashy, and a chorus of thrushes outdid its raucous call from the stable roof. It never failed, the smell of spring, the cold innocence of a new day for calling up her eternal spring of optimism. She remembered that Clara was unlikely to arrive to mother her children. She could do what she pleased with them; she could decide what was to be done about the farm. She could order a tractor, the way she felt, and start seeing about getting the electricity so that Flambards might be as well lit as Dick's new farm.

She was cheered by the feel of her new self and got herself

dressed and went downstairs. Mary was in the kitchen drawing up the fire, grumbling and muttering.

'We'll have breakfast in the dining-room, the four of us. Will you see to it? I'll go and get the children up, as Clara won't be coming any more.'

From the tone of her voice, Mary knew better than to pass any remarks. She went to lay the table, and Christina went upstairs, taking hot water for Dorothy and Mark in the guest-room. She knocked and went in. Dorothy was dressing, and Mark lay in bed looking as if he could well stay there for a week.

Christina was brisk.

'Did you sleep well? How are you feeling, Mark? Mary is cooking the breakfast now – I thought we could all eat together. You won't be long, will you?'

Mark groaned.

'Of course not,' Dorothy said.

Christina passed on to Dick and found him looking much the same as Mark, and as pleased with her information.

'A quarter of an hour, Dick,' she said sternly.

'I'm not sitting at the same table as that bastard.'

'You are, Dick, I'm afraid. This once – it will be the last time, I daresay. You owe it to me.'

She went and got the children their clean clothes and took them downstairs, and when Mary had the breakfast cooked and ready and took it in, everyone was in their place, polite and civil, Dick pulling out a chair for Dorothy, and Mark doing the same for her. She thanked him and he bowed and said, 'For you, my dear, anything.' Dick gave him a murderous glance from the head of the table.

Mark ate nothing but a piece of bread and marmalade but Dick tucked into two eggs and three rashers of bacon. They made cordial conversation about the weather for ploughing, the layout of the new stockyard and the feasibility of getting the electricity up the Flambards drive, and then Dorothy said she must go, for she had an appointment in London at noon.

She drove off with Mark in the Vauxhall. Dick stayed at the table with his cup of tea while Christina saw them off, and when she came back he said tentatively, 'I'll get back to the ploughing then. The men will be wondering where I've got to.'

'Very well.'

But he sat on, staring into his empty tea cup.

'What are you going to do?' he asked.

'I thought I would take the children for a drive if it doesn't rain. Tom really enjoyed it yesterday. I shall spend far more time with them now Clara won't be coming any more.'

'Are you angry – about Clara?'

'Not exactly angry. I don't want to see her again, that's all. What you do is your own affair, and what I do now is mine. We needn't really argue about it. We can discuss the implications when we are clearer in our own minds.'

'I know – what I've done ...' Dick spoke hesitantly, painfully, 'is wrong. But what – what you and Mark have – have between you – is – is sinful. It's against the church and against the law.'

'Do you think that I don't know that? We shall never consummate what we have between us, rest assured. I may be misguided, but I'm not what the church brands an evil liver, which is what you are suggesting. Save your condemnation for yourself. Plain adultery is a sin too, you know.'

Dick flinched visibly.

He got up to go, and Christina said, 'You can tell Clara she can come and collect her wages up to the end of the month. Then she is free to find herself another post.'

Dick went to the door. He turned just before he went out, hesitated again, and said, 'I didn't mean it to happen, Christina.'

270

'Nor did I!' Christina cried out after him. 'Nor did I!'

The anger broke in her then, surging uncontrollably, but Dick had gone and she could do nothing but throw two plates unerringly at the marble mantelpiece with a crash that brought Mary running.

'Oh, my, I don't know what we're coming to, I'm sure! Don't take it out on the china, Miss Christina, we've little enough as it is! Don't carry on so, my dear. They are none of them worth it in the end and that's the truth of it.'

But Christina, having stated her principles so forcefully to Dick, knew as she had known all along that standing by them was going to be unbearably painful, all the more so when Mark was being left on his own more and more by the errant Dorothy. When, after a drive to the seaside and back with the children, she called in at Dermot's on the way home, she saw the once optimistic house desperately in need of the woman's touch. Dorothy had lost interest and the welcoming, shining rooms now looked tawdry and unused. Mark appeared to live in the kitchen when he was alone and Christina found him there at lunchtime drinking a cup of tea which was all he felt able to keep down after the excitements of the previous day, sitting amongst a grim tumble of dirty dishes and unironed washing enough to depress even the most optimistic visitor.

'Where's your daily woman, for heaven's sake?' Christina asked, tying on Dorothy's apron and setting to work.

'She doesn't bother to come if Dorothy's not here. She keeps saying she's ill.'

'Someone's got to look after you – you've never been capable of doing it for yourself. Leave him alone, Isobel. Come and put these plates away for me. And Tom, you can get the broom out and sweep the floor, then I'll give it a scrub. Can't I make you something to eat, Mark? I'll boil you an egg, how about that?'

271

She had to quench her hopeless desires in a fury of domesticity. Tom and Isobel decided they were playing mothers and fathers, which made Mark laugh.

'Mothers and fathers! Who's your father, Tom? – Tell me that, my one and only.'

'Uncle Dick is my father.'

'Mark, Mark, stop it!' Christina scolded. 'It's not fair.'

But when she had occasion to go up to the lovely south-facing bedroom that she had once scheduled for the Russell nursery, her spirit faltered again and she had to launch herself into a demoniacal cleaning of the bath and the bathroom floor and a shining of the copper pipes to exorcise her frustrations. She could not stay with Mark any longer; it was beyond her capabilities to stay there seeing him despondent with his black eye and swollen lips and hungry, capricious stomach without wanting to kiss him and comfort him, so she finished and departed as abruptly as she had arrived, driving home with a crashing of gears, the children bouncing cheerfully beside her. That evening she sat alone by her fire, steadfastly not thinking of Mark alone by his, and as the days went past she recovered her senses, thrown by the night of discovering Dick with Clara, and built up an armour of steady, routine work, filling her days. She had the children to look after; she exercised Tiptoe steadily to teach him manners; she worked in the garden, she found a tutor for Tom, she made new curtains for the bedrooms, she practised her hill-climbing with Fergus, she taught Moonshine to lead and to be parted from Sweetbriar without fussing, she made cakes and polished the furniture. Sometimes she thought she was quite happy. She never went to Dermot's when she knew Mark was there alone.

She discussed the divorce with Dick.

'There is nothing else to be done, for you want to live with Clara. I will divorce you, citing Clara, and Clara will just have to go through the disgrace as best she can. It will be forgotten soon enough. Is that what you want?'

'It would be best, yes.'

'There is no point your coming home here any longer, if you agree. You can make your home in the farm. If we start divorce proceedings, we must live apart.'

'I don't want –' He stopped. 'Afterwards, I don't want your charity.'

'Afterwards, if I live here alone and keep the books, and you live at the farm with Clara and work as my farm bailiff, for wages, in charge of Flambards, I think that might work well enough. It worked before we were married. It can work again. I see no reason why not. Do you call that charity?'

Dick answered slowly, 'I call it charitable, on your part. No, not charity. I would count myself lucky, and Clara too. I would do my best for the farm.'

'That is why it suits me. I know you are a good farmer, none better. But I would *employ* you, Dick. If you don't like the idea, you must say now, I think. There cannot be two bosses.'

'No.'

Mark said, 'You're too bloody generous, Christina! He deserves being thrown out on his ear, not a job in a thousand like that.'

'That's for me to say! He only found another woman because I was fool enough to fall in love with you, and he knew it. It's time you took some of the blame.'

'Hmm, much good it did me! If you're the gaffer again, Christina, how about buying a tractor for Flambards? Dick needs to be brought up to date. If you tell him he's got to use one, he will. He can do four times the work with a tractor that he can do with a horse. He's crazy not to try it.'

'Yes, that's a good idea. But not from you, I think. From

Fergus. I will buy it, and Fergus will demonstrate to him how to use it.'

'You're wise. I'd drive over him. My selling technique – which as Fergus has told you relies on charm – would fail me. I sold five last month. We're doing very well, did you know?'

Gradually, with no home comforts to rely on, Mark had taken to working. Christina had noticed, and passed no comment, but it was a great satisfaction to her, to see Mark imperceptibly drifting into this congenial business with Fergus, not merely as amusement but with a genuine interest. Fergus told her, 'I'd be hard put to do without him now, it's a fact. I do the work at home, but it's Mark that goes out and gets it. All these way-back rural contacts – he knows everybody, and they all knew his father and his father's father before him, and they all think if a dyed-in-the-wool country squire like Mark is taking to the internal combustion engine it must be quite in order. It's something I could never have done. We're getting Maloney quite well trained as a mechanic now, and we are thinking of finding another man. And even the office – at this rate we shall have to get a secretary.'

'I am a trained secretary. Didn't Mark tell you? If you like, I could come and do that side of it. I'd like to.'

Fergus bought a typewriter and the small study at Dermot's was turned into an office. Christina took over the heaps of letters, bills, inquiries and order forms and turned the chaos into order in the way she had been taught before the war by Dorothy's father. She took to working in the office most mornings of the week, riding or driving over, quite often with the children. When Tom was not having lessons he went out selling with Mark or helped Fergus and Maloney and sometimes he worked on the farm with Dick, and was equally at home there, a bright, amiable and active child who accepted all his adult mentors with the same easy-going affection. He loved the racing-cars and to go on the hill-climbs with the Bugatti and the Straker-Squire made the highlights of his summer. At nine, he could drive the Bugatti round the field that had once been Will's old airfield. Christina, sitting on the gate with Isobel watching him, was overcome with an overwhelming sense of life's remorseless pattern, remembering old Mr Dermot running over the mown grass at the wingtip of his crazy aeroplane shouting instructions to Will in the frail cockpit. The place had seen it all before, and the ghosts were still there, Will coming up the grass amongst the buttercups laughing, the black hair and the dark Russell eyes, careless and excited – but it was Mark. Not Will.

'We've got another Captain Archie on our hands here! Malcolm Campbell and Co. will have to look to their laurels in another year or two!'

And Christina wanted desperately to embrace the proud father-figure before her, seeing all the intricate family ties growing out of their tangled past and wanting so desperately to have them firmly tied, the loose ends gathered into the knot that was denied them. But all she could do was summon Mr Perkins the family solicitor and start her divorce proceedings against Dick – which made no difference at all to her own situation.

'I suppose I ought to get divorced from Dorothy,' Mark said. 'She seems to have left me, have you noticed?'

'Yes. I have. But it's the ladies that have to do the divorcing. It's not nice for a man to divorce his wife.'

'It's not nice for her to have left me. She's in love with a Member of Parliament, did you know?'

'Really? How very smart. He wouldn't be very pleased if you cited him in a divorce case. It's the wrong profession for that sort of thing.'

'Even if I can't marry you, I shall have to sort things out with Dorothy eventually.'

'So that you can marry someone else?'

'God forbid. There is only you, Christina. There never has been anyone else at all, not even Dorothy. Give me a kiss. There's no law against that. God and King generously allow a chaste kiss.'

It was a summer evening and they were walking back to Dermot's together, merely because it was an evening for walking. The children were in bed; neither of them wanted to sit at home alone. The ground was dry and cracked and the warmth came up out of the hard clay beneath their feet and the soft pollen of the long grasses on either side of the track was brushed off on to Christina's skirts. They walked slowly, hand in hand. The sun was going down and the sky was flushed pink, a few clouds like flamingo feathers, the midges biting. They usually avoided occasions like this.

'But we're only flesh and blood,' Mark said savagely. 'Who made these idiot laws?'

'The Church. You're blaspheming. Don't spoil it, else we can't do even this. It's very unwise, you know it is.'

'Yes, I know. I ought to emigrate, I suppose. Leave you in peace, and you will forget me, and marry someone worthy, blast you.'

'I couldn't bear you to go away.'

'No, and I'm too idle to go. Give me that kiss.'

He turned her face towards him and put a hand under her chin and lifted her face. She hadn't the willpower to resist, reaching up to him helplessly. All the times they resisted made the few times they surrendered an agonizing frustration; it happened, there was no way of living like machinery, and it made the whole condition a hundred times harder to bear afterwards; the kisses were like sparks to bone-dry grasses underfoot. Christina was terrified – of herself more than of Mark – and tore herself away in a frenzy. It never gave the required comfort, the crumb of satisfaction which was all she thought she needed. Every time she thought she could be content, she could control herself where the time before she had failed, but it never happened. Every time it was worse.

'Christina, don't!'

Her agony of despair put Mark close to tears himself. 'There is no need to – for God's sake, it's not the end of the world!'

But in a sense it was, no life nor future stemming from it, and Mark knew it. It was very hard to see the funny side afterwards; Christina found it took several days.

Christina had a letter from Dorothy in London asking her to come and stay, and bring the children. She went, borrowing Mark's Vauxhall for the journey, which was an adventure in itself. Dorothy had a flat in Kensington, as smart as once Dermot's had been, and had tickets for the circus, plans for the zoo and a pleasant hired nanny to look after the children while she took Christina to see 'Chu Chin Chow' and listen to Nellie Melba at the Albert Hall. Christina did some shopping for some new clothes, declined to have her hair cut off as seemed to be the rage in London, and went to the Savoy to meet Dorothy's new friend over cocktails. He was suave and amusing, introduced merely as Jim. Christina, slightly bemused by the drink Dorothy had ordered her, heard Dorothy say, 'Christina is in love with my husband, Jim darling, who happens also to be her brother-in-law, which is why I asked you to meet her.'

Christina laughed, finding this amusing as related by Dorothy. The drink was really very potent.

'I thought she would be interested in the amendment to that bill your friend is drafting, the one you were talking about last week. You said there is a strong group determined to get it passed.'

'Which one is that, my dear?'

'The one with the dreadful name.'

'You mean the amendment to the Deceased Wife's Sister's Marriage Act so that it applies equally to a deceased husband's brother?'

'That's the one.'

'Well, yes, of course. We have great hopes, but there is a strong Church faction against. They do not like Parliament interfering in what they think of as their province, you see. But if we wait for the Church to change the ways of the world, we could well wait for ever.'

'Quite right,' Dorothy said firmly. 'Tell Christina what this bill amendment is for.'

'To enable a widow to marry her deceased husband's brother, which is at the moment unlawful. It is quite simple. The sad losses in the war have made it seem a sorely needed adjustment.'

Christina took another sip of her drink, thinking what a very pompous man – Dorothy was surely not going to stay with him long?... it then slowly dawned on her what the pompous man had said. She put her drink down quickly, before she should drop it.

Dorothy looked at her and laughed. 'Don't look so tragic! It is good news, surely?'

'We can't be sure it will be passed, I feel bound to reiterate. But we are certainly going to do our best.' Jim gave Christina a bland smile. 'You could perhaps be made happy by such a change in the law?'

Christina stared at him wildly. She could not speak, not trusting herself to make sense, the shock having given her palpitations like an old lady. She wasn't sure if she was going to pass out, or leap up on the table and scream with joy.

'Steady on, Christina,' Dorothy said anxiously. 'You're not going to faint? I wanted to give you a nice surprise. It's very hopeful, you must see?'

'I can't believe it!'

'Even if it's not passed this time, it must come before long.

The other way round – for a man to marry his dead wife's sister – was passed years ago, after all. So it must come.'

'But you –'

'I shall divorce Mark. I won't stand in your way.'

'Is it possible? He's done no wrong.'

'I'm sure I can think of something, don't you worry!'

'I can't believe it will happen.'

'There, that's why I wanted you to hear it from Jim himself – I knew you'd think it was just one of my stories. Tell her, Jim, it is going to happen.'

'With luck on our side, next year. Yes, certainly.'

'Do you hear that, Christina? Now stop being stupid. I wanted you to be made happy. Look happy, for goodness sake!'

Christina, never having dreamed of such an abrupt change in her fortunes, was unable to utter another coherent word for the rest of the evening, drifting through the crowded foyer of a theatre in a daze, seeing nothing of what was enacted on the stage, driving back to Kensington afterwards, staring silently, unseeing, out of the cab window.

When she went home, she told Fergus to tell Mark what she had found out, for she did not think she could make it sound sense. She had only just begun to believe it, after two days. The man had said it was not certain to be passed. 'But I am an optimist,' Christina remembered. 'I know it will be passed.'

The harvest had been taken in; the stubble gleamed white and gold and Mark had got the hounds fit again. Maloney had got Ragtime's weedy muscle up and his coat shining like the paintwork on the racing-cars. Mark was starting cubbing.

'It's my work, you understand?' Mark said. 'That is why Christina is going to marry me, because I've turned into a worker.'

'You mustn't kill yourself hunting – working, I mean – before I get round to marrying you.'

'No, that would be a shame. I'll try not to.' But Christina knew he would not change, any more than Dick had changed. And this time she would know better than to expect it. Mark had his business with Fergus, steadily making money, and she had Flambards and would run it with Dick as her bailiff, so that the two did not overlap. Dorothy, on one of her flying visits – and she stayed at Flambards, not Dermot's – suggested that, when they were married, Christina and Mark should live at Dermot's, not Flambards.

'Flambards has not been particularly lucky for you, when you think about it. It's full of ghosts and failures. It's too big and old-fashioned. But Dermot's – the business is there, and your land comes right to the door. You could just as easily manage the farm from Dermot's, and let Flambards off. It would make a new start. That upstairs room you liked so much – you said it was perfect for a nursery, didn't you? And you know Mark wants lots of children, just like himself . . . you know that. I don't envy you, Christina! Just imagine a whole brood like Mark.'

'Steady on!' Christina could not take it all in, Dorothy's casual recipe for her new life. 'There's a whole lot of things to be got through first – an act of Parliament, some tedious divorces . . .'

'Just routine, my dear. Nothing that matters. You must think of the practicalities. Fergus can marry that nice headmistress and live in the coach-house which can easily be converted into a house. Perhaps the headmistress would then like to run Flambards as a school – that's a good idea! Then you can have all those children of yours educated half-price –'

'You are mad! Whose life are you running? I think I should take a hand in yours. You're not going to marry Jim, I trust, when you're safely severed from Mark? He's much too serious for you, Dorothy.'

'You're quite right. I'm thinking of going back to nursing,

if you want the truth. I shall never settle down with a man, so I might as well settle down in a job. I was a good nurse, and I think I would like to run a hospital.'

'Yes, that would be worthy of your talents. You need something huge and demanding –'

'Because I am so bossy? Yes, I think so too. We're getting everything sorted out rather well, aren't we? Who's left? Dick?'

'You must leave Dick alone! I won't have you meddling there. I shall go down and talk to Dick about what's happening. He is entitled to know what his wife is up to.'

Her contact with Dick had been minimal, owing to the requirements of her solicitor, but after Dorothy had gone she rode over to the farm on Ceasefire. She went in the evening so as to find him in, hoping that she would not find Clara there too, but he was alone, washing up his supper dishes at the sink. He was surprised to see her.

'Is anything wrong?'

'No. May I come in?'

'Of course.'

She had sent messages to him with Tom, talked to him a few times in the fields about the work, the hiring of the threshing-machine, the men's wages, but she had not been alone with him since he had left home. He pulled a chair out for her at the table, still covered with a none-too-clean cloth. He did not appear to have much in the way of comforts, there being little evidence of a woman's touch about the place.

'Does Clara not come to you here?'

'No. She's gone away.'

'Where to?'

'She's working in Southend, in service, until the divorce is decided. We thought it better. She has her children to think of. It's not nice for her, the divorce.'

'No. Divorce is very squalid. Dorothy is divorcing Mark. It's disgusting, what they have to go through.'

'She isn't citing you?'

'Of course not, how can she? Mark has to go up to London and spend a night with a lady provided by the solicitor, in a hotel, and be surprised by a detective, also provided by the solicitor. Dorothy – to be fair – said he could proceed against her if he wished, for she could give him perfectly adequate grounds, but as she is applying for a post in a hospital, it would do her no good to be the guilty party. She would never be accepted.'

'Does she wish to marry someone else? Why does she want a divorce?'

'No. Mark wishes to marry someone else.'

'No! That's not true! He –'

'He is going to marry me. The law is going to be changed, to allow it.'

Dick was as stunned as Christina had been the night she had first heard the news.

'How can they change it? It is a law of the Church – Parliament cannot change such things.'

'They changed it nearly fifteen years ago so that a man may marry his dead wife's sister. What is the difference? If this law is passed and we are free to do so, we shall marry.'

'The Church will never condone it!'

'If it is passed by Parliament, the Church will be forced to condone it. And the children of the marriage will be legitimate. Oh, don't tell me what our neighbours will think of it, for I know already! I have been through it all before – for marrying you, and no law had to be changed to allow that! I know what I am doing, but I have never been ashamed of any step I have taken, and I shall not be ashamed of this one. I have never harmed my children. If it wasn't for them and the children we would bear I would live with Mark whether the law was changed or not. For *myself* it is the only true course to take. But I am no sinner, Dick, and if you would make me one, then you and Clara are no different – you must see that.'

'I am ashamed of what I have done, I don't deny it. And Clara too. We shall never be clear of it, not even when we're wed. But if you were to be happy too, it would make sense of it all, I daresay. I have a lot on my conscience, towards you, since I've been on my own and thought about it.'

'Well then, those are my feelings too. But there is no point in going over what has happened. We shall always have regrets, but if we have a future to look forward to – and I have now as well as you – it makes a difference.'

'I only hope it works out. You and that bastard, eh?'

'I can remember him saying exactly the same – you and that peasant, he said. He wished me luck.'

'I give you much the same chance! Fifty fifty. We didn't fail by all that much, Christina.'

'Perhaps not.'

'I can see where I went wrong, looking back. But there's no changing nature. There's one thing I regret above all else –'

'And me too.'

'Harry?'

'Yes.'

'I shall regret that child to my dying day. You and me, Christina – it will never happen now.'

'No, I feel the same. I think about him . . . oh, I think about him!'

'Well it's past. It's like you said, no good dwelling on it. I hope you'll be happy. I hope it'll work out this time. As long as you're the gaffer on the farm, otherwise I'll be handing in my notice.'

'No fear of that. Mark's no farmer. You might see him over here with hounds, that's all.'

Christina went to the door and stood looking down the

garden. It reminded her of somewhere else, its neatly hoed rows of spinach and young sprouts, the bright fire of the staked dahlias, and the clumps of herbs, a straggling lavender ... it looked like the Deakins' place, even to the duckpond and the young white ducks which had displaced the mallards. She smiled.

'I'll be going.'

Dick came with her to the gate, and then to the stable to help her with Ceasefire. He gave her a leg-up, just as he had done as a fifteen-year-old boy, shy and blushing. She laughed then.

'Do you remember? How we kissed that night in Sweetbriar's stable?'

'We've learned a bit since then, eh? Give me another for old times' sake, and we'll call it a day. There's no lawyers watching.'

Christina leaned down and kissed him tenderly on the lips, and rode quickly away, thinking firmly of her future. But when she turned round, going through the gateway into the dusking stubble fields, he was standing there watching her. She half pulled up, hesitated, then waved her hand. He did not move. She put Ceasefire into a gallop and headed him for Flambards, racing the glowing red ball of the sun disappearing behind the home covert. 'If I get to the stable yard before it goes, I am going to be happy. It is going to work. But if I don't ...' Fifty fifty, Dick had given her. She picked up her whip and gave Ceasefire a stroke down the flank and his hooves rattled on the hard clay. The childish game disturbed her; she laughed at herself, but would not let Ceasefire slacken. When she came to the gate into the home wood and saw that it was fastened, she knew she had no time to get off and open it, not if she wanted to be happy; she did not even trust Ceasefire as a jumper, but she shortened her reins and drove him resolutely at the obstacle, knowing even as she did so that it was dangerous, the light going and the ground so hard. What had Dick said? 'There's no changing nature.' But the sun was showing only a scarlet fingernail. Ceasefire jumped, and the dark wood swallowed them.

*The earlier books in the Flambards series are also
published in Puffins*

FLAMBARDS
THE EDGE OF THE CLOUD
FLAMBARDS IN SUMMER

Other titles in the Puffin Plus series